Far from [illegible]
The soil w[illegible] ambition springs.
Where humble worth neglected sighs,
And friendship but a foe's disguise,

Henry Man 1747 - 1799

Macello

Blake Detective Series, Volume 6

Jon Mason

Published by Jon Mason, 2025.

This is a work of fiction. Similarities to real people, places, or events are entirely coincidental.

MACELLO

First edition. October 23, 2025.

ISBN: 978-1916757127

Written by Jon Mason.

Also by Jon Mason

Blake Detective Series
Dance With the Devil
The Blooding of Brian Blake
Nemesis
Counting The Dead
Death in The Slushpile
Macello

Watch for more at www.jonmasonbooks.com.

'The damage to the pillar. Is that at right-angles or ...'

'Square-on, right-angles.' That was five shots in quick succession. A shot gun was bad enough, but this ...

The first to arrive at this scene was ACC Mithering with Detective Chief Superintendent Ollerenshaw, his deputy. Ex-Leicestershire. 'Sergeant Blake, causing havoc on your first day?"

I smiled. 'Good morning, sir. I'm afraid so. Old habits do die hard.' Introductions made he shook my hand and congratulated me on my second visit to the Palace.

Before I had a chance to talk them through the scene there was a shout. 'Sarge, the photographer wants to know if he can drive through to the Morris Minor?'

I glanced at Mr Mithering. 'Until Superintendent Wallace arrives it's your crime scene, sergeant.'

'Sir.' I turned and shouted up the hill. 'No, Tell him he'll have to drive round via Hartshead and Clifton.'

'Yes, he got that. Didn't look too happy.'

He'd live. The last thing you needed was for any extraneous traffic, foot or vehicular, to contaminate your crime scene.

I walked them through the scene: the advance warning signs were somewhat battered but genuine. The blue light on the grass verge was a Mickey Mouse affair that looked as though it had been fastened down with adhesive tape. The lens wrapped in blue cellophane – nevertheless, in the dark it would fool anyone who didn't get a close look. The ACC called PC Renton over to discuss the rifle slugs. 'I'm not interested in what you get up to on your leave, Renton,' he said. 'As long as it doesn't interfere with your ability to do the job.' The ACC hadn't heard of rifle slugs either. The hand print on the roof. The occupants. He knew far more than I did. Two detectives from Blackpool. DC's Jack Roberts and Cameron MacArthur. As to who the prisoner was and why he was there as yet unknown. But he did comment on the man's apparel and his watch –

so, not a robbery. Why the number plates had been removed was an attempt to slow the enquiry; however they'd left the excise licence in the windscreen.

'What are your thoughts?' DCS Ollerenshaw gave him a strange look. So did I. *Why are you asking a Sergeant?* He held his finger up. 'Wait. Go on.'

'When I first contacted Lancs County, sir, I had no idea it wasn't Wakefield until they asked me to confirm that Brighouse and Sowerby Bridge were in the West Riding. Then they told me who they were ...'

'Moment, sergeant,' DCS Ollerenshaw interrupted. 'Do you know how that was possible?'

'Not sure, sir. I think it's something to do with the manner in which radio waves oscillate between the ionosphere and the ground. The car just happened to be stationary at the right place. Apparently it works better at night.'

'So, had it been the same time on a June morning this wouldn't have been possible?'

'Quite possibly, sir,' they both nodded so I continued. 'They hadn't a clue about the journey and asked for the registered number. I gave it them from the excise license. They asked me if the occupants were DC Roberts and a DC MacArthur. I managed to extract their wallets. Confirmed MacArthur's Id but there was no warrant card in Roberts. Perhaps he dropped it when he was shot. Had that been me I would have had my warrant card handy as I approached what I believed to be a road accident. I've put the wallets on the dashboard. Incidentally, sir, that's how I got in this state.'

The ACC took one look at my uniform. 'You can't wear that. As soon as you're free go home and change. I'll authorise either dry cleaning or replacement.'

I nodded. 'Who ever carried out this assassination knew the route and the schedule. It had been organised in a hurry.' In answer to their puzzled looks. 'The blue light was cobbled together. The shooter has no compunctions about killing. It was obviously carried out very rapidly. But the big questions to me, sir, are who is pulling the strings? Why bring the car over here when they have the whole of Lancashire to play with.'

DCS Ollerenshaw gave Mr Mithering a quizzical look.

'You'll get used to him.' Mithering smiled. 'He's noted for it. Anything else, sergeant?'

'Sir, the occupants are not wearing seatbelts and no-one appears to have made any attempt to move. The first shot took out the driver. The shot passed straight through his skull and into the passengers' face. The second shot was for the passenger hence the debris both inside and on the outside of the door. The third shot was different. It was much more deliberate. The gunman leaned through the driver's window and, I think, placed the barrel against the victims face, or very close.'

'Why?'

'Because the powder burns are tight around the orbit, sir. There's no spread. Obviously the pathologist and forensic may disagree but that's my guess.'

'And the reason for the hand print on the roof?'

'The print is left-handed, sir.'

'Doesn't mean to say that the gunman is, does it .. However, it would be difficult if not impossible to fire the gun left-handed from that position. How many people involved.'

'Here, sir? Two. No more needed. Two lots of signs to put out. Park their car here where the blue light is, facing Brighouse, and wait. Stop the vehicle and whilst one is shooting the other is ripping the number plates from the vehicle. Then they get the hell out of it. But they were apparently interrupted.'

DCS Ollerenshaw narrowed his eyes. 'Guesswork or crystal ball, sergeant?'

'Neither, sir. It's inarguable that a shotgun was used.'

'There are no cartridge cases.' Said the DCS as he looked around.

'Not on the ground, sir. They've been picked up. However, there is one in the nearside footwell.'

'Just the one?'

'Yes, sir. Five shots were fired in quick succession. Driver, front passenger, rear passenger and the two spent rifle slugs in the road. Just before you arrived I checked. There is unexplained damage to that Morris 1000's offside.'

'And a sixth into the driver,' said Mr Mithering. 'You think this was a pump-action shotgun.'

'Yes, sir. It explains why there is only a single spent cartridge in the nearside footwell. I can't think of anything else that could do this.'

'And why you said they were disturbed. The gunman had his back to the traffic when the Morris appeared.'

'Yes, sir. And why they only had two men. A third would have been on the bend. The shooter would have been ready for him. He wouldn't have got that extra quarter mile.'

DCS Ollerenshaw laughed softly. 'I don't suppose you can describe them?'

'Not exactly, sir,' I replied and smiled. 'But we can estimate the height of the gunman.'

Five

Detective Superintendent Wallace area CID, DCI Hodgkinson Halifax and DS Donaldson, Brighouse arrived followed by the photographer. DI Peter Cartwright remaining with the Morris 1000.

Introductions complete Mr Mithering suggested that I take Detective Superintendent Wallace and the others through the scene. There were no questions. I went home to change. It was now half past eight. I managed to get Lucy's attention. She brought my spare uniform into the garage and kept Claire out of the way. The last thing I wanted was for her to come running to be picked up with my uniform still wet. That's one thing she didn't need to know about. My soiled uniform went into a clean paper potato-sack.

The traffic was worse than I thought. All the traffic that would normally drive along the A644 towards Brighouse was being diverted towards Huddersfield. The fact there was a major incident under investigation meant nothing to those who had no idea what was happening. Me being allowed through did not go down well. I got snapped by the press. An occupational hazard.

An hour after leaving I was back at the scene, so was Jack Hawkins, a biologist from the forensic science laboratory. 'You again,' he said and laughed. 'You ought to carry a Government Health Warning.'

The Coroner's Officer was in conference with Detective Superintendent Wallace. Technically speaking we were all Coroner's Officers; however, PC Jarvis was the area liaison officer: all Coroner's files went through him. The photographer had finished. The force

Plan Drawer was busying himself. A recovery vehicle and a hearse with three leak-proof coffins. Not a pleasant business. Mr Mithering and his deputy had also departed.

'Sergeant Blake,' a voice boomed as DI Cartwright made himself known. He hadn't changed. 'Creating havoc on your first day, Brian?'

I grinned at him. 'That's just what Mr Mithering said. I'm sorry to get you out of bed so soon, sir' I grinned at him and shook the outstretched hand.

'Don't worry about it,' he replied. 'The phone was ringing anyway. You were lucky, your house is just up the road if I remember right.'

'Mile and a half towards Leeds. Lucky for me it was all over when I arrived.'

We spent a couple of minutes catching up. He jotted his contact details down and invited us to his home.

'And the twins?' I smiled. He had no idea.

'Twins? You never mentioned them before, Brian.'

'Early days. In four weeks.'

His face split into a broad grin. 'Oh, definitely. Janet will play merry-hell if you don't come.'

Leaving the Coroner's Officer to his own devices Mr Wallace came over to us. 'Did I hear you say twins in four weeks?' He said with a beaming smile.

'You did, sir.'

'Many congratulations,' he said and stuck his hand out. 'That will be three?'

I took the hand. 'Yes, sir.'

'You like work, I'll say that for you. Look, many thanks for what you've done. Not least for protecting the scene. Plus, you've given us a good thirty to forty five minutes extra. But we can't deprive you of the perils of being a patrol sergeant any longer. I'll ensure that you're kept informed. There will be a press conference this evening, hopefully live on Yorkshire television. Should anything else come to mind contact Mr Cartwright. Oh! I'll also arrange for you to attend a joint meeting, the West Riding and Lancs County.'

It was ten fifteen. That was it for now. The scene had been roughly searched and I was allowed to drive through. A hundred yards away a dozen bobbies plus supervision waiting to carry out a full search of the road, riverbank - over the wall to the south, and surrounding areas. The aim, to find the three missing rifle slugs. My next call? To meet with my new divisional officer.

Six

Chief Superintendent Cartwright, no relation, was of the old school. He was six feet plus and must have been nearing age limit. He knew his own mind and didn't care for other people's opinions, especially if they conflicted with his own. He'd earned the right to impose himself on others by surviving as long as he had. It became very clear as I stood in front of his desk, that as a probationary sergeant I was on a short rein and my actions would be scrutinised in depth as long as I remained on his divisional strength and, or, until he decided otherwise. The fact that anyone could be promoted to the rank of sergeant with less than four years' service, unbelievable. And, in spite of a successful posting to CID immediately following my probation, if I thought that I could, on a whim wander off and become involved in this case involving the death of the two Lancastrian police officers I could think again.

Any breach of the Police Discipline Regulations, no matter how minor, would be reported. However, I would be allowed to express my opinions. The final point that he made concerned the house. Twelve months earlier, a decision was taken to standardise police housing stock. We lived in a non-standard house i.e. it was purchased for the police and not built for them. As a sitting tenant I was given first refusal. I was allowed to buy the house complete with its huge rear garden, for £1950.00. Mike Riley, an architect friend of Joe's drafted plans and our two bedroomed detached house became four bedroomed, two bathrooms, one en suite plus integral garage. We paid £950 from our savings and obtained a £1000 ten year mortgage, and, maximum rent allowance. The chief superintendent was of the opinion that I should live within the boundaries of the sub-division. There would be no excuse whatsoever for me not parading for duty on time.

That was that.

The chief superintendent waited until the door closed behind the young sergeant and smiled to himself. He picked up the sergeant's divisional file and read it again. He had to admit that he was impressed, but the trouble was these potentially high-flying officers thought they were wearing anti-gravity boots. It wouldn't do him any harm to have his wings clipped. Keep him grounded. He called Superintendent Valentine over the hill in Huddersfield. 'He's quite an impressive young man. But from what you told me it won't do him any harm to have his wings clipped.'

'I agree. He does tend to fly a little. What he needs to learn, is when ..'

I did get it. The chief superintendent's attitude. It took me back to those conversations that I'd had with DS Nicholson about two years ago. What I had achieved as a constable was in the past. I now had to learn to be an operational supervisor. I had to prove that I was up to a different job.

Seven

Inspector Marshall, fortyish, pleasant features and a firm handshake - plenty of nicotine staining. Five ten. Fifteen stone. Dark receding hairline with more than its fair share of grey. He was a sergeant short, gave me a warm welcome and joined me for a cup of tea whilst I took my meal.

'You don't mind if I call you Brian?'

'Not at all, sir.'

He nodded. 'What happened?'

'I can't really say. I saw the traffic signs and the blue light on the nearside verge. Then the car with its occupants. I've seen a few bodies but this was different. Two dead policemen and one other. But until the press conference I've been told to keep my mouth shut. No doubt there'll be a teleprinter circulation. One thing I can divulge is that from the blue light on the verge we're looking for some vehicle that could have been mistaken for a police car.'

He didn't press the matter but asked me about the medal ribbons. I told him what I thought he should know about Tadcaster.

He frowned. 'There's something that you won't or can't tell me.'

'Can't, sir.' I was saying nothing about the man who would have been my father-in-law being involved in espionage.

'And the BEM was for your part in Wainwright?'

'Yes sir.'

'Both hard won. Congratulations,' He stood and offered me his hand. 'Now, you're married with a young daughter.'

'Yes sir.' I was forced to smile. 'And twins due in four weeks.'

His face was a picture. 'You like hard work,' he laughed. 'I've got one of each but Robin was born five years before Caitlin. That's bad enough. Good luck.'

He commiserated on my ruptured appendix and not being able to sit my promotion exams the first time round. Apart from that he chatted about my short time in CID.

Food consumed we repaired to his office and talked about shift rotas and duties and how he organised them. there were four shifts but only three sergeants. The other two being Martin Chalkley and William 'Bill' Bentley. The shifts that the sergeants worked depended on how many were working on the day; that would please Lucy. Monitoring annual leave and the property store, would be my responsibility. He wanted a breakdown of outstanding annual leave by the weekend. That would be my first priority. I couldn't think of a different way to end my first shift at Sowerby Bridge than by providing the Inspector with his annual leave audit. At least everyone would know my signature.

Eight

The first editions were full of it:

Two Police Officers Amongst Four Slain In Ambush.

It could have been much worse. Lucy had heard little from me but the lunchtime news carried a longer report. Half the neighbours had been round to ask questions. You couldn't blame them; it had happened on their doorstep and they were apprehensive. They were waiting to doorstep me when I arrived home. 'I'm a uniform sergeant not a detective,' I told them. 'I only know what I'm told. I'm afraid that you will have to wait.'

I told Lucy what I could which wasn't much. It would be interesting to hear what had been discovered in the interim. Perhaps the press conference would enlighten us.

Wherever the venue was it was packed. BBC and Yorkshire Television broadcasting live and Granada camera crews plus umpteen reporters. ACC Mithering and Detective Superintendent Wallace held the conference. The format was as expected. A short statement and then a few questions, which may or may not be answered. Thankfully there was no suggestion that a police officer had been the first to come across the scene. Two detective constables from Lancashire, Jack Roberts and Cameron MacArthur, an unknown male and David Nevin, a heavy goods vehicle driver from Huddersfield were those who had been killed. There was no connection whatsoever between Mr Nevin and the occupants of the other vehicle. He just happened to be in the wrong place at the wrong time, with a request that the families be left to grieve in private at this troubled time.

Mr Wallace took over. 'The attack took place at approximately five fifteen this morning. Two men were involved. We know that the gunman was five feet six or seven inches tall. The second was powerfully built. Both were dressed as police officers sufficiently accurate to convince the two detectives that they were genuine. They used a vehicle similar to a police vehicle, again convincing the two detectives that it was genuine. We know that those responsible drove from the scene towards Brighouse. We would ask that if you drove along the A644 between Brighouse and Cooper bridge around that time, or, if you witnessed a dark coloured saloon car containing two men wearing dark clothing travelling in the opposite direction or anywhere in the area about that time, to please contact your nearest police station.'

The floor was opened for questions. Everyone had picked up on the fact that we knew the height of the gunman. 'How do you know, Superintendent? Do you have a witness?'

Mr Wallace smiled. 'Let's just say that we know. The individual concerned is where no-one who isn't supposed to know will find them.' So it went on.

It was crude but relatively simple and very unpleasant. You couldn't fire a shotgun into the car and cause the injuries that were apparent from the shoulder. It had to have been from the hip. It was a question of looking at the points of entry and egress of the rifle slug through Jack Robert's skull and extrapolating backwards. As I said, crude and unpleasant, but it suggested that the gunman was quite short. The five feet six or seven was suggested by Mr Wallace. In the circumstances it seemed reasonable.

Nine

Wednesday 20th September, 1968

0540 hrs. Wakefield Road, the A644 was clear. I introduced myself to the night shift and was met with questions about annual leave; actually it the same question from several mouths. 'Sarge, how many days can we carry over to the next leave year?'

'Five.'

It was generally accepted that, *subject to the exigencies of duty,* members of the departing shift could, within reason, leave as long as their replacement had arrived, particularly following a night shift. It happened. There was a panel of direct alarms mounted on the office wall. The alarm at Venners engineers, about a hundred yards away, activated. 'Sorry fellas, it's only ten to six hopefully we'll get you off on time.' There were a few groans and one dissenter. All bar one of the beat officers hi-tailed it for Venners whilst the radio operator contacted the keyholder. It was my intention to follow as soon as possible. However, one PC Charles Lassiter determined that he was going home.

'Sergeant. It's ridiculous. You've got the entire night shift attending and there's never been a genuine alarm at Venners. I'm going home.'

'Lassiter, you will attend and that is an order.'

'No, I'm going home.'

I held my hand out. 'Your pocket book.' I endorsed his book, cautioned him and set off for Venners with the words of the office clerk ringing in my ears. Chief Superintendent Cartwright would have his first report sooner than I expected.

'Charlie, what the fuck are you playing at?'

'It's ridiculous sending so many. I'll see you later.'

I arrived with Mr Venner who was wearing a jumper and tracksuit bottoms over his pyjamas, bizarrely he was wearing a pair of brown brogues without socks. An open window had been found at the rear of the premises.

It was genuine. Not exactly on New Scotland Yard's most wanted list but two fourteen year old boys, reported as missing from Elland the evening before, were in the works canteen hiding under a table. They had sneaked into the loading bay just before the works closed the evening before and got locked in. The open window was purely coincidental. They had wandered round the factory and found somewhere to sleep. When they woke up they found the toilets then opened the canteen door triggering the alarm. Mr Venner declined to take any action, just grateful that the boys had used the toilets and not the floor. The night shift got away five minutes late and the kettle went on. Of course I was questioned: Yesterday's incident. They were referred to the teleprinter that had been circulated during the night. What happened to Lassiter? Where had I served prior to Sowerby Bridge? No-one asked what service I had. And, although Keith Fleming, one of the older bobbies, recognised the George Cross medal ribbon, and remembered why, none of the others did. 'Look,' I said. 'Yes, I went to university. That doesn't make me a better copper. There are loads of good senior officers who started without a university education and still made it.'

'Yes, sergeant,' offered Keith Fleming. 'And there are just as many who made it because of funny handshakes as well.'

'That's true,' I said. 'But they still had to pass their exams.' It wouldn't do any good for them to find out that Lucy was the Chief's second cousin. 'It's all about attitude. Attitude is everything. The fact remains that you have to want it, and, be prepared to put the work in. If you're quite happy being a beat bobby, that's fine, nothing wrong with that. But I wanted more.'

THE BOYS WERE SITTING in the interview room until returned to grateful parents after breakfast with advice from the inspector as to what would happen if they did it again. Time would tell. A crime was recorded and written off: *Complainant declines to prosecute.*

The inspector called me into his office. 'Sit yourself down, Brian.' He indicated the chair opposite. In his hand the report that I'd submitted concerning PC Lassiter. 'And this is how it happened?'

'Yes, sir. Exactly as it says.'

He nodded. 'I shall go and see him before I submit it,' he said and smiled. 'How did you find it, submitting your first discipline report?'

'Easier than I thought, sir. I was annoyed. Anyone can make a mistake; it's part of the human condition. This wasn't. Call it defiance, dereliction, but it's unacceptable.'

'I agree. Over the past few months Lassiter has let things slide. I'll find out if there are any extenuating circumstances.' He put the report back on his desk. 'Now, tomorrow you'll be on your own. I've got a one-day course at Bishopgarth so Inspector Fowler from Todmorden will call in a couple of times. Probably at ten for a coffee, and then around three,' he passed me a letter. 'And have a look at this. It's from Councillor Martin. He's had a number of complaints re drunken behaviour after closing time. We're right on the edge of Halifax and the level of offences of drunkenness etc is rising. Have a trawl through the Offence Book. Put some figures together for me.'

Thursday was a quiet day. There was one prisoner. Carl Smith wanted on warrant for non-payment of fines; not backed for bail. He would be transferred to court for ten o'clock. Other than ensure he was breathing there was nothing for me to do so I dealt with the inspector's request. Made myself a list of the offenders for future reference. Sowerby Bridge was a busy little spot. Compared to last year's annual report we had experienced a twenty five percent increase in drunken violence, particularly on Thursday and Fridays. Not that it was high, just higher.

Inspector Fowler arrived at ten for his coffee and a chat. I cleared my in-tray. Went for a walk around the town and said 'hello', to Mr Venners. Showed my face in a few more places, get myself known and was home for half past two.

Ten

Mr Collins looked down at the woman, her face contorted, nails digging into his back. She was a head turner and could turn a trick. Insatiable. She could earn herself and Harry a ton of money. In a couple of weeks she would be saleable.

The phone rang. 'Bollocks,' he said and stopped.

'Aw, come on, finish me off.'

He looked at the clock. 9.30pm. 'Be quiet, Josie.' He rolled off and picked up the phone. 'Who the hell's ringing at this time?'

He froze at the voice. 'You screwed up. You were seen.'

'Harry?' Harry never rang in the evenings. 'Just a sec. I've got company.' He turned back to the bed. 'Time to go, Josie. Take your clothes. Get dressed in the bathroom.' He opened the top drawer in the bedside cabinet and passed two £5 notes across. 'Lock the door when you leave and no eavesdropping or you will regret it. Now go.' He watched admiringly as she padded across the floor. She was young and had a cracking figure. He waited until the door closed and looked through the curtains. Josie waved as she closed the gate.

'Now then, Harry. What's all this about? Who saw us, where?'

'I don't bloody know. Don't you watch the sodding news?'

'No, as it happens I don't. Why? What've they been saying?'

'You've made the nationals and the telly. Two men, the gunman was five six. The second powerfully built. Dressed as coppers and driving a look-alike police car.'

'Harry, that's bollocks. There are no witnesses. At least non left alive.'

'The coppers gave out your height, five six. They're positive. They've a witness in hiding. I paid you a lot of money to do that job and I haven't got value. Get it sorted.' Harry was big on value.

His mind was working overtime. It was true, topping a copper carried a hefty premium and he had done two. 'Okay, okay. But it's going to take time.'

'I don't give a flying fuck. Just do it.' The line went dead. Harry Field smiled to himself. Collins was useful and had done some good work for him in the past, but there was a limit to permissible cock-ups. Collins was not unique.

Collins checked the clock once more. There was no point rampaging around at this time and drawing attention. Chris could wait until morning. He poured himself a stiff scotch and paced.

10.00AM. 'Chris, are you sure you haven't said anything?'

'Positive, Mr Collins. Not a dicky.'

'You haven't been out on the piss shouting your mouth off?'

'No, I haven't had a drink. Goin' out tonight though,' he added with a grin.

Chris was a good lad. Not the brightest button but was prepared to do what he was asked. 'Good lad. Don't say anything. Just listen and let me know. All right? And go easy with the dosh.'

Eleven

Friday, 22nd September, 1968

The Oak Room, Police Headquarters, Wakefield. 10.00am

As a mere sergeant my name had been at the bottom of the list. I was in exalted company. Two chief constables, one deputy chief, one assistant chief – crime, one detective chief super, two detective supers, two DCIs *et moi*. I didn't need to know any names. I just called everyone, Sir. The only people I didn't know were from Lancashire.

The purpose? A discussion around the circumstances of the event and an exchange of the latest information.

The chief constable commenced proceedings. 'Good morning gentlemen and welcome to Wakefield. Would it be that the circumstances had been better. Detective Superintendent Wallace is the officer in the case from this end; however I will ask Detective Superintendent Molloy to start the ball rolling. Mr Molloy?'

The officer sat three down from the chief boxed his notes and sat forwards. 'Thank you Mr Barton. The handcuffed man in the rear of the police vehicle had presented himself at the front counter of Blackpool Central police station at 7pm on Monday 18th September. The date prior to the incident. He was described as being in a *worried state*. He asked to speak with someone from CID, refusing to divulge his personal details or reason for attending. He is still unidentified. His photograph has been circulated nationally via Police Reports and Police Gazette. There is no record of his fingerprints. Neither was there anything in his possession that could identify him. He was taken to an interview room where he spoke with DC Jack Roberts for ten minutes. Then left unsupervised for fifteen minutes whilst DC Roberts left the station. On his return they spoke for a further two minutes after which the man left without speaking. No record of his attendance at the police station had been made in any of the station registers or in the communications room. Strangely enough no record was found in the officer's pocket books.

At eight fifteen DC Roberts left the station on enquiries. According to his wife he called at home and told her that he was going on urgent enquiries in the Wakefield area and would be back when she saw him.

Mrs MacArthur said that Roberts had called to see her husband at eight forty pm. Her husband left with Roberts telling her that he would be home in the early hours.

Mrs Fothergill, owner of the Albany Guest House, Knowle Crescent, Bispham, said a man giving the name Graham Smith, who spoke with what she described as a London accent, had booked in around three pm that afternoon. He had no luggage. He left to go for a walk shortly afterwards asking where the police station was. He returned at eight thirty pm and stayed in his room until they were awakened at two am. He was arrested, handcuffed then driven away by two plainclothes officers. She identified them from photographs as DCs Jack Roberts and Cameron MacArthur. She had no details of the vehicle they used.

Nothing was heard from any of them until Sergeant Blake contacted our control room by radio. I understand that was a fluke of physics. Nevertheless. Enquiries are on-going across Lancashire. So far nothing.'

Detective Superintendent Wallace took over. 'The first intimation we had was the call from Inspector Duckworth in your control room. Thankfully, Sergeant Blake was able to protect the scene. One shotgun cartridge case was recovered from the footwell and two spent rifle slugs were recovered from the road surface. In all probability the weapon used was a pump-action shotgun. We are hoping that forensic examination may be able to match the impression on the cartridge case with a specific manufacturer; it will take some time. We have ongoing enquiries with those firearms dealers who supply rifle slugs. They're intended for big game e.g. red deer; there can't be that big a calling. There were partial prints recovered from the case but badly smudged and of no evidential value.

Nothing of value has been recovered from the light that had been affixed to the roof of the car or the blue cellophane rapped round it. The light itself was battery operated and old but serviceable.

The registration plates are still missing.

One interesting point, the front nearside tyre impression taken from the grass verge have been identified as a 6.40/700SR Michelin ZX, the tyres the car left the factory with. The front offside as a 165R14 Michelin XAS. The marks found on the tyre show that it has a bent or worn-out suspension component. It displays a pattern of diagonal scallops. This was only received this morning and has been circulated nationwide, although the car is probably a scrapper. Enquiries are being made at local vehicle dismantlers.

We have ongoing nightly traffic checks along the A644 through Brighouse and along the roads through to the Lancashire border. So far nothing.'

'Mr Wallace,' said Mr Molloy. 'Are you in a position to identify this witness that the Press have been banging on about.'

'In a word, no. The fewer people who are aware the better.'

Eventually the conversation died. The Lancashire County officers accepting the fact that the location of our mysterious witness would not be released began to straighten their notes until Mr Mithering spoke. 'Sergeant Blake, you've been sitting there, thinking, for quite a while. You were first on the scene have you anything to add to the conversation?'

There were a few askance looks in my direction as if to say, why are you asking a uniform sergeant, although no-one had asked why I was there. Before I could speak the door opened and the chief's secretary informed Mr Barton that there was a phone call for Detective Superintendent Wallace in the chief's office. A Commander Jameson, Metropolitan Police.

'Crack on, sergeant,' said Mr Mithering. 'Don't wait for Mr Wallace.'

'Very well, sir,' I took a deep breath. 'You've seen the photographs, gentlemen. Traffic was very light. When I arrived dawn was breaking. After the Police Accident signs the first thing I saw was the blue light on the nearside verge, then the Ford Zephyr and its occupants. It was when I noticed the rear seat occupant in handcuffs and the police radio I realised the implications. He was wearing an Omega wrist watch, so it wasn't robbery. In my mind it had to be targeted. Did they want to make sure there were fewer witnesses. Whoever was pulling the strings, the killer knew the area, the route and the time. That someone was decisive, had immediate access to everything he required and had no scruples with killing. That road is usually busy and the perpetrators knew they couldn't just hang around; it was coming light. So who did DC Roberts call when he left the station. If he didn't call anyone why was anyone there? Who were they expecting to rendezvous with and where? It obviously wasn't where the killing took place otherwise they wouldn't have required the subterfuge. And the rifle slugs. It was PC Renton, one of the traffic officers, who recognised what they were. I'd never heard of them. They come under Part 1 of the Firearms Act 1937 so, in theory, the shooter should have a firearms certificate.' There was a ring of laughter as I continued. 'I think that's a moot point.'

Mr Wallace returned and sat down. 'Finish what you were saying, sergeant.'

Just one last thing, sir,' I said. 'What was dangled in front of them to make it worthwhile in throwing their careers away? And what is the going rate for topping a copper?'

Detective Superintendent Molloy smiled as he broke the silence. 'Ever thought about CID, sergeant?'

'Yes, I would like to get back into CID, sir.' A comment that raised a few eyebrows as well as smiles.

The detective superintendent leaned forwards elbows on the table, looked at me, frowned and pointed. 'Sergeant,' he said. 'George Cross and the BEM. That's an impressive pair of decorations. You're the Blake from the Wainwright case?'

I smiled but before I could respond ACC Mithering did. 'Yes he is.'

'And the BEM is for the Wainwright case?'

'Yes sir.'

'The George Cross?'

I looked across at the Chief. 'As long as it is in the public domain, sergeant.'

So I told them, receiving a brief round of applause.

'I'd like to know what you can't tell us.'

'So would everyone else, sir.'

'Sorry, Mr Barton. But I'd like a chat with the sergeant later.'

'Certainly, Mr Molloy,' the Chief replied to laughter. 'Just as long as you're not trying to poach him.'

The room settled. 'As you're aware,' began Mr Wallace. 'That was Commander Jameson, the Met Major Crime Unit. Our unidentified rear seat passenger may be one Kenny Summers. Never been in trouble. Not so much as a parking fine. Bookkeeper to Harry Field. Into haulage, brothels, casinos, off-course bookmaking and protection. A busy man. DCI Hodgkinson and I are leaving for

London on the one o'clock train from Leeds. Yes, we are,' he confirmed in answer to the DCI's puzzled look. 'Secondly, and even more interesting is that hand print taken from the roof of the car, although there aren't enough points to confirm identity and put before a jury, there are enough for our purposes. The owner is one Nicholas Nickleby, as in Charles Dickens. Apparently his father was a Dickens nut. Even more interesting is the fact that Nickleby died in a road accident nine years ago whilst being pursued by the police. This was on the A104 at Buckhurst Hill, north out of London. He was wanted for the murder, by strangulation, of a prostitute. There seems to be a conflict somewhere. Normally the prints would be destroyed once death has been confirmed. The fact that the Met still have them is a bit of a cock-up. They are now looking though Police Gazette references for Nickleby where there may be photographs. They're also trying to trace his mother and sister. Commander Jameson assures me that the offence file will be resurrected and that a new warrant will be obtained this afternoon. Any questions?'

There was silence. I was surprised that no-one had made the link. 'Yes, sir,' I said. 'If the rear seat passenger was this Kenny Summers, and he had the protection of Harry Field, who could frighten him enough to take a one-way journey out of London? And, if that was Harry Field himself, what had Summers done? What links does Field have with Blackpool?'

'Bloody good questions, sergeant,' said Mr Molloy. 'Once we get the answer to the first we can try to answer the others. Are you sure we can't tempt you across the Pennines?'

'Thank you, sir, but I'm happy with the white rose.'

There were no further substantive conversations. The meeting broke up into a series of chats. Detective Superintendent Wallace and DCI Hodgkinson left to catch the London train. I had just been buttonholed by Detective Superintendent Molloy when Mr Barton caught my eye. 'Sergeant, a word.'

I made my apology and followed the chief into his office. 'I know that you would like to immerse yourself in this enquiry but I'm afraid you'll have to complete your twelve months probationary period.'

He did sound regretful. 'I'd be disingenuous if I said that I wouldn't, sir. However, you never know, the shooter had very good local knowledge so the mysterious Mr Nickleby might just live on my patch.'

THE MYSTERIOUS REAR seat passenger had been identified as Kenny Summers, bookkeeper to Harry Field. There were rumours aplenty but little fact as to why he had ended up hand-cuffed and dead in the West Riding in the rear of a Lancashire County police car.

On the Friday morning, Doreen Roberts and Kirsty MacArthur were transported across from Blackpool to identify the bodies of their husbands. I understand that the mortuary staff had taken all necessary steps to ensure that evidence of the entry and egress of the rifle slugs were covered.

At 2pm the same day, Harry Field accompanied Gwen Summers, a former holder of the Miss Brighton title to the identification. However, on arrival she declined to see her husband. The fact that Harry Field had known Kenny Summers since he was fourteen was accepted by the Coroner to establish identity.

Twelve

I hadn't worked a full week on shifts for over twelve months. Here I was on six to two evenings. Seven on the bounce. This was number four. Thursday. Payday. As before I took over from Bill Bentley. Martin Chalkley, was on annual leave. It was a good nick with the odd exception. We had one of the new UHF radio systems in the sub-division to see how it coped with our huge area and terrain. As expected there had been a bit of probing. They wanted to see who I was. Tonight could be interesting. The report I had prepared for the Inspector indicated that Thursday was attracting too many young men who wanted to drink too much and relied on low numbers of police officers to have a good time. Should the promised rain occur that might not be an issue. They didn't like scrapping in the wet.

First half I took the supervision car and sought out the late turn officers. Asked them questions about their beat. For my benefit not as a test for them. Apart from a road accident at the top of Tuel Lane, dealt with by traffic, it was very quiet.

Meal at 9pm and paraded the night shift at 9.45pm. The same officers that I had worked with the preceding week. Keith Fleming was on Town Beat so I accompanied him. There were also a couple of special constables, I had them patrolling as a pair.

10.30pm. The rain held off. It was busy. As you would expect most couples going out for an evening would choose Friday or Saturday. Tonight's revellers were, for the most part, male and not all of them youngsters. After being suitably lubricated it was on the rowdy side but not so much that there was a danger of a breakdown.

We were standing opposite The Wagon, an unaccompanied young lady, coat pulled tightly around her, collar up, hurried passed as the door opened and five young men were ejected by the licensee. 'I've told you you're barred.' Accompanied by raucous cheers and fist waving.

'Oh Christ! That's all we need.'

'Trouble?'

'With a capital T, sarge. From left to right. Michael Frazer. Clive Batley. Gregory Martin, his father's the Councillor who wrote that letter about drunkenness. The big one is Chris Grogan; a bloody handful when he's pissed. The other one is Vernon Willis, he usually drinks in The Heifer in Mytholmroyd, I'm surprised he's mixed up with them.'

Local knowledge was a great tool. 'We'll just keep an eye on them for now,' I said and kept pace as the group ambled along Wharf Street towards the Town Hall. Then Martin spotted the girl. 'Just look at the fuckin' arse on that,' he shouted to more cheers and fist waving from his acolytes. 'How much do you charge darlin'. Come on.' The girl looked apprehensively over her shoulder the began to run. Martin and the others followed suit.

We legged it after them. 'I'll take Martin and Grogan. You grab one of the others.'

'For Christ's sake be careful. Just look at 'em, sarge,' Fleming said as Martin grabbed the girl's sleeve. The pedestrians in front scattered. 'They're like a pack of bloody hyenas.' The girl screamed. Swung her arm breaking his grip.

'Come on I'll give you a free ride on my foreskin, sod the others,' she screamed as Martin grabbed her sleeve again and tried to drag her into an alleyway.

I was a yard ahead of Fleming. He had his staff drawn and ready to use it. I barged between Martin and the girl breaking Martin's grip and pushed him away. Turned to the girl. Late teens, pretty and visibly shaking. 'Are you all right?' She nodded.

'What's your name?'

'Catherine Swift.'

'All right, Catherine, just wait there. I promise you'll be fine.'

Fleming, holding his staff in plain sight, was facing all five of them arranged in an arc in front. They were hyperventilating and uncertain what to do next. 'Caution them and tell them they're under arrest.'

'What offence, sarge?'

'Common law riot.'

He glanced at me. I nodded. Before he could speak Martin became agitated. 'Go bollocks. We've done nowt. Get 'em Chris.' He was obviously a leader of men.

The aforementioned Chris grinned as only a drunk can and raised his fist. I hit him with a double straight punch to the belly. He folded. The dirty bastard vomited on my shoes. Martin only needed one. He joined his acolyte on the deck both of them whinging. Fleming had his prisoner under control. The other two just stood there gawping like idiots. I pointed at them. 'Stand just where you are,' I said. 'If I have to come and find you this is what will happen.' I pointed to the two on the floor. 'Understand?' They both nodded.

The two special constables hurried up as a traffic car arrived, it's beacon reflecting in a dozen office windows. Both crewmen jumped out. 'Everything all right, sarge,' said the driver asked looking round. 'We had a report of a large punch-up,' he paused and stared at the ground. 'Is that Grogan?' he said pointing at the prostrate acolyte.

'It is.'

'What did you hit him with, a club?'

'Just a fist,' I said and smiled.

'If you say so.'

Keith Fleming laughed. 'It's true, just a fist.'

'You two,' I said to the Specials. 'Get these two unattached cuffed-up and walk them to the station. Arresting officer PC Fleming. Offence, common law riot. Oh, I suppose I'll be booking them in when I get there.'

'There's no-one else, sarge,' offered PC Fleming. As he put the cuffs on his prisoner.

'Fair enough.' I indicated Catherine Swift to the driver. 'This is Catherine. She's had a bad scare. Run her to the nick will you. And you,' the observer. 'Get Martin cuffed and walk him in. Can you manage to walk so far?'

'Everyone's a bloody joker these days,' at least he laughed. 'Yes, sergeant, that I can manage.'

Including washing the contents of Grogan's stomach from my shoes it took an hour to get everyone booked in. PC Fleming took a statement from an embarrassed nineteen year old Catherine Swift. I rang her parents and explained what had happened. Her father wasn't happy that we had taken a statement without him being there. I don't think she would have appreciated that.

Keith Fleming and I sat in the canteen keeping a cup of tea company whilst we made our pocket books up. An almighty din erupted from the public counter.

'I have the right to speak with my son,' someone shouted. 'I demand access.'

He was aged about fifty, five ten and wearing a good suit – at midnight? 'What seems to be the trouble?' I asked. PC Farrar the night radio operator breathed a sigh of relief.

'I want to see my son.'

'So I heard, And you are?'

'You know dammed well who I am,' he said.

'If I knew who you were I wouldn't be asking. So?'

He looked me uncertainly up and down. 'You must be new. I'm Councillor Martin. Now, can I see him?'

'In a word, counsellor, no. He's an adult and, he's drunk.'

His demeanour changed. The politician coming to the fore. He smiled as only politicians can. 'Sergeant,' he said. 'You know what it's like, you're young yourself. Work hard all week. Get paid on Thursday. Go out for a drink with a few friends and, how shall we say, overdo things a little.'

'He certainly overdid things. However, according to your son, counsellor, he is unemployed and, has been for some time.'

His eyes narrowed. 'Well, are you going to bail him?'

I glanced at the office clock. 'That will be for the magistrates to decide later this morning.'

'Surely that can't be necessary for a simple alcohol related offence? Can I ask what the charge will be?' He sounded apprehensive.

'Common law riot.' It was my turn to smile.

'WHAT! Don't you realise, sergeant, that we politicians and the police have to work together. Surely there is another less confrontational manner in which this little issue can be settled. And, remember that your remuneration comes from the people of Sowerby Bridge.

That was just plain silly. 'There is a small financial precept on the rates bill,' I said, 'but the vast amount of funding is from central government. And, with respect, if you're thinking of threatening me with loss of my job I would remind you the police are not the employees of any local authority. We make our oath of allegiance to the Sovereign, not a politician. We are Crown Agents. Now, If you have nothing further, counsellor, I have a statement to type.'

He gave me a filthy look and stormed out of the station. 'Is he always like that?' I asked PC Farrar.

'If he can't get his own way, Yes, sarge. But tell me, did you really only hit Grogan twice?'

I smiled and nodded. 'Yup.'

'Can you teach us?'

'I'll teach you karate, no problem. What I won't do is teach you punches and kicks in isolation. You could end up hurting yourself or causing serious unintended damage to someone. So, if you want to learn let me know.'

He looked quizzical. 'Can you demonstrate what you did?'

'Sure.' I had him stand in front of me. I demonstrated the stance, posture and the punch at full speed. Rewarded with a 'bloody hell. How do you punch so fast.'

'Practise,' I said and grinned.

Perhaps I shouldn't have but I called the Argus and left a message for Alistair MacDonald. It was a little bit cryptic but he seemed to like cryptic messages.

Thirteen

09.30. Wednesday. The prisoners were in the court cells. The Prosecutions' staff were running round in circles. Sergeant Peters, the prosecutions sergeant and I were in the Chief Super's office. He put the file back on his desk and read the report I'd typed regarding Counsellor Martin's visit before handing it to Sergeant Peters. His eyebrows lifted as he handed the report back. 'About par for the course, sir,' he said.

'Indeed. In view of who is sitting this morning I will take this case, sergeant. It's time I got some more practice. And put Sergeant Blake on the rota.' Another baptism of fire was to take my turn as prosecutor. That should be fun.

Sergeant Peters smiled. 'Yes, sir,' he said and left the office.

I was in the process of following when the Chief Super called me back. 'Well done. It was the right decision. You're a martial arts instructor?'

'Yes, sir.'

'Tell me about these punches you administered.'

'It's called a choku zuki – a straight punch.' I demonstrated in slow motion then at normal speed. Then the double I'd used on Grogan.

'And you used the same on Martin?'

'Just one, sir. Two would have been excessive. With Grogan I wanted to make sure he went down and stayed there.'

'I see. And Fleming?'

'Did very well, sir. He identified them. Based on that I made the decision to deal with Martin and Grogan myself and told him to grab one of the others. That was Fraser. Whilst I was making sure Catherine Swift was physically unhurt, he was facing them down.'

'Very well. Let me have a full confidential report as to what happened.'

The magistrates were in. The prisoners produced looking slightly dishevelled. There were surprised looks when Chief Superintendent Cartwright took the prosecutor's spot in court. Perhaps the Bench realised just how seriously we were taking this case. Then a man wearing the ubiquitous suit stood.

'Your worships, I am Dominic Grey of Blackstone Sharp. We have been appointed by Gregory Martin's father to act on his behalf …'

Gregory Martin was having nothing of it. 'Your Worships, my apologies for interrupting but I have already spoken with Mr Grey. My father can spend his money howsoever he likes. I want nothing to do with him.'

'Your Worships. Mr Gregory is a young man and requires professional advice, would it be possible to request a short adjournment for that purpose?'

The Chairman of the Bench, a fire-breathing retired army major, Draco Hambleton. 'Mr Grey you have already spoken in private with the defendant, Mr Martin. I assume he refused to have you represent him. He has just spoken in court reinforcing that view making his wishes clear. There will be no adjournment. Mr Clerk, if you please.'

The Clerk to the court stood and read out the charge. Mr Grey settled and took notes.

All pleaded not guilty. Whether that's because they all thought they were, or because pressure had been applied I don't know, but it was a trial.

Chief Superintendent Cartwright stood. 'Your Worships, with the exception of readings of the Riot Act which came into force in 1715, there can be no greater threat to the Queen's Peace and safety of the populace than riot. The Common Law offence of riot requires that three or more, with common purpose, use or threaten violence, disorder, or cause terror to the public sufficient for a person of reasonable firmness of mind to fear for their safety, and, resulting in a disturbance of the Peace .. Your Worships. At approximately 10.30pm of the evening of Thursday ...

I would now like to call my first witness. Catherine Swift ... '

From our point of view it was plain sailing. Sergeant Peters told me that Catherine Swift gave her evidence bravely, if nervously. Not surprising considering the circumstances. In fact, it was probably her nervousness that leant weight to her testimony. PC Fleming and myself had given evidence on numerous occasions, perhaps on this occasion the potential of serious harm to Catherine Swift notched it up several degrees.

In a trial where a defendant is not represented they may make a statement from the well of the court without being cross-examined. Give evidence, when they may be cross-examined, or stay silent. In this case Martin and Grogan stayed silent. Frazer, Batley and Willis made statements, all along the same lines: That they had gone out for a drink and come across Martin and Grogan. When those two got a bit noisy in The Wagon the landlord had turfed them all out. Once outside they became wrapped up in Martin's behaviour.

After thirty minutes the Magistrates found all the defendants guilty.

Batley and Willis were fined £20 each payable within twenty eight days. They were the ones who stood around gawping. Frazer received seven days in Armley. Martin, who incited Grogan to attack us, and Grogan who suffered, six months. That was a result. They got a speech from the Chairman of the Bench. Had a bit of a stately pile somewhere up the valley. Behaviour of this sort would not be tolerated. The court would take a dim view of any future occurrences. Woe betide anyone foolish enough to ignore his advice.

He complimented Catherine Swift for her courage in giving evidence in what must have been the most harrowing of circumstances. He would be writing to the chief constable about our behaviour in what he described as hazardous circumstances.

I'd spotted Alistair MacDonald whilst I was giving evidence. Afterwards, we were having a chat in the foyer when Inspector Marshall strolled up. I introduced him to MacDonald. 'He's a reporter with the Argus, sir. Been dogging my footsteps since the Wainwright case.'

'Since the explosion at Buy Smart, you mean. Never gave me a thing.'

The inspector smiled; he had other things to talk about. 'Sergeant, normally in circumstances like these I would say work a nine to five. However, in view of what's happened I want you to work six two as listed, just in case. Put the hours on your card.'

'Yes, sir,' I didn't need any slips, turned and shook hands with MacDonald. 'It's good to see you again. I'll see you sometime.'

Lucy was a bit miffed at my having to return to work but there was nothing I could do about it. Plus I put any overtime on my time-off card and not for payment. They can't tax time off. That extra time-off might be handy in a few weeks.

We made the Northern News: *Five men were convicted of the ancient offence of Common Law Riot at Halifax West Riding Magistrates Court today. Gregory Martin and Christopher Grogan were each sentenced to six months imprisonment. Michael Fraser to seven days imprisonment. Clive Batley and Vernon Willis each fined £20. Councillor Martin, father of Gregory Martin and leader of the Conservative Group on the Calder Valley Council was unavailable for comment.*

Perhaps it was the extra four officers shipped in by the Chief Superintendent, but it rained all evening. Maybe even that it was plastered across the front pages of the Courier and the Argus but the town was flat that night. There was no trouble at all. How long that state of affairs would last was anyone's guess.

Fourteen

Liz Vernon read the letter for the tenth time and wondered. Looking at the clock, the feeling of tension in her stomach heightened and her heart skipped a beat as she heard the crunch of the gravel.

Giuseppe 'Gus' Massimiliano dismounted, swung his 750V Moto Guzzi Ambassador onto its stand and pocketed the key. Lifted the panniers and looked at the house for the first time. Took a deep breath exhaling slowly. Two steps, pressed the bellpush and stepped back, waiting.

The door opened slowly. After all these years she was standing there, face wreathed in smiles and just as beautiful as he remembered.

That smile took her back a quarter of a century. All tension and tiredness drained from her body. Her memories flooded back. An extramarital affair; refreshed every twelve months for almost ten years. Her husband less than a mile away. But Gus was roman catholic and trapped in a loveless marriage. Nevertheless, he knew how to pleasure a woman. And if she were honest she was pleased when she found out she was pregnant; a lasting reminder that kept her going until the next years TT races. A secret she dared not divulge; to anyone.

That first letter she received from Gus, postmarked Napoli, turned her brain inside out. And now he was here. In the flesh. She smiled at the thought.

Panniers on the floor, he turned and locked the door. 'How is the mother of my daughter?' he smiled as he clasped his hands behind her back.

She reached up, hands behind his head pulling him forwards into her waiting lips. 'Better now,' she whispered. 'And, you're a grandfather.' His eyes bulged. 'Claire is three and the twins are due in a few weeks.'

They parted. 'Twins?' The look on his face said it all.

She smiled. 'Twins.' She took him by the hand. 'I'll show you to your room.'

PROPPED ON HIS ELBOW he looked down and smiled. If only things had been different. Caterina was very religious when they met. When Sofia was born she decided that sex was for procreation and that sex for pleasure was a sin. Probably because Caterina's father was a priest, and rumoured to have fathered several. That reminded him of the Italian proverb:

Putting your faith in a priest is like trying to catch the wind in a net.

Sofia was a sickly child and died from pneumonia when she was three. That had ripped his heart out. The congregation trotted forth the usual platitudes: *She is safe in the arms of Jesus. She has gone to a better place. It was meant to be,* they all said, for all the good that did. *Stavano dicendo stronzate.* Caterina decided there would be no more children.

He had been to the Isle of Mann for the TT races every year. Bill Vernon was a genius. But every night, racing the next day or not, he was drinking, leaving Liz on her own to look after their son, Gerald. He met them all and became friends. A friendship that was refreshed every year. It was his second visit to the TT, Bill, as usual was carousing with his friends. Gus was chatting to Liz and his story came out; she invited him to their room where they had sex. Liz welcomed him every night, It became a beautiful interlude for eight, or was it ten years. However, even when Liz missed the

TT the following year because she was nursing Lucy he assumed she was Bill's. It was when Lucy was seven and Gerald nine they decided it was too dangerous to carry on. They decided to end their affair. Rather than risk any problems, should there be a random meeting, he travelled to the far side of the island, to Peel. After a couple of years he ceased to attend altogether.

But, it was not until that day when Lucy and Brian had ended up in the police station on Capri, because of the altercation involving Angela D'Agostino and Antonio Bruni. The day when he had shown them the photograph taken of him with the family the year Bill had won the Senior TT race, and Lucy's divulging the information regarding Bill's death that the memories surged into his mind. Caterina's death from a stroke three days before changed everything. He was free. But how would Liz feel? Was the passion they shared have lasted. Now, he knew the answer.

'A penny for your thoughts?'

'When did you realise that Lucy was mine?'

'When I was late. Rumours were circulating that we were spending too much time together. Bill and I had a blazing row. Eventually I managed to smooth things over. We hadn't had sex for a couple of months and I lied about my dates. Things calmed and we resumed marital sex; although it was more perfunctory than romantic. When it became obvious he couldn't prove anything he seemed to just let things go. Lucy's birth sent him over the moon. All suspicion died. That was the year I missed the TT ... When did you realise?'

'Only after Lucy and Brian left the island. I couldn't get her out of my head. Especially her grasp of Italian. I had her date of birth from the file and dug out the dates of the TT's for that year. It fitted. Almost exactly forty weeks. But I couldn't do or say anything.'

She smiled and stroked his face. 'When do you have to go back?'

'I have to leave Sunday morning.'

She put her hand over his mouth. 'Shh. Lay on your back. We've some catching up to do.'

She felt him enter, the ripples of pleasure signalling what was to come. He was a big man and filled her completely. It was as if time had stood still. Placing his hands on her breasts, with eyes closed she began to raise and lower ...

THEY WELCOMED SATURDAY in the same manner they said goodnight to Friday.

Gus surveyed the breakfast table and the full English. 'I could get used to this,' he said, watching the egg yolk spill across the bacon.

She couldn't help smiling. What must be going through his mind? After the realisation, the journey north and the past 10 hours. Her hand on his, she smiled when he looked at her. 'Gus, not that I'm complaining, far from it, but you haven't come all this way just to share my bed, have you? What are you hoping for?'

His heart began to sink. 'No, Liz. I wanted to know if the love we shared all those years ago had lasted. I think it has. It can't happen for a while but I was hoping that you might ...'

'That I would marry you?'

He nodded. 'Would you?'

'I would,' she noticed the look in his eyes. 'But, there are so many questions to be answered before I could make a final decision. If I had no ties it would be a different matter.'

He sighed. 'I understand. It was foolish of me to think it would be simple.'

'Gus, you are welcome to my bed, anytime. I promise you there is no-one else, now, or likely to be in the future. Come on let's get breakfast finished and the rest of the day is ours.'

Their conversation stopped as the front door opened. A little voice shouted. 'Grandma, where are you?'

Liz smiled to herself. 'Claire, there's a present for you in the dining room.'

'Thank you, Grandma.'

Liz turned to Gus and smiled. 'Unexpected but welcome. You're about to meet your daughter and granddaughter. Wait here. I won't be long.'

Liz beamed at Lucy, currently supported by Brian's left arm. 'I didn't expect to see you before the birth; it's only ten days.'

'Can we sit?' Lucy indicated the dining room.

'Of course ... Steady, Claire,' Liz said as her granddaughter ran into the hallway carrying a large box.

'What is it?'

'It's a Duplo, you can build things with it, like Lego but bigger.'

'Will you open it for me, please.'

Liz reached forward. 'Claire, there's someone in the kitchen who will help you. Let mummy sit down.'

'Ok, grandma,' Claire headed for the kitchen.

'THAT'S BETTER,' SIGHED Lucy as she sat. 'What's going on, mum?'

'What do you mean, dear?'

'There's a stranger in the kitchen who you are happy will help Claire. A new Moto Guzzi 750 on Italian plates outside, and from the rain it's been there all night.

You've never mentioned anyone from Italy, and the only one that Brian or I could think of was that Carabinieri sergeant, Massimiliano, we met during our honeymoon on Capri, who just happened to carry a photograph of our family in his wallet. And you're trying hard not to laugh. So...?'

CLAIRE RAN INTO THE kitchen and stopped when she saw Gus drying the breakfast pots. 'Hello, I'm Claire. Are you a friend of Grandma's?'

He gazed at her taking in every inch. The blonde hair just like Liz. The blue eyes and other facial similarities. The summer dress, white ankle socks and brown shoes. A bundle of energy; as different from Sophia as it was possible to be. 'Yes, I am.'

She held her present out. 'Will you help me to get this wrapper off?'

'There.' Gus put the wrapper in the bin and passed the box to Claire who smiled.

'Will you play with me?'

'I'd be delighted. We can build something here, behind the table.'

'GERALD AND I KNEW ALL about the rows during TT week. He always woke us up. And he hit you.'

'Once or twice.'

'A day. And he stunk of cheap perfume. Other women?'

'I suspect so. It was safer not to say anything ... No, don't look at me like that. Everything was in his name. I was totally dependent on him. If I'd walked out we would have been destitute. However, things did get better.

Lucy nodded and squeezed Brian's hand. 'Sorry, mum. I shouldn't have gone on about it. But what you're trying to tell me is you and Gus had an affair during TT week, and I'm the fruit of that liaison?

'We renewed the affair every year for almost ten years.'

'What? And you never let on, even to Gus?'

'How could I? Bill would have thrown us all out. Gus was trapped in a loveless marriage and his wife was a staunch roman catholic and would never have agreed to a divorce. He didn't know about Bill's death until you met on Capri, and his wife died only recently.'

'From your smile and Gus's presence, the spark is still there.'

'You have no idea. When I received that first letter from Gus, the Italian postage stamp and Naples postmark I couldn't have dreamt what was inside. I've read the print off those letters. When I heard the doorbell and saw him standing there last night it was if it was yesterday.'

'And your dates are correct?'

'They are. Gus checked as well, comparing your date of birth from the statement you made and an old TT calendar.'

'And that's why he wrote?'

'Yup.'

'Have you thought about the future?'

'Yes, but I'll tell Gus first.'

'All the years that Dad, or should I say Bill, caused problems. Deep down do you think he knew?'

'Possibly, but that's an unanswerable conundrum. Now, shall we go and have a chat with your father?'

GUS WAS IN HIS SEVENTH heaven.

'You are silly, you have to overlap the bricks so they don't fall over. I'll show you, watch me.' With great care Claire built her wall, Gus disturbed by the sound of footsteps in the hallway.

'I've got to stand up now, Claire but carry on building.'

Liz, Lucy and Brian were watching from the doorway. 'Liz, thank you for giving me such a beautiful daughter and you Lucy, for a beautiful granddaughter. You are like three sisters, could I have a photograph of the three of you?'

'Of course you can,' said Liz.

'Do you want to sit, |Lucy? When are the twins due?'

'Ten days.'

'First, I think a hug for my new father.'

'After Sophia's death I never thought I would have this opportunity,' he said as he enveloped Lucy in his arms.'

'Mummy? Shouldn't you be doing that with daddy?' A small voice piped up.

They all laughed and looked towards Claire who was peering over the table.

'You like Granddad Joe, don't you?' said Lucy.

Claire nodded vigorously.

'How would you like another one?'

'Another Grandad Joe?' She said and frowned.

'No,' Lucy smiled and put her hand on Gus's chest. 'This one is called Giuseppe, or Gus.'

Claire ran round the table, stopped and looked up. 'Are you really,' she paused looking up at her mother, questioning.

Lucy smiled. 'Go on, Claire. You know the words.'

Claire turned to Giuseppe. 'Are you really ... mio nonno?'

Gus, unreal feelings lancing through his brain, smiled at his granddaughter, with her blonde hair the spitting image of her mother, and crouched. 'Meraviglioso. Wonderful. Si Principessa, I really am.'

Claire's face creased in thought. 'Does that make you my mummy's daddy?'

'Yes, it does.'

Claire thought for a moment and beamed at him. 'Okay. Will you read me a story?'

The smile was in danger of becoming a fixture. 'Principessa, I will read you hundreds.'

'I think I like Giuseppe better than Gus, nonno. I'm going to call you nonno Giuseppe, like Pinocchio's daddy.'

This was going to be magic. Tears rolled down his cheeks. 'No, Princess, his name was Geppetto.'

Claire paused and frowned. 'Was it?' then she smiled. 'Oh yes ... why are you crying?'

He crouched. 'Tears of happiness, Princess, I am happier now than I have ever been.'

She threw her arms round his neck. 'I love you, nonno Guiseppe.'

'I love you too, Claire.'

She leant back and looked him in the eye. 'Nonno? Will you read me a story, now?'

'Of course, Princess,' he said and stood. Claire perched on his right arm. 'Which one would you like?'

'Pinocchio!' she shouted in his ear.

'Pinocchio it is.'

Liz stepped across and put her hand on Gus's shoulder. 'The answer is, yes.'

Fifteen

The tone was measured and controlled, but for how long. 'You've been very quiet for the last week. What have you got for me?'

Mr Collins hadn't been dreading the call but information concerning this witness was as scarce as an honest politician, and Harry had a short fuse at the best of times, and he knew a threat when he heard one.

'Harry, there's nothing, honest. I've checked with my contacts. The local lot are just plods, couldn't find their own pricks with a map. I've called in favours from the Press, but if I put too much pressure on the coppers it'll draw attention. They'll start to ask why.'

'What about this copper you were talking about a few months back. To do with Venners. Lancaster wasn't it?'

'You mean Lassiter. Cold feet. Got himself into trouble with the new sergeant . Don't worry he'll keep his trap shut.'

'He'd bloody better. Give his chain a good yank. Remind him he doesn't want me as an enemy. Now, this new sergeant, tell me'

'Never seen him. His name's Blake, keen, got some sort of medal ribbon. involved in that big case a couple of years ago. Multiple bodies and a bent senior police officer. He's handy, him and another copper locked five up for riot, including Chris Grogan, got him six months.'

'I thought Grogan was hard.'

'He was pissed.

'Is he married?'

'The sergeant? Yep, with a young daughter. First copper on the scene, on his way to work ...'

'... It's got to be him. There's fuck all else,' interrupted Field.

'Harry, it can't be, there was zilch. Only the guy in the Morris 1000 and I took care of him. It could be there is no witness and the police are trying it on.'

The thinly veiled control slipped. 'That's fucking bollocks and you know it. Your neck's on the line as well as mine.' He paused and a smile entered the conversation. 'He's got a wife and a daughter you said? That's leverage, now get it bloody sorted, or I will.'

ONE LAST KISS. LIZ waved Gus on his way. All being well he would return in five weeks.

The answers to the questions: If Liz were pregnant he would want the name on the birth certificate to be Massimiliano. The baby, if there was one, being born in England.

They would split their time between Naples and Boston Spa. Neil Greeley, already deputising for Liz would be brought further into the managerial team.

They could be married in a civil ceremony in England, living apart until he drew his pension in two years. It would be a strain but worth it.

He had a legacy from his father equivalent to £100,000, hence the Moto Guzzi, and prize money thanks to the Italian Lottery of 400 million lira; almost £250,000.

Liz would give Gus a roving commission, checking on her thirty seven franchises.

I HAD MY FIRST TASTE of prosecuting the following Wednesday, Sergeant Peters called the day before court to deliver the prosecution files. I took them home to read. All guilty pleas. Sergeant Peters stayed for the first half dozen and then left me to it. It was a quiet baptism.

Sixteen

PC Neil Farrer, the late turn radio operator-cum-office clerk called across. 'How's your wife, sarge? Two weeks isn't it?'

I laughed and wandered into the front office. 'It is, and she's fed up,'

'My wife was fed up with our last. She's insisted that two is enough.'

'It would be for me, but she's happy to have more.' I patted my stripes., 'These will help financially.'

'Yes, I suppose they will .. This karate class at St Martin's Church Hall, you've spoken to the Inspector about, can anybody join?'

I grinned at the well-padded office clerk. 'Yup, you fancy it?'

There was an answering grimace. 'I don't know so much, but my kids might.'

'As long as they're over ten.'

'Andrew's fifteen and Kath's twelve.'

'That's ok. When I can't make it, my step-father, Joe will step in. Clive, my little brother and his girlfriend will probably be there.'

'When's it start?'

'A week on Thursday. 7pm. 2/6d. (Two shillings and sixpence – 12.5p now) All the funds go to the church.'

He looked puzzled. 'I thought you ...?'

'I am, but we're renting their hall. No doubt there will be those who disagree on principle about martial arts being practised on church premises. So ...'

He nodded and picked up his mug of tea as the phone rang.

'Finish your tea, I'll take this.' I could hear the row as I lifted the phone. 'Sergeant Blake, Sowerby ...' I snapped my fingers and pointed to his message pad and began to write. 'When was this . . There'll be someone with you very shortly.' I handed him the phone. 'Ring CID then Force Control. Till snatch at Speedy Fuel in West Street. They've got one, the other made off in an A reg cream Vauxhall VX 4/90 with dark side-stripe. Firearm seen.' I reached for the mike. 'PC Wilson. Sergeant Blake. Till snatch at Speedy Fuel. One male detained. Get round there and report back. Report of firearm seen. Let me know if they have it, or if it's with the second man ... Vehicle made off towards Wharfe Street. An A reg, cream coloured Vauxhall VX 4/90 with dark side-stripe. If seen report direction of travel. No heroics.'

'Speedy Fuel, Brian?'

'Yes, Colin,' DS Greatorix and DC Turner dashed out of the door.

'A mad sixty seconds, Neil.'

'Yup.'

'PW Weatherly, over.'

'Go ahead, over.'

He could hear PC Napier's voice in the back ground. 'Just pass the bloody message; it's urgent.'

'PW Weatherly, pass your message.'

'Never mind. Napier! A similar car going like the clappers has turned right into Wakefield Road. Cut across the traffic and took a hit to the rear nearside. Might have a flat ...Just a sec.' There was a screech and raised voices. 'That was the Halifax car. He's after the Vauxhall. I'll sort this bump out.'

'All received.'

Neil Farrer was back in touch with Force Control ' ... You got that? Right that one's yours ... No, we still don't know if there was a firearm or where it is .. I'll call and let you know ... cheers.'

'DS Greatorix, over.'

'Go ahead, Colin.'

'We've got the firearm. It's a big bugger. First World War Webley revolver 455 calibre, fully loaded. Prisoner's new to me. Ended up on the deck with a sixteen stone HGV driver sat on his chest. Poor sod could hardly breathe.'

'Oh dear, how sad. Wheel him in, I'll be waiting. ... Sergeant Blake. For information. One in custody and we have one firearm.' I put the mike down. 'Neil, call Force Control. Tell them we have the revolver. Or at least *a* revolver. I'll be in the cells.'

'PC Napier, need a recovery for an A40 Farina from this bump. Front end stove in. Get 'em to expedite, the Wakefield Road junction is half blocked.'

Seventeen

'Who's the arresting officer?' I said as our new guest was brought into the cell area; wrists cuffed behind.

'I am, sergeant,' said PC Lassiter.

'Has he been searched?'

'Only cursorily.'

I looked the prisoner in the eye. 'We're going to take the cuffs off. You will put both hands flat on the desk, shoulder width apart whilst we carry out a search. Is that clear?'

'Fuck off.'

I put my pen on the desk and walked round to the prisoner's side. 'Don't do anything stupid.'

His look and tone were scathing. 'Think I'm scared of you?'

'I don't care whether you are or not. Don't do anything stupid.' I nodded to PC Lassiter who removed the cuffs.

It was the deep in-breath that let him down. Before anyone else could react he swung round with his right fist clenched, aiming for my head. I was faster, blocked the forearm and applied a chokehold. He froze. 'I said, don't do anything stupid. You will find it impossible to talk. Do not try and move or I won't be nice.' I nodded to PC Lassiter, who since our run-in had been as good as gold. 'Take his jacket off and empty the pockets.'

DC Nigel Pagett pushed through the door, took one look and smiled. 'What?'

'Later,' I said. 'Jean's pockets, waistband, belt off. Then laces and a pat down.'

'Driving Licence, sergeant,' Lassiter held it up. 'I'll go check it with M.O.' He left the cell area.

Apart from a dirty handkerchief there was nothing to identify our visitor. 'Right. This time take notice. And if you're thinking of having another go when I'm not here, this lot are quick learners. When I let go put both hands on the counter.' He did. I took a Detention Sheet from the drawer. 'Name?'

'It's in the driving licence.'

'I dare say there is a name in the driving licence. Just tell me.'

He smiled exposing us to a stream of bad breath. 'Mickey Mouse.'

'When were you born?'

'1st January 1905.'

'And your address?'

'Disney World.'

He was five six, unruly dark hair, brown eyes, dirty broken finger nails and numerous tattoos. Wearing worn blue jeans, green work shirt, brown socks and black boots.

Mickey Mouse was placed in a cell. The driving licence, issued in the name of Patrick O'Brien, had been reported as stolen in Manchester.

Fingerprints were summoned to try and obtain Mickey Mouse's fingerprints from the counter.

Officer in the case: Detective Sergeant Greatorix.

MY OFFICE DOOR CLOSED. PC Napier and PW Weatherly standing in front of my desk. 'What happened? Why didn't you pass the message?'

PC Napier made as if to speak. I held my hand up. 'Weatherly? Don't you want to be a police officer?'

'Yes, sergeant. But it didn't seem right. We didn't know for certain.'

'Didn't they teach about suspicion at Bruche? Armed robbery at a filling station. One man in custody. One firearm recovered. A vehicle made off from the scene with one male occupant. A similar vehicle turned right at high speed into Wakefield Road causing an RTA. That should be enough to make anyone suspicious.'

Before she could answer a grinning Neil Farrar tapped and stuck his head round the door. 'They've got him, sarge, taking him to Brighouse.'

'Great. Where?'

'He ran out of road at Lister Bridge.'

'Injuries?

'One slight. Vehicle probable write off. I've turned a garage out and DS Greatorix is going to Brighouse.'

'Arresting officer?'

'Will Kendrick.'

'Ok Thanks.'

The door closed. 'You probably heard the screech when I was talking, sarge,' said Napier. 'That was Kendrick.'

I nodded and looked at Weatherly. Janet Weatherly had joined the previous week. A nineteen year old from, of all places, Westleigh. Her parents were friends with Jenny Sendrove, a DC from the Wainwright case and the reason she wanted to join the police.

'Weatherly, If you and Napier hadn't been there the incident wouldn't have been brought to a conclusion so quickly. Even if he's not the second male involved in the robbery, he has questions to answer. The chances are that he is the one ... Well done,' I said to Napier and flicked my head towards the door.'

'Thanks sarge,' he said and left.

'Not you.' Weatherly paled. 'You've only been out of Bruche for a week. Nevertheless you're expected to behave in a professional manner. This was a very serious crime involving a loaded firearm. You can't afford not to take action,' I held my hand out. Your pocket book.'

'Am I in trouble?' she passed it to me.

'I'll put this down to inexperience. If you want to have your appointment confirmed, you'll have to improve.' I endorsed the pocket book: *Guidance administered.*, and handed it back. 'You need to be more proactive; I want to see more in your pocket book. There's no need to go mad, stop a few vehicles, especially older ones and get round the local motor cyclists. Get some documents produced, parking offences. Get something moving. Show the inspector and the chief super that you're alive.'

Eighteen

Peter Cartwright kept me informed regarding any progress. Harry Field was stalling, or so it was believed. We, the Met and Blackpool were digging. Our telephone conversations were short. We paid them a social visit the following week under strict instructions: No talking shop. Lucy was less than one week away from her due date. The twins were oblivious; they hadn't seen a calendar. Fortunately, Peter's wife was a sister in midwifery at the Royal Halifax Infirmary (RHI). So, if anything happened ...

Lucy's waters broke in the early hours two days later. By arrangement Lucy was carted off to the RHI by ambulance. I let the nick know before ferrying a very sleepy Claire across to Huddersfield. Thence to RHI arriving just in time. Lucy gave birth to Douglas Joseph Dante, 5lbs 8ozs, at 2.45pm. Arthur Michele, 5lbs 2ozs, six minutes later. They were identical. We'd discussed names a lot. Complicated by my biological father, Douglas. In the end Lucy decided: Dante and Michele being Gus's middle names and Arthur being Joe's.

I thought they might have shooed me out of the delivery room but I was lucky. I stayed and we held hands during the entire procedure, Lucy making valiant attempts to crush mine. It helped us both feel better, I thought. Stitches inserted she was handed both boys whilst I took a photo, despite her saying she felt like a wreck. Her smile cancelled any thought of that. Wrist bands attached whilst the boys were in their cribs, names clearly displayed. We didn't want to get that wrong.

I was substituted by the two grandmas plus a fleeting visit by Joe. I slipped Claire in to see Lucy and her new baby brothers. She was miffed that she couldn't jump on the bed as she did at home. Her assessment? 'They're boring, not doing anything.'

Jen arrived so I left Claire with her and bought Lucy some flowers from the kiosk, then home for a shave, a bite to eat, call work and Peter Cartwright. I'd set the alarm whilst I had a nap. I slept through and woke up as everyone returned from the hospital. Evening visits were husbands only.

I'd never seen as many flowers. Over the next two days the visitors had to be curtailed. The Spartans arrived en masse. Clive, sixteen next, with Caroline his girlfriend from school and strangely enough now member of Joe's karate school, plus half the Wainwright team including Superintendent Valentine, in uniform. Three sisters, two of them pregnant. Norman, Gerald, Marianne and Olivia. It had been quieter in the nick following the riot.

Lucy was allowed home after five days. The twins had to stay a little longer. How long? Open-ended. I went back to work two days later, my first task being a report to Personnel notifying the increase in family.

Nineteen

Mum was with Lucy and our growing brood. I was in the St Martin's Church Hall with Joe, Clive and Caroline. All in our Gi's.

'Any idea how many?' said Joe.

'At least half a dozen. Beyond that I couldn't say.'

'Individual tuition?' said Caroline.

'Could be,' I said and laughed as the door opened and a group of a dozen teenagers entered, mostly boys each carrying sports bags.

'Is this where we learn Karate?' said the leading boy as Niel Farrer entered followed by a girl and boy.

'See you in about an hour,' he said.

'Not stopping, Neil?'

'Dad exercise? You must be joking,' said the girl.

'I did wonder,' I said and laughed. 'You must be Kath and Andrew.' They nodded. 'I'll see you at work, Neil.'

'Ok. Back in an hour,' He said, laughed and left.

I turned to the others, 'To answer your question, yes, it is. Are there any more coming?'

'They said they were,' replied the boy as the door opened and another eight boys entered followed by another who stood out. He was black.

'All right, everybody,' the room quietened. 'Because this is the first session there will be no charge. From next week it will be 2/6d. All the monies will go to the church for use of the room ... Caroline, will you take the girls and show them where to get changed, please.

Clive? And if you're all observant you will have noticed we are all in bare feet.'

'Good turn out,' said Joe as they left, chattering ten to the dozen.

'For now. We'll see what time does,'

Always a stickler for doing things right, Joe began a register.

Most were wearing football or gym gear, with three wearing Judoki. Before I could say anything else two men aged in their thirties entered. I recognised them from their photos; two PCs transferred from Todmorden under a cloud. Thomas Williamson and Bruce Knight.

Williamson spotted the black lad, Cameron Douglas, and made a beeline for him. 'You can get out for a start,' he said jabbing his right forefinger.

In two paces I was between them. 'I run this class, not you. What's your problem?'

'He's trouble. The entire family are. He's going.'

'That's my decision, not yours. Cameron, have you ever been in trouble with the police?'

'No, my brothers have, I haven't.'

:It'll come,' said Williamson. 'Give it time.'

'How do you know this, anyway?'

'He's a copper.'

'Why you cheeky young sod,' said Williamson stepping forward into my raised my left hand. 'Take your hand off me.'

'You walked into my hand. Back off. Now.' He stepped back.

'If you're a policeman you'll have a warrant card. Let me see,' I held my hand out. Knight produced his and I nodded. 'Force Standing Orders are quite clear. You will carry it at all times and produce it on demand. So?'

With a bad grace Williamson produced his warrant card.

'Williamson, just transferred from Todmorden. I've one of these but mine is bigger. Now, Cameron is staying but you're not. Please leave. Clive, escort this gentleman to the door.'

'Come on, Bruce, I need a pint,' he said as he turned towards the door.

'You can go. I'm staying if that's all right.'

'It is.'

'Suit yourself,' Williamson stormed out of the door.

'Go with Clive,' I said. 'He'll show you where to get changed.

The door closed behind Bruce Knight I turned to see that all the kids had clustered round Joe.

'If it's going to cause trouble I can leave.'

'Cameron, the only trouble was caused by my colleague. You came here to learn karate. I can't make you stay but you're here. Stay for the session and then make your own mind up.'

He nodded and smiled. 'OK.'

Bruce Knight returned in football gear.

'Right, a bit of exercise to begin, get those muscles warm. Clive?'

He frowned then laughed. 'Thanks! It's duck walking.'

'Ladies behind Clive, the rest of you join in. If you fall over, laugh, get up and continue. Everybody does one lap. Crouch as low as you can.'

It always works. Breaks down inhibitions and loosens the atmosphere. Then burpees, press-ups, squats and sit ups followed by stretch and rotations.

One boy, Thomas, was rubbing his stomach. 'And I thought Anderson was a sadist.'

I smiled at him. 'You're leaving?'

'No way. I just didn't expect that.'

'You can always do it at home. Getting fit takes time. The fitter you are the more you will get out of it.'

He grimaced. 'I'll have to.'

'Ok, form lines. Ladies at the front. Leave a yard between the rows and either side ... A few rules. I know this is a church hall but it is also our training room. We refer to this as a Dojo, a translation from the Japanese – place of the way – a journey. The first step on your journey into karate. We're not going to get into philosophy, but we do use Japanese. All commands and counting will be in Japanese. All punches, kicks and blocks are named in Japanese.

Respect and courtesy. Boxers touch gloves. In karate we bow, but, you never take your eyes off your opponent. When we enter and leave the Dojo we bow as a sign of respect ...

... Before we begin, a short demo. Clive, A front kick, a Mae Geri. Yoi!'

The demo was met with gasps.

'Have you ever used karate as a policeman?'

'Yes, Cameron, many times.'

Kath laughed and joined in. 'He had to go to Buckingham Palace where The Queen gave him the George Cross.'

I had to laugh. 'Wait 'til I see your Dad.'

'Can you tell us about it?'

I took a deep breath and sighed. 'I took a firearm off somebody who was going to kill me.'

'Wasn't that dangerous?'

'It was. but not as dangerous as being shot.'

'You couldn't expect to keep it bottled up for ever, Brian,' said Joe with his hand on my shoulder. He turned to the group. 'There were four of them, Brian, my daughter Anne, Lucy, that was the night Brian proposed to her and now his wife, and Lucy's mother.'

'And that is as much as I can say. The rest is covered by the Official Secrets Act. And, you're wasting your own time. Come on, line up.'

The rest was a breeze. Enthusiasm doesn't enter in to it. The odd parent arrived with five minutes to go. 'Right, remember your square yard and practise what you can. See you next week. If I have to work then Joe or Clive will be in charge. And don't forget to ...?'

There were twenty replies. 'Bow to the Dojo. And bring 2/6d.' They walked out laughing.

'That went down well,' said Clive. I couldn't disagree.

'Numbers will begin to drop off slightly after a month if it follows the pattern,' said Joe. 'It will find its own level. But it's a good start.'

'I expect so. Who's coming for a coffee?'

'And to see the twins,' laughed Caroline.

Twenty

A fortnight had passed since the murders and from what I could glean we were no further forward. Yes, there had been many pieces of information concerning dark coloured cars and car occupants in dark clothing. But nothing that lead anywhere. Neither Lancs County or Blackpool Borough made any progress with the phone call made by DC Roberts. What no-one could have known was that the phone call was made from the office of The Golden Cascade, a local amusement arcade and Field's latest provincial acquisition, in his deceased wife's maiden name. Still, there were enough detectives throughout Lancashire, Yorkshire and the Met working on this and sooner or later there would be something. When, was anybody's guess. At least there could be no bleating that we should hand it over in entirety to the Met.

AS FOR ME, I WAS DOING ok. The hardest thing I had to do was make a decision. Getting out of bed in January is exactly the same manoeuvre as it is in June, it's only the temperature that's different. So what's the problem? If you make a mistake and the world doesn't stop turning, what's the problem? I remembered the advice that Calvin Yates, my inspector at Westleigh gave me. *If those of a higher rank disagree they will tell you. Bear it in mind for future reference. The worst thing you can do is nothing, especially when you should be doing something.*

Twenty-One

St Martin's second session. How many would turn up?

The first group had been singing the praises. We had enough for a second group.

'You take the first lot, Brian. Myself, Clive and Caroline will look after the others.'

'Ok. I'll borrow Caroline for five minutes, if you don't mind ... They're all here apart from Cameron. Will you take the money and complete the register.'

'Sure.'

Cameron burst into the room. 'Sorry I'm late.'

'Glad you're here.' I said and motioned them to gather round. 'I've split the class. Give your money to Caroline then get changed. Put your clothes in your bag and bring it back here. Off you go.' They trooped out.

It was noisy. 'CAN I HAVE YOUR ATTENTION, PLEASE?' The chatter stopped. 'Thank you. I will be taking the group that was here last week; at the far end of the room. The rest of you are under the supervision of Joe and Clive, with help from Caroline.'

Duck walking under way with the usual tumbles and laughter, one of the new group, a tall well-built lad about eighteen walked across. 'I came to learn karate, not that, ' he indicated the duck walkers with his head. 'That's for bloody kids. Wendy,' he said raising his voice, 'come on we're going. I'm not stopping here for this crap.'

Wendy, a tall slim attractive girl, aged about sixteen, stood. 'I told you Gavin, you're too fond of telling me what I can and can't do. I dumped you last week, now leave me alone.'

'I decide when we split, not you. Come on.'

I stepped in front and faced him. 'The first thing you need to learn karate is self-discipline, and that includes doing the warm-up like everyone else, part of which is duck-walking. If you're not going to participate, leave quietly, now. Wendy wants to stay. Leave, or I will eject you.'

'Think I'm frightened of you?'

'You should be,' Bruce Knight appeared at my shoulder. 'Gavin Earnshaw,' he said with an amused smile, 'he isn't wearing that black belt for show. Not learned your lesson yet? It's time you grew up and realised the world doesn't revolve around you and your father. Do yourself a favour and leave. Don't cause any trouble.' Earnshaw stormed out.

'Old friend?'

'Unfortunately.

I glanced at Joe and nodded. 'Does anyone else have any problems,' he said .'Because if you have, now is the time to speak.'

There was a loud chorus of No.

'Good. Shall we continue?'

I returned to my group. 'All right, back to waddling. And Wendy, see me before you leave.'

'How was that?' I said as they stood.

'You're still a sadist,' Said Thomas.

I grinned .'Better?'

He grimaced. 'A bit.'

'Good. Forget what they're doing behind!' I said, echoed by Joe. 'A reprise on the straight punch, no step, just the punch. Make sure you can see ... Ok. Right fist clenched. Between belt and ribs. Left hand extended, elbow bent. The object is to deliver the punch *through* the target. In this case through the stomach to the solar plexus. The power of the punch coming from the snap. ... see ... Cameron can I borrow you a moment?' He stepped forward looking worried. 'Don't worry I'm not going to hit you. If I deliver the punch straight it lands there.' I put my fist just below his diaphragm. 'If the fist too high,' I put my fist level with my ribs, 'but I'm aiming for the same spot this is what happens . ... The wrist rotates but bends downwards; the force traveling through the wrist joint and not through the forearm, risking an injury.' I dropped my fist below the hip bone. 'This happens if I have my fist down here. The shoulder rotates and it turns into an uppercut. Everybody got that?. ... Ok, thanks Cameron. ... Right, ten punches, five either side: counting in Japanese. So when you deliver the first punch pull your left fist into position. In slow time ... Yoi .. Hajime, ichi „ni . san . hold it . Carol, Dave . your hands cross. As the punch is delivered by the right fist the left is drawn back for the next punch and so on, ok?'

'Yes, sensei,' they said together and grinned, I reciprocated. 'Yoi. Hajime , ichi .ni ... ...

'That was good. Technique, technique, technique. Get it right and the rest will follow. In your own time. Don't forget to count.

'Excellent. Now, Kumite. Literally, grappling hands. Practice against an opponent.' There were a few worried looks. ;No-one is going to get hit. Caroline?

With Caroline facing me I told them. 'Caroline has been practising for almost two years and gets private tuition from Clive. What we're going to demonstrate is more advanced than you will do, but it is what can be achieved, with practise. I'm going to deliver a right punch. Note how the block is delivered. Watch her feet as well. I looked at Caroline. 'Yoi.'

She nodded.

I delivered the punch at half speed. Caroline stepped forward but rotated bringing her right arm across knocking my arm out of the way, kept rotating driving her left elbow into my abdomen just below the sternum. Then completed the rotation driving her fist towards my jaw, pulling the punch at the last second.

'That was a soto uke, an empi uki, and choku tsuki. You've all got that?' I said and grinned.

'Every single word, sensei,' said Cameron, to a chorus of laughter. I had wondered how Cameron would be received, so far, so good.

'You will,' I said, demonstrating. 'What you're going to practise is a right punch, a choku tsuki and a left hand inside block, soto uke, immediately following through but pull the punch. When you have both done that, a left punch and block .. First and third rows turn to face your opponent. You will deliver the first punch. There will be no contact, thanks Caroline.' She returned to the other group. 'Yoi ... Hajime.'

'Yame.' They all relaxed. 'Well done everybody. Did you enjoy that?'

'Brilliant,' was the general comment. 'Go home and practice. And what three words are the most important?'

The chorus spoke. 'Technique, technique, technique, sensei.'

I had to grin. 'Good. Remember the Gedan Barai and the basic kata. Get the timing right and keep it slow to begin with. And consider purchasing a Gi. See you next week.'

Carol, Sally and Wendy came over. 'I'd like to buy a Gi. £5 wasn't it?' Said Sally.

Yes they are, Joe imports them, have a word with him. But a good decision, it will feel totally different when you're wearing one.'

She nodded, 'But ...'

'There's a problem?'

'Mmm, my Dad, he thinks this is a church youth club.'

'He doesn't know?'

'He was a prisoner during the war, the Burma railway.'

'I can see why that would be a problem.' 20,000 allied prisoners died constructing the Railway of Death as it was known. Learning Karate would be anathema to her father.

'Look, Sal,' said Wendy. 'I'll look after it for you. You and Carol can train at our house; my mother won't mind. A girls only group, and I'll have a Gi as well, please. How about you Carol?'

'I was going to leave it, but go on then, in for a penny.' Happy, they went to join the queue.

Bruce Knight wandered across having placed his order. 'How's it going, Brian?'

'In here, ok. But considering the numbers very well, Bruce. 'It's early days, but you never can tell. The fact that there's a commitment by investing on a Gi is a positive sign.'

He paused and nodded. 'I read about your George Cross, Congratulations, it sounded hairy.'

'Very,' |I said with a grimace.

'Can you say anything about the offences under the Official Secrets Act?'

'That's easy. No.'

The girls were leaving. 'Oh, Wendy, a minute.' She wandered across.

'If there is any more trouble with Earnshaw let me know. Don't try and sort him out by yourself, leave that to us.'

'All right, sensei, But he won't dare come to the house and cause trouble. My dad would sort him out.'

'Ok, just be aware. His type often don't understand the meaning of the word,

no!'

Twenty-Two

The next morning I was returning to the station and stopped outside the local newsagent. I'd run out of Polos - my addiction. Purchase secured I headed for the car. A few yards away an elderly pedestrian walking with the aid of a stick stumbled and went down on his knees. He was chuckling to himself as I crouched beside him. 'Bloody hell, nicked at my age. Help me up, lad, please.' He was still unsteady on his feet. I helped him into a nearby coffee bar and sat him down and ordered two coffees. The lady behind the counter smiled as she ran the steam through the milk and turned to my casualty. 'In the arms of the law again, Tommy. I thought you'd given all that up.'

'Just the once for old times', Mary,' he laughed and grimaced as he stretched his left leg, 'but this one's wick.

So, my new acquaintance had history as well as a sense of humour. He had the look of Robert Newton: ruddy complexion, chubby cheeks and a twinkle in his steel grey eyes and would have made a passable Long John Silver. I got his story. In his youth he could outrun and outclimb any police officer in the valley. They always caught him in the end and he'd been sent down on more than one occasion. Early one morning whilst breaking into a warehouse via the roof he slipped, fell fifteen feet and broke several vertebrae. Of late he was finding walking difficult. He suggested that I talk to Sergeant Chalkley about his past. I asked him his full name.

'Thomas Grogan.' He stared at me, unblinking. 'You're the sergeant that thumped my grandson.' It was not a question. I looked at him quizzically. 'Christopher's not a bad lad but there's something wrong. I'm glad you did it. A bit of time inside might make him think. No great shakes at school, no qualifications but has a job helping out a bloke named Collins, a bit of a dogsbody. Slips me a few quid from time to time so I can't complain, but he'll never tell me what he does, only that he helps Collins out. But, and it's a big one, he has far more brass in his pocket than he ought.'

When I booked Grogan in he gave his occupation as a driver, he had a current full driving licence for non-articulated heavy goods vehicles.

'It's no secret, can't stand Collins. Yes, I've been a wrong un in my time but I've never hurt or threatened anybody. Collins has a reputation, arrived in this area over five years ago, nobody knows a thing about him. Talk about tight lipped? He started cropping up in pubs and at events as far into Lancashire as Burnley and Haslingden. Elland and Brighouse t'other road. He's good wi' people and always stood his corner. But hasn't any what you would call *friends*. Nobody knows his first name, always Mr Collins. He rented a house at Mytholmroyd for a couple of years then bought a piece of land at Norland and built himself a big house, well, big for round here. After twelve months he started buying, but he's never had a job, and nobody has a clue where his money comes from. Whatever he's bought it was always at his price.'

Mary came across and joined in. To be honest it began to sound like a conspiracy theory.

Thomas Grogan continued. 'Jeffrey Needler's father, Gordon, had owned the scrapyard in Todmorden. He was killed when a stack of cars had unaccountably collapsed. Collins bought it for a song a month or so later. Dorothy Naismith, she owned a newsagents and post office outside Hebden Bridge, had been held up at gunpoint and sold out to him. Over the last three years there were eight other examples of incidents that resulted in Collins taking possession of established businesses along the Calder Valley, following some mishap.'

There had been others, perhaps not as dramatic. The police and fire brigade investigated but nothing found.

It was interesting background information but . 'Thank you for the information, but?' I paused and looked questioningly at them both.

'You're new here,' Tommy said.

'You're not tainted, sergeant,' Mary added.

What? That was quite an allegation. 'Off the record, care to name names?' It had to be a sergeant or inspector, although Inspector Marshall seemed to be above the kind of chicanery they were suggesting.

'Look where they buy their cars.' That was interesting. I'd noticed a few of the bobbies bought their cars from Riverside Motors. Did Collins own that?

'Has he made an approach to buy you out, Mary?'

'Not in as many words, although he suggested that it might be in my best interests to consider it. That didn't last long, I'm too small, got his eyes on bigger fish. Ginny works for me on Saturdays and in Venner's canteen during the week, told me Collins was there, had a blazing row with Mr Venner about money. Everyone heard it.'

I was mulling things over when Tommy Grogan pointed at my medal ribbons. 'I've read about you, Sergeant Blake, they don't give those away like Green Shield stamps.'

He seemed to think I could make a difference. How, I wasn't sure although I might be able to set their minds at ease. 'No promises,' I said. 'Would the people concerned talk to me?'

'They'll talk to me and Mary, maybe you, but not in uniform and not around here.'

I left them in the coffee shop still chatting. About what I could only guess. Something Mary mentioned stuck in my mind, "*When you meet him take note. He smiles a lot but it never reaches his eyes. He's a cold fish."*

I finished my paperwork and walked to speak with Mr Jenner. 'I don't know how you found out, sergeant, but yes, he paid me a visit, and it was acrimonious. Collins knew I'd lost a big order and to be honest it has hurt. There'll be no overtime and it's the run up to Christmas, it'll hurt my staff although I'll ensure they get their Christmas party. Collins made me a derisory offer for the business. Not that it was for sale. It was an insult. I told him I wouldn't sell and threatened to have him thrown out. Then he got personal.'

'Did he make threats to you, your family, staff or the factory?'

Jenner nodded. 'Implied not explicit. He smiled and said "*Be careful*.' There was nothing you could put in front of a court.'

I left telling Venner to let us know if there was any further contact with Collins that concerned him.

I took the enquiry to Inspector Marshall. The next two days should have been my days off. I put them on my time off card and worked in civvies. I spoke with eight former business owners impacted by Collin's approaches and, whilst I sympathised with their dilemma there was this hint of conspiracy theory running through the story. Collins, as unpleasant as he might be, was simply an opportunist? Nevertheless I would keep in contact with Thomas Grogan who still wanted me to do more. I explained that the more noise I made the greater the risk of Collins finding out I was digging into his business affairs.

As an afterthought I rang DS Martindale, I'd met him during my Junior CID Course, he was a student on the Senior Course and now a DS on the Fraud Squad. I asked him if he had any contacts at Companies House, explaining my interest and gave him the facts that I had. He expressed an interest and promised to keep in touch. I asked how many businesses had Collins as a director and any co-directors.

Twenty-Three

10.30. **Back in harness once more.** Outside it was cold and wet, a north wind whistling down from the moors, miserable.

'Sarge?' Neil Farrar, the radio operator's questioning tone dragged me from my typing.

I looked up. 'Yes?'

'Got Mrs Hathersage from The Beeches, Wakefield Road on the phone, says her husband has an incurable disease. Two years ago the doctor told him it will kill him in about three years; motor neurone disease she called it. But he's dead and she thinks it's suspicious.'

The Hathersage family moved in a circles that had the capacity to cause problems, especially if what Mrs Hathersage had told PC Farrar was accurate. I took the call. 'Mrs Hathersage, my condolences. Sergeant Blake, is there anything else you can add to what you've told PC Farrar?' There wasn't. Call concluded. 'Where's Weatherly?'

'With Colin, Sarge, junction Wharf Street and Church Bank.'

'Tell them to wait there I'll meet them in two minutes.'

Since my *guidance* she had improved. However, she'd never seen a dead body; this would be a baptism of fire. There is no opting out. And as coroner's officers we had to get it right first time. It was a two minute drive. Right from Bolton Brow into Wakefield Road. A half mile on the left.

The Beeches was a scaled down version of a Georgian great hall, complete with portico and all the trimmings. Inside was like a museum. If these were genuine pieces there was serious money involved.

There were three permanent staff. Mrs Phillips the housekeeper and cook, John Phillips the gardener, her husband. They lived in a cottage in the grounds and were due back that evening after a couple of days away. Lastly the maid, Verity, mid-twenties, five three, brunette, pleasant looking, and wore no rings. Her mistress was in the Drawing Room sitting on a chair gazing out of the window, smoking. I would guess that Mrs Hathersage was in her early to mid-forties with a fuller figure, brown permed hair and wearing a red dress with matching shoes. Introductions complete I asked Mrs Hathersage to explain what she had told me on the phone again, which she did without embellishment. PW Weatherly made the notes.

Doctor Olivier, a new doctor from the private practice she and her husband used, called on spec and found her husband dead in bed. Calling without an appointment was non unknown but a rare occurrence. Although death was the natural outcome of the disease, Dr Mellor, their neurological consultant, had informed them that the process would take three years, not two. Doctor Olivier had given her a death certificate timed forty minutes earlier. She had not known of the existence of this Doctor Olivier until he arrived. I asked if I could see her husband. She had Verity show us up to her husband's bedroom. As I walked up the stairs I asked the maid to describe what had happened.

'I answered the door and the doctor was standing outside.'

'What sort of car was he driving?'

'I couldn't see a car.'

'No car at all?

'No, sir. I did step outside but there was nothing.'

Strange. 'Talk me through what happened next.'

'I took him to Mrs Hathersage and waited by the door. Then she told me to take the doctor to her husband's bedroom. The bedroom door was closed as it had been at ten o'clock when I cleared his breakfast tray.'

'How long before?'

'I'm not sure exactly, perhaps thirty minutes. Then the doctor told me to leave so I went down stairs to the kitchen.'

'You didn't see into Mr Hathersage's bedroom on that occasion?'

'No, sir.'

'Did the doctor close the door after you left?'

'Yes, I heard it close as I was going down stairs.'

'What happened next?'

I was taking Mrs Hathersage some tea when the doctor came downstairs. I heard him tell her that her husband was dead.'

'How did she react?'

'She said thank you to the doctor and poured herself a cup of tea. I showed the doctor out. When I returned she was calling the police station.'

'What did he have for his breakfast?'

'His favourite, sir,' a smile drifted across her face. 'Poached smoked haddock and two poached eggs. When I took it up he was sitting up in bed reading. And he had been smoking, although he wasn't supposed to.'

'Where is Mrs Hathersages bedroom?'

'Across the hallway.'

'Did she see her husband this morning?'

'No, sir. She usually saw him around eight pm when he settled down for the night.'

'And to the best of your knowledge the last time she looked in on him was eight pm yesterday?'

'Yes, sir.'

The bedroom door was open. Mr Hathersage slept in a double bed against the left hand wall. An oxygen cylinder with mask next to the bed. A table to either side. On the nearside table several photographs, an ash-tray, packet of cigarettes - Kensitas, and a lighter, two pairs of spectacles in open cases. On the far side-table a telephone and an open hard-backed book face-down and, out of reach. Mr Hathersage was slumped against his pillows, covers straight and pulled up to his chin. An odour of cigarette smoke hung in the air. 'I hope you're taking note of what you can see,' I said. but PW Weatherly was transfixed. 'Once things get moved you can't put them back where they were.'

'What am I supposed to be looking at, sergeant?'

'Remember we are coroner's officers and Mrs Hathersage reported her husband's death as suspicious. You are the first officer on the scene. You take in everything. The open door. The oxygen cylinder and mask. The photographs, cigarettes and accessories although he's not supposed to smoke. Two pairs of spectacles. The telephone. The open book. The state of the bed. Look at Mr Hathersage and tell me what you see.'

There wasn't a sound.

'All right, don't worry. In bed there's a grey-haired elderly man, bald on top, laid back against the pillows, covers pulled up to the chest. Arms outside the covers. His eyes are closed. He has the pallor of alabaster. His lips are blue. There are no lacerations to the face or other signs of assault. He is not wearing glasses but there are two pairs on the table; probably for normal vision as well as reading. We shall need to speak with the doctor to see if he took them off and why. If he was reading when the maid saw him. Was it the doctor who put the book where it is now or could he do it? Just what you see. It builds a picture in your mind. We don't move bodies but one of the things we can do is this. Do you remember from your first aid training what you were taught about checking the eyes?'

'Yes, sergeant. To see if there is a reaction to light. If the person is dead the pupils will not react.'

'Well remembered. Now tell me what you see. 'I stepped across to the body and gently raised his right eyelid. 'Well?'

'The pupils didn't react.'

'Correct, now take a closer look. What *can* you see?'

She leaned forwards. 'Little red dots?'

'Correct. Not a good sign. They're called petechiae and an indication that further investigation is required. Now check for a carotid pulse.'

'But?'

'Still check. He won't bite.'

'Well done,' I said as she straightened. 'These are the things we have to do. Next time you'll understand. It won't be a big deal. Make sure you write it in your pocket book. If in doubt see me. Now, find Verity. Sit down with her and take a full description of the doctor. Her personal details and routine. And Mr Hathersage's routine. All in note form and not as a statement.'

'Yes, sergeant.'

I left her to it and called the station from the phone in the hall. PC Farrar answered. 'Is Sergeant Greatorix about?'

'Colin, Brian Blake. I'm at the Beeches. Duncan Hathersage is dead. Appears to be asphyxiation of some description. Can you get the circus rolling'

'I heard, any suspects?'

'Some mysterious doctor from their private practice. If you've no objection I'll give them a call.'

'Be my guest. I'll get things rolling here and see you shortly.'

I went into the Drawing Room to speak with Mrs Hathersage. She took one look at my face. 'It's true isn't it? He is dead?'

'I'm very sorry, but yes, he is.' She took the news well.

'Can you tell me how?'

'At the moment, Mrs Hathersage, I can't. There will have to be a post mortem examination to establish that.' I could tell that she wasn't enamoured by the thought. 'Your husband was dying, have you any idea who might want to harm him?'

'Off hand, sergeant, no. He was in business for many years and made some enemies, but none that I can think of who might wish him physical harm.'

I asked her for the number of the medical practice and dialled from the telephone in the drawing room. I spoke with the Practice Manageress, Mrs Pepperell. Yes, they had a Dr Olivier in the practice. I told them that Detective Sergeant Greatorix or one of his colleagues would call back later in the day. Whilst I had the opportunity I asked Mrs Hathersage for a description of Dr Olivier. She was reticent, telling me she hadn't been in his company for long. I persevered and also took possession of the death certificate ostensibly signed by Dr Olivier.

I took another look in the bedroom and the en-suite bathroom. Nothing in the bathroom that gave cause for concern. But an ornate plaster cornice in the bedroom caught my eye. Clumsily I backed into the bed. There was a clatter. A photograph mounted in a ten by eight inch silver frame, of four young men in RAF uniform all astride motor bikes. It must have been under the bed clothes and the jolt dislodged it. What it was doing there was anybody's guess. But the photograph was interesting, very interesting. The motor cyclist on the right had sergeant's stripes, was now dead in bed facing me. The second from the left, the last time I saw him was much heavier. He had been recalled to prison. Initially sentenced to life imprisonment for murder by beating someone to death whilst wearing a spiked knuckleduster. I arrested him my first month on the job whilst he was out on licence. He was intending to wreak vengeance on his former arresting officer, then sergeant now Inspector Meadowcroft. I got in his way. He'd tried to remove my head. There was no mistaking Vivian Smedley's nose and eyes. The other two I didn't know.

Mrs Hathersage set me straight. She'd met them all at the end of the war, before she was married. The motor cyclist on the left was Nick Collins, the same Mr Collins I'd heard so much about recently. He was a cold fish, no humanity in his eyes. The second she knew as Viv, who she thought was uncouth. That I could believe. The third Bryan, with a 'y', but she knew nothing else about him. The reason her husband had the photograph was that he wanted to contact them after an absence of over twenty years. She didn't want to speak to Collins so I offered to do it for her. With her permission to copy the photograph I placed it in my briefcase. *Was there a joint history? Were there any further connections.* Doctor Fuller, the police surgeon arrived introduced himself to Mrs Hathersage and went upstairs accompanied by me. I wanted to know more about motor neurone disease. Having confirmed death he left passing DI Cartwright, DS Greatorix and DC Foster in the Hall on our return.

'That's Smedley?' queried the DI when I showed them the photograph.

'What do you intend?'

'See Smedley first. Then Inspector Meadowcroft. He and Smedley have history. Get the photo copied at HQ Studio. Then go see Collins, find out if either Smedley or Collins know the whereabout of the fourth rider, Bryan. With a bit of luck Collins will touch the glass at least once.'

DS Greatorix's face split into a broad grin. 'Crafty sod.'

The DI and DS Greatorix already knew Mrs Hathersage so made their presence known and offered condolences. Her three children, two sons and a daughter were en route to join their mother. It was explained that an examination would be made of her husband's bedroom and photographs taken. Her husband's body would be removed and a post mortem examination carried out to confirm the course of death. DS Greatorix and DC Foster would take statements. Enquiries would be made with Doctor Olivier. Subsequently a file would be submitted to the Coroner.

DC Foster was taking a statement from Mrs Hathersage. The remainder were sharing a bedroom with the corpse. 'Right, Brian,' the DI lead off. 'You've got the temperature of the water, what do you think?'

'It's crazy, sir. It appears contrived and, had things been slightly different I would have said it was a mercy killing.'

There was a startled, 'That's a wicked thing to say, sergeant.'

'Young lady,' the DI turned on PW Weatherly. 'You've been out of training school for less than two weeks. You haven't earned the right to have an opinion never mind express it. You're here to observe, listen and learn. When we want your opinion we'll let you know. Do you understand?'

A very guilty looking PW swallowed hard. 'Yes, sir, sorry.'

'Good. Whatever you hear in this house you will not repeat to anyone outside it, civilian or police. Anyone. Clear?'

'Yes, sir.'

He nodded to me. Attention now on me she relaxed. 'Doctor Fuller called it Amyotrophic Lateral Sclerosis - ALS. This being the most common of four types. It affects the brain, spine and muscles of the arms, legs, mouth and lungs. No known cause therefore no cure. Over time progresses, accelerates and is inexorable. He described it as diagnosis to death in three years.'

There was silence for several seconds broken by DS Greatorix's 'Nice.'

'He said it was not a pleasant way to die. The first symptoms are tripping over fresh air, an inability to hold things, subsequently the muscles of the mouth and the respiratory system would be affected. Mr Hathersage had the disease for at least two years so should have lived for at least another year. The petechiae explained why but we would have to wait for confirmation until after the post mortem examination. The maid said she brought his breakfast up; his favourite meal, quote: Poached smoked haddock with two poached eggs. She cleared the breakfast tray at ten when he was reading and smoking a cigarette.'

DS Greatorix scanned the bedside.' But, if he has, or had, difficulty in manipulating small articles could he still manage to use a knife and fork, smoke cigarettes safely and turn the pages of a book?'

'Or swallow,' added the DI. 'Plus there are two pairs of spectacled folded and in their cases. And, the book is on the opposite side of the bed and out of reach. Which is why you said it appeared contrived.'

'Yes sir.'

'Hmm. Well at the moment we have this Doctor to see. Mrs Hathersage and her maid are providing mutual alibis. However, nothing is spoiling .. Thanks for that Brian. I'll let you two get off.'

'On final point, sir.' I turned to PW Weatherly. 'Did you say that the maid described the doctor as looking like Steve McQueen?'

'Yes, sir,' she held her pocket book out to the DI.

He scanned the entry and smiled. 'Quite detailed,' he said.

'It matches what Mrs Hathersage told me,' I handed him my pocket book.

'Too closely if you ask me. But we will wait and see what the pathologist has to say tomorrow.'

PW Weatherly looked worried. 'Am I in trouble, sergeant?'

'No. That was Mr Cartwright's way of pointing out that you have to leave your emotions out of the way, consider only the evidence. Then you can draw conclusions and that takes experience. But remember what I told you. Mrs Hathersage reported that in her opinion the issuing of the death certificate as being suspicious, which it is. Now, what enquiries do we have to do?'

We spent the remainder of the short journey discussing how the case might progress. At the station I helped her complete the

Sudden Death report and her pocket book. She kept a copy for future reference.

I brought the inspector up to speed including my relationship with Smedley, and secured permission for a prison visit.

Twenty-Four

An hour later and in civies I was escorted into the Deputy Governor's office. Graham Sidebottom, the same person I'd spoken with during the Wainwright case, stood behind his desk as I entered. 'Sergeant? We've met before.'

'We have, sir. The last time it was ...'

'Zebadiah Coch,' he ejaculated and smiled. 'But that was less than three years ago. And now you're a sergeant. That's very good going.'

'Thank you.'

'Might I ask why you wanted to speak with Smedley? He had TB and died less than an hour ago. Was it an urgent enquiry?'

'Not at all. During the last war Smedley was an RAF Dispatch Rider and a member of a small team. We have a photograph of the group and I recognised him. I was hoping he could identify the others.'

'You recognised Smedley?'

'I arrested him and the reason he is back inside.'

'You did?'

'On my own.'

'In that case you earned those stripes.'

There was nothing further to be gained. Thirty minutes later I was drinking coffee in the Hecton canteen.

'Sergeant, with less than four in ...'

'Just.'

'Splitting hairs, Brian. That's going some. The sky's the limit. Now, what can I do for you?'

I slid the photo across the table. 'Who do you know in here, sir?'

'Smedley?'

'He died this morning. I was on my way to see him but too late.'

'The world will be a better place.'

I couldn't disagree. 'He had TB. I understand he was a shadow of his former self, Is there anyone else?'

'No, is it important?'

'I knew that you knew Smedley. I wondered if you recognised anyone else.'

'Should I?'

'Not really. The others are Collins, Bryan with a Y, and Hathersage.' I pointed them out.

He laughed. 'Collins and Bryan with a Y don't mean anything. I came across a Hathersage some time ago, lives in your area, something to do with haulage.'

'He's the one. Died this morning. We're looking into it.'

Twenty-Five

10.40 **Norland.** It was a new house, certainly different; cut into the hillside giving it the appearance of having a third floor. Had it been on the level it would have been a dormer bungalow. A garage at the base with a steep drive to a parking area at the rear. I didn't have long to wait as a small man, around five feet six tall, mid-forties with light brown wavy hair over his ears and collar answered the bell. Wearing a sky blue tracksuit. He looked me over a couple of times. Full of nervous energy. He stared at me and smiled, but as Mary had said the smile didn't trouble his eyes. He thrust his hand out, 'Sergeant,' he said pleasantly. 'What can I do for you?' He stepped back and invited me in. 'I've just brewed some coffee,' he said over his shoulder. 'Have you time for a cup?' Very user friendly.

The kitchen was ultra-modern. The living room furniture likewise, Scandinavian and elegant. Hung on the wall were a couple of panoramic photographs of the moors, where they were taken I don't know. I parked myself in the chair he indicated. He sat opposite.

I took a sip of coffee. It was good, definitely not instant. I put my mug on an adjacent coffee table.

'Now then, sergeant, what's dragged you up here?'

'I understand from Mrs Hathersage, Marcia Hathersage, that you were a long-time friend of her husband.'

Collin's face clouded over. 'Well, yes. It was a shock to find them up here. We served together during the war as RAF dispatch riders. But, you said *were* a friend. Has something happened?'

'I'm afraid he was found dead in bed yesterday morning.'

The look of shock seemed genuine. 'I knew he had been ill for a long time. Was it his heart?'

'I can't say, Mr Collins. There will have to be a post mortem examination. The reason I'm here is at the request of Mrs Hathersage.' I took another sip of coffee, reached down and took the photograph from my briefcase and handed it to Collins, who very kindly left an imprint of his right thumb on the glass. He studied the photograph; a broad grin appeared. 'Good grief. 1943. That dredges up some memories.'

'Over the past few days, Mr Collins, her husband has been looking at that photograph and telling his wife that he'd like to get in touch with you all once again. She knew you and her husband but wasn't too sure about the two in the middle. The one next to you she thinks was called 'Viv', other than that all she could only recall that he was uncouth.'

Collins laughed and tapped the photo with his left forefinger. 'Vivian Smedley, 'Viv'. Uncouth is one way of putting it. It'd be more accurate to say that he was as rough as a bear's arse. But, he was a genius with bike engines. That's a fact. For all I know he's still in clink. He got involved in a scrap and killed a man, fourteen or fifteen years ago. He got life. I haven't heard about him since, sorry.

'Thanks. I'll chase it up. The last one. Bryan, with a 'y'.'

Collins nodded and left another left forefinger print on the glass – that was good of him. 'Yup, Bryan Forbes. Marcia was his girlfriend but Duncan decided he was the better man. It got quite nasty. Duncan got him on some trumped up theft charge. Bryan got six months. Almost got kicked out. There's no love lost there. But he left Marcia with a present.

'You mean?

He nodded. 'Yup. Before the split she ended up shagging both of them. His eldest isn't Duncan's, it's Bryan's.'

You wouldn't think it to see her now. 'Did he know?'

'To the best of my knowledge he didn't and Marcia didn't let on. As for his whereabouts, the last I heard he was operating a motor cycle courier business in Birmingham. That would be a good place to start.

I thanked him, relieved him of the photo frame and put it back in my briefcase.

He paused. 'Sergeant, rather than you take it back I ought to go and see her. I could do that. Save you a journey.'

There was no way I was going to lose that thumb print. 'It's all right but thanks for the offer, Mr Collins, but I need another statement from her. I can kill two birds with one stone. Besides, no disrespect intended but she did ask me to take care of both photo and frame. I don't think she would be too thrilled if I handed it to you.'

His expression slipped for a micro-second then he smiled. 'As you wish, sergeant,' he indicated my cup. 'Would you like a top-up?'

I declined, made my apology and left to be greeted by the sun putting in an appearance. Mr Collins standing in the front window watching.

Fifty yards below Collins' I'd noticed a detached house set below the road on the opposite side. Whilst driving back I noticed a young lad, about twelve, leaning over the gate and waving his arms. He was tall, brown collar length hair, wearing a yellow check shirt and blue jeans. Was something wrong? I stopped at the entrance to the drive and exited, as a man about forty, probably the lad's father, arrived and put his arm round the boy's shoulders. 'Arthur,' he said, ''you mustn't do that. It might cause an accident. Sorry, sergeant but you're new.'

'New?'

He smiled. 'Yes, he hasn't seen you or this car before.'

'You collect new things do you?'

Arthur nodded. 'What's your name?'

'I'm Sergeant Blake, and you're Arthur.'

'What's your name?'

Arthur's father smiled. 'I'm afraid he doesn't do surnames, sergeant.'

'Ah. My name's Brian,' I said and smiled. 'And you're Arthur?'

'Yes,' he pointed at my supervision car and, to my astonishment rattled off the specs. 'That's an Anglia Super 123e: 1198cc engine, 4 speed all synchro gearbox, 48.5 bhp at 4800 rpm, all round drum brakes, top speed 82 mph and zero to 60 in 21.6 seconds, weighs 1692lbs, and does 31 mpg.' He looked at me and grinned.

I had to laugh. 'That's very good. Do you know all cars?'

He nodded.

'You're lucky you got the shortened version,' his father laughed. 'Conversation is difficult for him, sergeant, but he can look at something once and remember the details.'

'Can I sit in it?'

'Not today, Arthur, sorry. I have work to do.' He looked disappointed. 'I promise you can sit in it when I have time, all right?'

'Come on Arthur let the sergeant go. He's a busy man.'

Bill had arrived early and I had a couple of calls to make including telling Lucy I'd be late.

Twenty-Six

'Excuse me, sir, can I have a private word?'

Commander Richard Jameson of the Metropolitan Police stopped and turned. 'DS Stacey, isn't it? A bit irregular? Shouldn't you're first port of call be your DCI?'

'It's a bit awkward, sir.'

'It's about your DCI?' Jameson prided himself on his accessibility but for a DS to bypass the entire chain of command. That was unusual. 'You'd better come in.' He sat behind his desk and motioned the sergeant to the chair opposite. 'Well?'

'It concerns DCI Frobisher and Harry Field, sir.'

'I'm listening.'

'The wife and I took the 9.45am from West Acton this morning, sir. Most of the traffic's gone by then. We were in the middle coach and the train was less than half full. On the opposite seat further down and next to the door was Harry Field.'

'Field was on the tube? How well do you know him?'

'When I was in uniform I took the misper when his wife disappeared.'

'She was never traced, was she?'

'No, sir. But there was no evidence so ...'

'I see. Does he know *you?*'

'I doubt it, sir. I was younger then with a beard and I had more hair.'

The Commander laughed. 'Didn't we all?' Then?'

'We stopped at North Acton. I could see the DCI on the platform; he sat next to Field.'

‘And there was plenty of room?’

‘Yes sir, there were only half a dozen in the carriage. They got into a huddle. I couldn’t hear what they were saying but Field took an envelope from his inside pocket. If I didn’t know better I’d say that it contained cash. That’s what he usually does. Seed money. Used notes. Go to one of his bookies put the money on what he says and collect the winnings. Goes through the books. A lucky punter.’

‘And it would be a foolish man who took the seed money and ran.’

‘It would indeed, sir.’

‘And you heard nothing.’

‘Not until we pulled into East Acton. The DCI put the envelope in his inside pocket and tapped his jacket twice with his left hand. When he stood and waited for the doors to open I heard Field say, “Don’t forget.”

The DCI replied. ‘The six dog. Got it.’

‘He didn’t see you?’

‘I was reading a newspaper someone had left. Plus he never looked down the carriage. Had Field recognised me and mentioned it to him, I think he would have looked.’

The Commander nodded. ‘And that was all and just the one stop?’

‘Yes sir. And there’s a meeting at Romford tonight.

‘Good point. Do you know if Field got off the train?’

‘Holland Park, sir.’

‘Anything else that springs to mind?’

‘A DCI and Harry Field, sir, it’s not going to be £50.’

‘Agreed. And thank you. What are you doing for the rest of the day?’

‘It’s our wedding anniversary tomorrow, sir. I managed a couple of days leave. We’re on our way to meet our respective others.’

The Commander looked puzzled. 'Of course, the twin brothers who married twin sisters on the same day. Congratulations.'

Hands shaken DS Stacey left the office. The commander slid the door sign to DO NOT DISTURB. 'Mrs Andrews,' he said when his secretary answered. 'No calls, even if it's the Commissioner.'

The next call was different. 'Bob, Commander Jameson. I want twenty four hour obs on DCI Frobisher with immediate effect, open-ended. I want someone so close that if he farts we know what he ate. Is that clear?'

The laughter rang down the line. 'Yes, sir. He's been about a bit but I'll find those he doesn't know. And, if you've no objection, DI Bellamy, Linus. They're joined at the hip. You never know."

'Good, and there's a good chance he will not only visit one of Harry Field's bookies but he will be at Romford tonight for the racing.'

'Leave it with me, sir. I'll keep you posted.'

Twenty-Seven

Detective Chief Inspector Alexander Frobisher had done well from providing extra-curricular services to Harry Field. His bank account in the Channel Isles, his pension supplement was growing nicely. But this was a first and he didn't like it. The trouble was that when you took Harry Field's money, whether you knew what Harry wanted or not the contract was sealed. You did not renege. Not if you wanted to see your next birthday. There were £1000 in used notes in the envelope wrapped with a postal sleeve. The simple message scrawled in Harry's childish hand: *Sgt Blake, Sowerby Bridge, terminate.* Frobisher knew the bet had to be placed on the 6 dog in the last at Romford that night and, use Harry's bookies in Camden Town. It was always the same, the bet to be placed ten minutes before the start. The odds would determine the payoff. He still didn't like it. He picked up the phone and dialled.

'Bellamy.'

'Linus, come into the office and close the door.'

DI Lionel 'Linus' Bellamy, a six feet, fifteen stone former bare knuckle fighter, closed the door and stared at his friend. 'Problem?'

Frobisher pushed the note across the desk.

'A copper? Fuck! How much?'

Frobisher opened the top drawer in his desk so that his friend could see. 'A big one at Camden. Six dog. Last at Romford tonight'

'A grand on a dog? Same arrangements. You go to the race I'll see to the money?'

'And it had better all be there. No syphoning anything into your back pocket. They will count it and you know what to expect from Harry if it isn't right.'

'All right. It was the once. A bullseye. It'll be straight. When's he want it done?'

'Within two weeks.'

'Where's this Sowerby Bridge?'

'God knows.'

Bellamy picked up the phone and dialled. 'Information Room.'

'Colin, Linus Bellamy. I'm doing a quiz and I'm stuck.'

'Reading the Beano again, Linus?'

'Aren't you the funny one. Where in God's name is Sowerby Bridge?'

'How the hell should I know? Just a sec,' Inspector Colin Jackson held the phone against his chest. 'Greaves,' he called across the room. 'You're the Met quiz boffin. Where's Sowerby Bridge?'

PC Geoff Greaves paused in mid-sentence and released the talk key. 'Up in Yorkshire near Halifax, sir,' he replied and continued with the call.

'Did you get that, Linus?'

'Yeah, cheers.'

'How did you pass your education exam?'

'Like you, I cheated.'

'What was all that about you bloody idiot?'

'You wanted to know. I didn't. I asked.'

Frobisher took a clip of messages from the hook on the side of his desk flipped the top five over and passed them across. 'Have you forgotten these? That has to have been that psycho Nickleby, or Collins or whatever he's calling himself. Kenny Summers, two DC's from Lancashire and that lorry driver who shouldn't have been there. Let's hope that your little query doesn't jog too many memories in a couple of weeks. Our first call is on Collins.'

Twenty-Eight

After grovelling to the DCI in fingerprints and explaining my request, I completed the paperwork, left the glass from the photo frame in his care, then crossed the second floor of HQ CID block for an identical performance with DI Mathers in the studio – I wanted an additional copy of the photograph for myself.

Next, a visit to a picture framers in the Bullring. A new piece of glass for the photo frame. I would have the copy photo tomorrow. The answer to the question – *was either of the prints left on the glass by Collins, the right thumb or left forefinger, on record.* That might take a little longer.

At 8.30pm Superintendent Wallace called me at home; something he'd never done before. My heart beating a little faster. 'Sergeant,' there was a hint of humour in his tone. 'I'm sorry to trouble you at this time but I've had a call from Fingerprints. You left the glass from a photo frame with them earlier today. You asked for a couple of prints to be checked. Why?'

The first question that jumped out at me was, why the interest, except that I hadn't followed the correct procedure. But that didn't necessitate a detective superintendent calling me at home. 'Have you seen the photograph, sir?'

'The photo behind the glass? No, I haven't.'

'You're aware of the suspicious death in Sowerby Bridge?'

'Yes, Hathersage. It's to do with that case?'

'Yes, sir. I bumped into Hathersage's bed and the photo frame fell out. It must have been pushed under the covers. Dated 1943. Four young men in RAF uniform. Dispatch riders. I recognised

Hathersage as the one on the right - a sergeant. The second from the left, Vivian Smedley, had done time for murder. I arrested him my first month in the job. I didn't know the other two. Mrs Hathersage identified the one on the left as Nick Collins a local businessman from Sowerby Bridge who has an unsavoury reputation. She also claimed, and I'm now certain that she lied, that she only knew the other as Bryan, spelt with a 'Y'. I wanted to know if there were any other links to Smedley.'

'That's all?'

I was confused. 'Yes sir, is there a problem?'

'Not exactly, but how many points of similarity do you require when comparing fingerprints?'

Strange, I thought. 'Minimum twelve, sir.'

'Correct. Now, that fingerprint you acquired and left with Fingerprints this afternoon? In particular the left forefinger. There are ten when compared to the handprint lifted from the Ford Zephyr. You've found the shooter.'

Now my heart was racing. 'Collins is Nickleby?

'Yes, congratulations. The silly bastard wasn't wearing gloves. They've been sent to the Met for comparison and confirmation against Nickleby's.'

'Collins' first name is Nicholas, or Nick.'

Twenty-Nine

Attendance was lower than had been expected. The forecast of snow might have been responsible, nevertheless there were about 1500 present. The car park was full. Everything from bangers to rollers. The well-heeled, as usual, in the restaurant. They had their own betting platform. The regulars in front of the grandstand. Cheek by jowl. Shoulder to shoulder. Everyone was going to make a packet. Frobisher was, he didn't know about anyone else. Hot dogs, pies, teas, coffees, hip-flasks. The atmosphere ramped up as the dogs for the first race were led out and paraded. Selections made and bets placed. Amongst the crowd and in the Commentary Box a few select were watching the watchers. Two were photographing those of special interest.

The last race was due. Frobisher had two winners out of the first ten races leaving him £10 out of pocket. Now was his time. The same man who had been behind him in the queue for every race took his place again as Frobisher placed £100 to win on the six dog at odds of 40/1. It came fourth. 'Bastard!' was the comment as he pushed his was out of the stadium.

LINUS BELLAMY ARRIVED at The Betting Field, Camden, at ten minutes past nine. The last race due at twenty two minutes past. There were three die-hards studying form and the obligatory cheap-looking blonde tart in her fake fur hoping to relieve some fortunate punter of a few quid, but not for him. He put the money on the counter and slid it beneath the safety screen. '£1000 to win on the six dog in the last at Romford,'

The manager smiled, took the money and passed it to the young woman at his side. 'Check it, a Grand,' He looked up and nodded to the blonde who stood and sauntered up and put her arm round Bellamy's waist and smiled.

'A grand on a little doggy,' she said in her sexiest voice. 'My, that's a lot of money and odds of 40/1. Why, with your sake that's £41,000. Are you going to show a girl a good time. We could go up west, or if you prefer somewhere quieter, my place is only a two minute walk. I'll take all your cares away. Help you sleep like a baby.'

He managed a grin. 'We'll see.'

The girl returned. 'It's all there.'

'There you go,' he said and slid the betting slip across. '£1000 on the six dog next at Romford, odds 40/1.'

The clocked ticked. The speaker crackled and burst into life: '9.22 at Romford. First No. two, second No. three.'

'What!?' said Bellamy. 'But ...'

'Yeah!' one of the punters, a slim man in his thirties dressed in bib and brace overalls punched the air. 'That's a single and a fivefold. What a night.' He walked the few steps to the counter and pushed his betting slips under the screen.

The manager smiled at him. 'Well done.' He turned away and took a calculator from a desk drawer.

The slim man turned to Bellamy. 'That's tough luck. I wish I had that sort of money.

'Yeah. Cheers,' Bellamy looked sick.

'Here you are, sir, that's £87.15 including your stake. We'll see you again sometime, I hope.'

'You certainly will. Cheers,' he said as he turned to leave.

'And this is yours,' the manager pushed a parcel under the screen to Bellamy. 'It's all there.'

The slim man turned back looking from Bellamy to the manager. 'I don't understand. He's only been in two minutes and had one bet. I won; he lost. Is that cash?'

'Nothing to do with you,' the manager replied. 'It would be best if you left, now.'

'But ...'

The blonde put her hand on the slim man's arm. 'Please, you've had a good night. Just leave. Nothing's happened.'

One of the two remaining punters stood, knocked the other on the leg and waved his thumb in the direction of the door. The man took one look at the knife in the other's hand and left; the doorbell clanged in confirmation. The slim man was about to speak when the hand on his left shoulder and the sharp stab of the knife in his back made him catch his breath. 'You heard what the lady said, it's time you left. Don't talk, don't look round and don't come back.' For the second time in a minute the doorbell sounded.

Linus Bellamy was confused. Harry wanted a job doing so it was unlikely that anything untoward would happen but what was next?

'Isn't this nice, the three of us, shall we go for a little stroll. Come on Carl.' The woman looked over her shoulder at the manager. 'Thanks Jimmy.'

'You're welcome, Yvonne.'

Yvonne linked arms with the two men. 'Linus, why don't you pick your parcel up, you don't want to leave that now do you?'

Thirty

The four men in the car watched. DC Vernon Grant focused the Nikon's telephoto lens on the betting shop door, clicks recording the exit as one man came out and hurried towards them. 'That leaves three, sarge,' DC Robert 'Bob' Green winced. 'Bellamy, Yvonne – whatever her name is and Carl Edwards.'

Detective Sergeant Anderson said. 'She uses Yvonne Richards but her name is Edith Ramsbottom,' the others laughed. 'How's your back?'

'Not good but I'll live.'

'Get it checked out later. Edwards can suck for a wounding as well. Vernon, here they come.'

Yvonne Richards, Linus Bellamy, Carl Edwards bringing up the rear. 'Bloody hell, there's £40,000 in that package Bellamy's carrying?'

'Well, Jimmy Moss said it was all there. A grand at 40/1. So?'

'Who's Field want killing? Bellamy and Frobisher are his personal hit team? This is not good.'

'Ok, slowly. Stop!' the DS said as a royal blue Rolls Royce, indicating right and brake lights on pulled to the offside and stopped. 'That's Field's car and we can't hear a bloody thing.'

'Oh, look. Harry's here,' said Yvonne as Field drew up alongside. The driver got out. She unlinked arms and turned to Bellamy. 'I think I'd better take this,' she said placing both hands on the package. Bellamy let go without a comment. 'Why, thank you, Linus.'

She sauntered across handing it to Field through the open window.

'Thanks Yvonne,' said Field. 'Tell me, is it true what they say about ladies who wear fur coats and their underwear?'

She grinned in return. 'Why Harry, you bought it for me. Would you like to find out?' She leaned forward giving him a peck on the lips.

'Hop in.'

She smiled and walked round the car as the chauffer opened the door. 'Thanks Pat.' The chauffeur nodded.

'Linus,' Harry beckoned. 'Nothing up front. Two weeks is the contract. Get it concluded and it's yours. All of it.'

'Yes Harry. I understand.'

'You'd better know that the weather forecast for that area is for some unseasonal heavy snow. There are no excuses. If you're late, you're late. Be warned.'

'And if you're late you're mine,' sneered Edwards.

'Who do *you* think you're talking to?'

'A bent copper,' sneered Edwards.

Bellamy spun round. 'Listen, shit for brains, you're walking the streets because of me, remember that.'

'Well if I go down you'll be welcomed with open arms.'

He thrust his face close to Edward's and spat the words out. 'You think you're hard sticking a knife in that punter's back. You're not. If I have to put you down it'll be in concrete. Back off.'

'Enough! Linus, before you go, did you know Alex was putting a bet on tonight. He put a ton on the six dog.'

'His own money?'

'Not mine. You'd better get off and make arrangements.' Bellamy nodded and walked away. 'Carl, don't antagonise Linus. You're out of your depth. He meant what he said.'

'But.'

'No buts. Understood?'

'What do you make of that?'

'Thieves falling out, sarge?'

'Between Bellamy and Edwards, I agree. Knife or no knife he'd crucify Edwards.'

'Nothing lost there. No, I meant Bellamy handing over the package.'

'Probably no up-front payment. Get the job done first whatever it is. If it's £40k it's not surprising .. Got your shots, Vernon?'

'Every single one.'

'Let's go.'

DC Bob Green slumped to his right. 'What the ... Bob!. Bob! Andy, Bob's collapsed. Sec ... Carotid pulse rapid, barely discernible.'

'Frank, nearest A & E.'

Frank Sillitoe, former road traffic officer dropped into second gear and accelerated. 'University College, Euston Road.'

'He said what? He doesn't trust us, that's obvious.'

'Alex, when did he ever trust anyone? That's not important. What matters is what happens in the next two weeks. Harry mentioned that heavy snow was forecast for the north of England. Yorkshire is what, two hundred and fifty each way plus time to do the job? Where's your road atlas?'

Fifteen minutes of studying the atlas it was decided. 'Pity they haven't

Finished the M1. We'll have to go A1 and cut across through Pontefract, Wakefield and Huddersfield.'

'Call Collins, get this Sergeant Blake's home address.'
'Let's hope this snow holds off. We're gonna need street maps of these

bloody one-horse towns.'

Thirty-One

Commander Richard Jameson, Detective Chief Superintendent Paul Yelland and Detective Inspector Robert Charles formed a sombre group at 8am the following day at the University College Hospital , Euston Road, London.

'Bob, what happened?'

'Green had a good night, sir, five winners and five-fold when ..' He looked at the Commander. 'Yes, you can mention his name.'

DCS Yelland gave them both quizzical looks.

'When Linus Bellamy..'

There a forceful ejaculation from the DCS :Bellamy's involved?'

'Hold on Paul, carry on.'

'Yes, sir. Linus Bellamy came in and put a grand on the six dog in the last at Romford.'

'Christ. What odds?'

'Forty to one.

'Did it win?'

'No.'

'But he still paid out.'

'He did.'

'This was at The Betting Field in Camden? ... Field and Bellamy?'

'It gets better.'

'Frobisher?'

'Yes, go on Bob.'

'Green backed the last winner and had collected his winnings when Moss pushed a large parcel across.'

'Cash?'

'Yes, sir. Green played the offended punter when Yvonne Richards came across suggesting he'd had a good evening and should leave, Edwards came up behind and stabbed him in the back. Green left the bookies and joined us. Told us about the stabbing but appeared all right until he blacked out.'

'Sir, you told me where this information came from but, do you know where it's leading?'

'No, Paul. Field is spreading his wings outside of London but Frobisher and Bellamy are under surveillance; so far they're still in the capital.'

'Right, sir,' said the DCS. 'Edwards for murder and other three conspiracy to murder. Separate stations.'

'Wait one,' said the Commander as Professor Stewart the pathologist arrived.

'Good morning Commander, gentlemen, Out of bed early this morning.,' he said with a wry smile. 'Follow me and we can get started.'

'Post mortems are never good at the best of time,' said DCS Yelland. 'But one of our own, especially in these circumstances ... He'd just passed his exams and his wife was expecting their second in a couple of months.'

'That is terrible,' said the professor. 'Will she be looked after?'

'She will,' said the DCS. 'But nothing will compensate.'

'Quite. Turn him on his left side, please.' Whilst the orderlies were rolling Green's body the professor said. 'Was he an athlete? he has the look.'

'Yes, he was, professor said DI Charles. 'A county-class miler.'

The professor nodded. 'You can see the entry point here. He pointed to the wound and inserted a probe. 'You can see the angle of entry, depth ... approximately three inches. A blow delivered with considerable force.' Photographs were taken. 'On his back please.'

Several minutes later the professor continued. 'You can see here, this severed blood vessel is the right renal artery, renal vein and other vessels.'

'I think we have seen enough professor,' said Commander Jameson.

'Thank you, gentlemen. The initial report will be on your desk this afternoon. I will have samples taken and analysed. The results forwarded as soon as possible.'

DI Charles was en route to see DC Green's widow. Commander Jameson and Detective Chief Superintendent Yelland were engrossed. 'Paul, this is the best chance we've had to knock Field off his perch. I'll get onto the Home Office and arrange for a phone tap. I'll leave the execution of the raids to you.

He nodded. 'Sir, I'll obtain search warrants for all Field's establishments, including his clubs. I'll visit him personally; and refresh our relationship. A simultaneous hit on everything at 12 sharp should rattle him.'

PAUL YELLAND SCRUTINISED the group in front of him. All seasoned detectives, not all of whom batted for the same team. 'There you have it gentlemen. Bob Green was one of ours. We know who we are looking for and, if he follows his usual pattern Edwards will not come quietly. But I want him in one piece. From this minute nobody, and this includes all of you, will make any phone calls or indulge in any conversation with anyone not engaged in this operation. If you need a piss, tie a knot in it. There will be no deviation from these instructions.

This is a search and arrest operation for the four suspects. I hope I make myself clear ... On the first strike of 12.'

Thirty-Two

The Mess Room was packed. 'All right, settle down.' Detective Superintendent Wallace waited for the hum to stop. 'Sorry we don't have a better photograph but we're waiting for one to be sent from the Met. You will know him as Mr Collins first name Nicholas or Nick. Some of you have bought cars from his garage and, during those or subsequent transactions I hope that information to which you, as police officers, have been privy, has not flowed the other way. However, Collins' real name is Nicholas Nickleby, as in the book by Charles Dickens.' He paused noting the startled looks on several faces. 'He was reputed to had died in a road accident north of London nine years ago. Obviously that is false. The operation this morning is to arrest him for the murder of Gloria Rodgers by strangulation in Brixton, London, on 12th August 1959.

You will work in pairs. One local officer and one detective who does not know the area. For those who make the arrest, because we will find him, he will be given the reason why, cautioned and cuffed behind. Those officers will not, under any circumstances, divulge any information including answering any questions he may ask. I trust you understand. There will be no mistakes. Inspector Marshall.'

He stood and checked his list. 'PC Dryden you will be working with DC Cavendish ...'

'Excuse me sir, can I have a word in private, please? It is urgent.'

The detective superintendent looked at the worried face. 'PC?'

'Lassiter, sir.'

Serious concern was draped across mine and Superintendent Wallace's faces. PC Lassiter looked guilty. I leaned forward and whispered in the superintendent's ear. 'Sir, the Chief is my wife's second cousin.'

Superintendent Wallace stood back. 'Really?'

'Very well, you'd better make sure your family is safe.'

He followed me to the door. I headed for the sergeant's office. He spoke to Inspector Marshall. 'Who is working with PC Lassiter?'

'DC Kidd, sir,' he said and pointed at a solitary officer standing at the rear.

'Very well, take Lassiter and Kidd off the list,' He looked at the DC. 'Kidd, in here please.'

Door closed; DC Kidd looked around in particular at the miserable uniformed officer. 'Kidd, it appears that PC Lassiter has been in collusion with Collins for some time, including providing the home addresses of several officers, including Sergeant Blake. Take him to an interview room and, under caution, take a comprehensive statement, from the beginning, after which he will remain.' He turned to Lassiter and held his hand out. 'Lassiter, your warrant card. You are suspended from duty.'

Thirty-Three

Damn! The line was engaged. Eventually. 'Anne, is everyone all right?'

'Yes, why? We've just had a friend of yours here, shall I go and catch him?'

I had a nasty feeling. 'What friend?'

'Nick, something.'

'Collins?'

'Yeah, that's him. Shall I ...'

'No,' I interrupted. 'Under no circumstances, he's no friend.'

'But .'

'Anne take Jen, go and wave him off and note the vehicle he's using: make, colour and number if you can. See where he goes.'

'But ...'

'Please, don't waste time.'

'Ok. Lucy's here perhaps you'll explain to her.' In the distance I heard Anne cajoling Jen. 'Come on Brian's given us a job to do. Mind your feet you don't want to give birth in the doorway.'

'Brian, what's going on?' Lucy's voice taking up the conversation.

'Hello, love. Collins is no friend of mine and his visit had nothing to do with friendship. I want you to get some suitcases ready in case we have to move in a hurry.'

'Brian, what's happening?'

'Sorry, I can't be specific but Collins has been acquiring home addresses. I think he was confirming where we live.'

'You think that we're some sort of target'

'That's a possibility.'

'Anne's back, I'll put her on.'

'Well, Mr Mysterious, it's an F reg beige Beetle. R-Y-G but I couldn't see the numbers. It turned right at the White Gate. Satisfied?'

I had to laugh. 'One more thing, please. Bob up to the front bedroom so that you can see the end of Slipper Lane, that's the one higher up on the other side of the road. Stay away from the glass but see if that car or Collins make an appearance.'

'You want me to play Secret Squirrel?'

'You've always wanted to help in a police enquiry. Go easy on the nuts.'

'Oh, ha ha.'

'Brian?'

'Yes, Mum?'

'Lucy seems to think you and the family are in some sort of trouble.'

'Would it be possible for Lucy and the children to come a stay for a week or so?'

'You think that it's necessary?'

'Not sure, but I'd like them out of harm's way.'

'I understand. Of course they can. We'd love to have them. How urgent is it?'

'I'll know more when Anne gets back.'

'She's here now.'

'Brian, I saw the beetle before it reversed almost out of sight. That man is sitting on the front offside wing looking at the house.'

'Ok, this is what I want you to do ...'

Thirty-Four

'Yes sir. According to my sister he'd been there ten minutes or so and was leaving when I rang. Either verifying what Lassiter had told him or as a warning.'

'Show me on the map.'

Superintendent Wallace, Inspector Marshall and DS Greatorix standing close behind I pointed out the landmarks. 'Cooper Bridge, Three Nuns, White Gate. Far Common Lane and this is Slipper Lane – joins Far Common Lane to the A62. My house is there, last house before the White Gate, opposite side. Collins was parked outside my house facing Huddersfield.'

The front door crashed open as a traffic officer dashed through. 'Sorry sir,' need a leak.'

His colleague followed laughing and nodded towards the disappearing back. 'Half-pint bladder, sir.'

It was a demonstration in high speed driving. Even faster than his dash to the gents. And it was the route that had to have been taken by Jack Roberts and Cameron MacArthur. I suspect that we were faster. As we approached Brighouse the call came through - Collins and his VW Beetle had left Slipper lane and observations were requested. Static road checks were established. We reached the A644. Road check two hundred yards towards Cooper Bridge. With two-tone horns and blue light in full swing we made good progress down the centre of the road. We were about the same position as the Morris 1000 saloon was parked on the day of the incident.

'Stop! it's there,' John Wilson dropped the anchor, slithered to a halt and upset a couple of drivers. 'There, between those two artics,'

I tapped the co-pilot, Will Kendrick, on the shoulder. 'Come on.' As we decamped the driver radioed in. 'Whiskey 86 suspect vehicle seen A644 600 yards Cooper bridge side of Brighouse. Sergeant Blake attending.'

Now nothing pointing towards Cooper Bridge was moving. Everyone watching us, especially when the reversing lights of the traffic car came on accompanied by a couple of annoyed, 'Make your bloody minds up!'

The inbound lane to Brighouse was creeping. The VW registration number RYG471F between two fully laden artics. The driver wasn't Collins but was staring through the windscreen, eyes fixed on the vehicle in front. It didn't matter about the driver being Collins, this was the vehicle Anne had seen. Who was he? I tapped on the driver's side window. He ignored me. I tapped again, no change. I leaned forward and looked at him through the windscreen. 'Stop this vehicle,' I shouted at him. He revved the engine, ignored me and edged forwards.

The driver in front stuck his head out of the window. 'Problem officer,' he

shouted.

'Stop your vehicle.' I got the thumbs up. The hiss of air brakes meant the

VW was going nowhere.

Behind, Will Kendrick was telling the driver of the second artic to close up.

The driver of the Beetle just kept revving the engine. Two beat men ran up. 'All right, sarge?'

Neither knew the driver of the VW. Occupants of the outbound traffic were

beginning to gather. The drivers to the rear were starting to express their displeasure. 'Right, get this other traffic moving. We don't need an audience.' I banged on the side window. 'Turn the engine off and get out.' Once again he ignored me. I drew my staff. I banged on the window, again. 'Turn the engine off and get out of the vehicle or I will put the window through.' No response. Glass might be tough but *lignum vitae* is harder. I turned sideways-on. Shielded my face with my left arm and swung the truncheon. Safety glass shatters into small pieces so there is less chance of injury through flying splinters. It didn't disappoint. The driver's lap glistened. I flipped the door release, opened the door and dragged the driver out of the car by the collar of his windcheater.

Slowly the audience was being dispersed but one man saw different. 'This is

not a police state. That was outrageous!'

This was the last thing I needed. A vicar with attitude. 'If this had been a

police state, reverend, I would have shot him, stop making fatuous remarks, please leave.'

'You are a rude and impertinent young man. I shall report you to your chief

constable.'

'Are far as pertinence is concerned, reverend, this is my job and not yours.

But write to Mr Barton, please. My name is Blake, B-l-a-k-e.' I turned to one of the beat officers. 'Escort him back to his car and advise him that if he is not on his way within thirty seconds he will be arrested for obstruction.' Hopefully that would get rid of him and the backlog of traffic. A movement caught my eye as a Traffic motorcyclist paddled down the centre of the road. Will Kendrick was nearby, 'Will, Get details from both these lorry drivers, we can get statements later.' He nodded. I turned back to my prisoner. 'Right, what's your name?'

'Michael Doohan. I've done nowt why the rough stuff?'

'We'll see. Whose vehicle is this?'

'Mine, why.'

'What's the registered number?'

'Dunno, just bought it.'

'And the documents?' He shrugged.

'Hello, Pat,' the motorcyclist arrived. 'In trouble again. You promised me the

last time was the last time.'

'He said his name was Michael Doohan.'

'His uncle, Doohan runs the site. This is Patrick McGurk.'

'All right, enough,' I said and cautioned him. 'Patrick McGurk I'm arresting

you for assisting an offender, under the Criminal Law Act 1967.'

'What? I've done nowt. What offender?'

'The man who was driving this car less than thirty minutes ago is wanted for

a serious offence. Work it out.'

I thanked the two lorry drivers and with McGurk cuffed to one of the beat

officers and transported to Brighouse by Will Kendrick in the Beetle I re-joined PC Wilson for my journey home informing Force Control what was happening.

I cleared the spare land on the Leeds side of the White Gate and called home for a quick cuppa. John's observation compared our house to a maternity ward. Anne pointed out that if Frankie had been in the UK instead of studying for her Doctorate at Harvard it would have been more complicated. John produced the photos of his three children and was adopted by Claire who brought her new favourite book – The Last Dragon Ryder by Graeme Sylverton. She was developing a penchant for older men in uniform.

I took the opportunity to call Superintendent Wallace and join the dots. DS

Greatorix was en route to Brighouse to interview McGurk. The VW was awaiting fingerprint examination. We were diverted to check the back roads to Sowerby Bridge. As for me, I had a little bribe to deliver.

Thirty-Five

'And you say that this youngster keeps a record of all vehicles that go to Nicolls' house?'

'Yes sir, plus any new vehicles he hasn't seen before. And he seems to know the specs of everything with an engine, an amazing memory, as I found out. Plus he only uses first names.'

'Really?'

'His father told me Arthur doesn't communicate well, but I can vouch he's a clever lad.'

'If he's a memory like that he must be.'

'I asked Dr O'Keefe, our divisional police surgeon, about him but without an examination he was loath to comment. He said it could be a form of what he called autism. What they used to call an *idiot savant*. Not well understood.'

'It's not a mental illness then?'

'No sir, it's something he was born with.'

'All right lets go and have a chat with Arthur. See what he has to say for himself.

Arthur was out of the house in a flash. His father close behind.

'Wow. That's a Volvo 122S,' said Arthur hanging over the gate.

'Arthur, come down. Let the sergeant and his friend in, come on.'

We were seated in the living room when Malcolm Truelove arrived with the coffee. 'White with two for you Mr Wallace. And a black with no sugar for the sergeant. Orange juice for Arthur and tea for me. Now then gentlemen how can we help?'

Detective Superintendent Wallace took a sip of coffee, placed his cup on a nearby coffee table and smiled. 'Arthur, what can you tell me about my car?'

Arthur looked at him. '

What's your name?'

'I understand you only use first names. Is that correct?' Arthur nodded. 'Well, I'm a detective superintendent and nobody is allowed to know my name. If I whisper it, you must never tell anybody. Do we have a deal?'

We all knew that his name was Richard, so this was a test. Arthur nodded. Information imparted. 'It's a Volvo 122S. 1782 cubic centimetre engine with 4 inline cylinders. It has a top speed of 92 mph and can do zero to sixty in 14.4 seconds. It develops 86 horsepower at 5400 revs per minute.'

'That's brilliant, Arthur. He beamed a smile at the young boy. 'Now, could I see that notebook of yours. The one where you write down all the car numbers?'

Arthur looked at his father. 'Nip upstairs Arthur and bring it down.'

'Mr Wallace, before Arther comes back please don't try to take his book. If you do he'll become very upset and the rapport you're developing will be lost, and you won't get it back.'

'Would he hold it so that we can see it?' I said.

'That shouldn't be a problem but I can't always be sure how he will react.'

Arthur arrived clutching his notebook. 'Arthur, stand in front of the sergeant and his friend and open your book so that they can read what you've written, please.'

There were page after page of vehicle registration numbers. 'How many numbers have you, Arthur?' I said.

He grinned. 'Three hundred and sixty. Sixteen to a page and I'm on page 23. Another eight and the page will be full.'

'Do you ever write the same number in more than once?' said Mr Wallace.

'What would be point of that?'

So it was not a diary of attendance. We both laughed. 'You remember every single number?'

He nodded.

'So, your book is opened at page eight,' said Mr Wallace. 'Can you tell us the third, fourth and sixth numbers?'

At last Arthur smiled. 'The third number was an Austin 7, JX 6840. The fourth an Austin 8, GVH 248 and the sixth ... a Volkswagen beetle 462 VUR.'

'Very well, I'm convinced,' said Mr Wallace. 'We need a copy of those pages. No, don't worry, Arthur,' he said when Arthur recoiled. He turned to me. 'Is the divisional photocopier working?'

'No, sir, but there's a new one in HQ Admin, behind the Mail Room.'

'Arthur, how would you and your father like a ride in a big police car?'

Thirty-Six

We drove into HQ carpark. 'Whose are all the cars?' Arthur's eyes opened wide.

'They belong to the people who work here, Arthur,' I said, 'but don't try to remember them all, otherwise we won't get the job done.'

We alighted outside the rear door to the Admin block.

'This doesn't look like a police station,'

'It's the back door that only important people use,' said Mr Wallace.

'It looks untidy.'

'It is, but that's not important, shall we go in?'

I opened the rear door as the chief was leaving. 'Sergeant Blake, I heard about your problem. Is everyone safe?'

'Yes, sir.'

'Good,' he turned to look at Arthur. 'And this is the young man you told me about. Mr Wallace?'

'Yes, sir.'

The Chief smiled at Arthur. 'Would you open your book so that I can see, please.'

The chief's eyebrows raised a notch. 'I see, and you know all these numbers by heart.' Arthur nodded. 'Remarkable ... Very well gentlemen, I will leave you to it.'

'Who was that?' said Arthur as the Chief headed for his Staff Car.

'That's the chief constable, Arthur,' I said. 'Everybody's boss.'

'What's his name?'

'Nobody knows, we all call him, sir,' I said.

Arthur looked miffed and frowned. 'That's not a name.'

'I know but that's the way it is,' I stopped and looked at the clouds. Shall we go, then we can get you home before it starts to snow.'

Apart from a few grumbles from the Admin Sergeant about indulging children in their hobbies it went smoothly.

Katherine, the operator, had Arthur stand on a box of paper so that he could see. She explained how to position his book for each page and a happy Arthur finished his task.

'But you promised,' said a crestfallen Arthur.

'I'm sorry, Arthur. But they decided that, in such a small space it would be dangerous, but there is something else to thank you for helping us.'

'Is that the garage, over there?' said Arthur pointing as a patrol car exited the workshop. 'Can I have a look inside?'

A couple of mechanics glanced in our direction as we appeared in the doorway. Arthur pointed at the nearest car; it's bonnet up. 'That's a Mk II Austin Westminster 110,' he said rattling off the specs, '4 speed manual gearbox. Maximum speed 102 mph. 0-60mph in 13.3 seconds. Standing quarter mile 19.4 seconds. Develops 120 brake horsepower at 4750 rpm.'

''That's very good,' came a voice from the rear. 'Where did you learn that?'

'I buy him motoring mags and he remembers everything,' said his father.

'That's a great skill. I wish I could.' He turned and walked away.

A two minute walk through the CID block towards the back staircase, eliciting the comment, 'Recruits are getting younger and smaller these days,' from a smiling officer in shirt-sleeves.

Up the stairs to the first floor. 'Just wait here,' said Mr Wallace and entered the Force Control Room; the Duty Officer, Inspector William "Bill" Rydal. 'I know it's an odd request Bill but the chief has no objections providing it's ok by you ... Arthur is eleven. He doesn't know it, but he's given us some information that could be vital in tracing a murderer. He's autistic with a photographic memory. He's not a brilliant communicator, but he is a very bright lad.'

Inspector Rydal nodded. 'Ok, sir,' he paused and leaned backwards. 'Terry, anything of any import running.

'Just the gold run for the Bank of England, sir.'

'OK, you're going to have a visitor.'

Under curious eyes we followed Inspector Rydal crowding into the small room, for the most part occupied by a large radio console with two policemen, one with a radio mike and the other a pad of yellow message forms. Both facing the wall with a huge map of the West Riding of Yorkshire and surrounding areas. Arthur stood between them devouring the map.

The radio operator turned to him. 'Hello, my name's Terry. What's yours?'

'Arthur,' he said without shifting his gaze.'

'Shake hands,' said Terry holding his hand out.

Arthur shook hands.

'My name's Nick. Hello Arthur,' said the other offering his hand.

'Hello,' he said, broke contact with the map, shook hands. And pointed to the console. What are all those switches for?'

'We call them keys. This one,' said Terry fingering the one on the left is ....'

'What was Arthur doing?' I said as Arthur peered over Terry's shoulder. 'It looked as though he was trying to absorb the map in its entirety.'

'He probably was doing just that,' said his father. 'He doesn't appear to read as such, but, he does absorb a lot of detail.'

Before anything else could be said there were two calls from the office. 'Report from Ambulance of a multiple RTA A639 Barnsdale.'

'Fire Brigade also en route.'

'I'm sorry,' said Inspector Rydal. 'You're going to have to leave.' He probably wasn't sorry at all. 'Did you enjoy that, Arthur?' he said as Arthur's father rounded him up and Terry began calling the Pontefract cars to attend.

'Yes, thank you .... Is somebody going to die?'

Inspector Rydal half-smiled. 'Hopefully not. But it is a possibility.'

Thirty-Seven

Thirty minutes later we dropped Arthur and Mr Truelove at their home. Mr Wallace shook hands with them both. 'Thank you for these, Arthur,' he said showing the copies of Arthur's notes. 'They could be very useful.'

He nodded. 'Could I have another ride, someday?'

Everyone laughed. 'I can't make promises,' said Mr Wallace. 'And now I have to get back to work, sergeant?'

'Sir, do not turn round. I've seen someone at the kitchen window across the road.'

'Mr Truelove can I use your phone, please?'

'Of course, superintendent. Come on Arthur, let's put the kettle on.'

'Sergeant?' the Superintendent said as he crossed the threshold and glanced over his shoulder. 'Where? Oh Christ!. Your phone Mr Truelove.'

It took thirty seconds for me to reach the door which was slightly ajar. Stepping inside, adjacent to the sink was a large suitcase secured with a leather strap. Sounds of somebody moving around in in the lounge. *Was he doing a runner?* A soft metallic click. I opened the door and stepped inside. Whether he was breaking the shotgun down for easier transport, or trying to assemble it, I don't know. I wasn't going to waste time asking him

I stepped forward. 'Nicholas Nickleby .'

'Who?

'You heard. Nicholas Nickleby, I am arresting you...'

'What the fuck are you talking about?'

'Arresting you on suspicion of the murder of Gloria Rodgers on the 12th of August 1959. You are not obliged to say anything but anything you say may be used in evidence.'

'What's going on. Who the fuck is Nicholas Nickleby when he's at home?'

I took the gun, a Lipari pump-action shotgun, from him. 'Turn round.'

'What the hell's going on and who the chuff is Nicholas Nickleby. You've made a fucking mistake.'

'Someone has,' I said. Safely cuffed I took him to the door. Superintendent Wallace and PC's Fleming and Napier were running up the drive. A double-manned Traffic car and Inspector Marshall pulling up.

I got a look from the Superintendent that said: *One of these days*!

'Sir, this is Nicholas Nickleby. Arrested on suspicion of the murder of Gloria Rodgers on the 12th August 1959, in Brixton.'

'Any trouble?'

'No, sir. Just a denial that he is Nickleby.'

'Understood,' he turned to the two Traffic officers. 'This man is Nicholas Nickleby, arrested on suspicion of murder, transport him to Halifax Borough cells; they are expecting you. When you notify force control that you are en route, mention neither his name or the offence. Is that clear?'

'Yes, sir.'

'He will probably give the name of Nicholas Collins but book him in under the name of Nickleby; with Collins as an alias. Arresting officer Sergeant 547 Blake. Fleming, you go with them.'

'And Fleming, in view of Nickleby's links with the local police nobody but nobody talks to him. I want to know if anyone does.'

'Sir,'

Nickleby and escorts left for Halifax. Nickleby no doubt wondering what his future held.

'I'll take the shotgun, Brian.' I handed it to Inspector Marshall.

'It's a Lipari pump-action, sir.'

'Pump-action?

I nodded.

'I know there's no rifling but perhaps forensic can match the firing pin to the cartridge cases we found.'

'That would be nice,' I said

'Napier, I want you on the door. Keep a pocket book entry of anybody who enters the building. Time in and out. You can start with Sergeant Blake. Inspector, one on the gate to keep the rubberneckers away.'

'Yes, sir. I'll arrange a rota and reliefs.'

Three further cars arrived. Detective Inspector Peter Cartwright, and the second containing DS Greatorix with DC's Turner, Kidd and Cavendish. In the third, Martin Chalkley, my relief sergeant and Bruce Knight. Inspector Marshall left to police the sub-division and a promise to tell Lucy that I might be late.

I refreshed my relationship with Max Cavendish. Bruce Knight was on the gate chatting with Sergeant Chalkley. The four DC's despatched to local enquiries. I took Superintendent Wallace, DI Cartwright and DS Greatorix into the bungalow.

'Before we begin, sir, and before I forget, again. It's about a lad I locked up in the riot case,'

'Is that relevant?'

'I believe so, His name was Chris Grogan,'

'Christ, he's a pain in the arse,' said Colin Greatorix.

'He got six months and can't be long before he gets out. I was talking to his grandfather ...'

'Tommy? He was another pain in the arse. Best climber I've ever come across.'

'Until he fell and broke his back. Told me Chris worked as an odd-job man for Nick Collins, no educational qualification but had a non-artic HGV licence, and too much money in his pocket

'The HGV details need checking out,' said DI Cartwright.'

'What point are you trying to make, sergeant,' Superintendent Wallace was becoming tetchy.

'Chris Grogan is not the sharpest knife in the box, sir, but I would think he had the brute strength to rip the number plates off the Blackpool Borough police car. If that is the case, he is at least guilty of being an accessory after the fact for the murder of the three in the car; possibly the Morris Minor as well?

The superintendent nodded. 'We know that two shots were fired at the Morris Minor. If it was Grogan, after the triple shooting he would know what was likely to happen to the driver. May even had pulled the trigger.'

'My thoughts entirely, sir. Six months inside is one thing, but he's potentially looking at four life sentences.'

The superintendent turned to the DI. 'Find out Grogan's release date. We need to interview him whilst he's looking forward to some fresh air.'

There wasn't much I could add to what I'd seen inside Nickleby's bungalow. Only the case in the kitchen, and show where I had arrested him

I left to type my statement of arrest as the snow began to fall.

Thirty-Eight

A folder slid off my correspondence tray. The Hathersage file shuttered across my desk, the photograph on top. '*Christ,*' I said to myself, It never bloody rains.

'Birmingham City Police.'

'Good morning. Sergeant Blake, Sowerby Bridge, West Riding. I'm trying to trace someone we know had connections with a sudden death we're looking into. The last I heard he was running a business in Birmingham.'

'Do you know which division.'

'Sorry, I don't.'

'Big place. Hold the line, sergeant.'

Seconds later. 'Sergeant Blake. DI Riley, I hear you're looking into a sudden death. How exactly can I help?'

'It concerns a team of RAF Dispatch Riders from the war. A Sergeant Hathersage, and three aircraftsmen: Forbes, Nickleby and Smedley ... ... '

'... I agree it does sound contrived. Bryan Forbes. Right, I will let you know as soon as possible. I'll send you a telex. What's your service number?'

'547.'

'Right, but before you go. I take it you are the same Blake that arrested Donald Palmer?'

What? 'Yes I am, sir?'

'Oh, I replaced him at Pannal. The Commandant, Chief Superintendent Sanderson was singing your praises. It might be a three year attachment but it's a good career move. At least it was for me.' I made my excuses, typed my statement and left for Salendine Nook.

Thirty-Nine

Field took a quick look at the half dozen coppers, some in plain clothes, waiting behind the chief superintendent. This didn't look good. 'Mr Yelland?'

'All right,' the DCS glanced over his shoulder. 'You know who we're looking for.' The waiting officers raced passed him. He turned to face Field. 'I have a warrant to search your premises. Similar warrants have been issued by the magistrates to search any and all of the premises in which you have an interest and, as we speak, they are being executed.' He handed Field the warrant.

'That's not very friendly. But you never were kindly disposed toward me.'

'You can only serve one master, Harry. I made my choice.'

'So you did. But this seems a lot of fuss. What's it all about?'

'The punter that Edwards stabbed in the back at your bookies in Camden last night.'

Yes, unfortunate that. I heard about it.'

'He's dead.'

'Is that why you're looking for Carl.'

'The man he stabbed was a police officer. Is that clear enough. I will turn London upside down and God help anyone who gets in my way.'

The blood drained from Field's face. 'Sorry, I didn't know.'

Probably didn't care either until it interfered with your business.

'Tell me who you are looking for, I might be able to help.'

'Very well. Apart from Edwards, I suspect that we might already have the other three in custody by now. They are Yvonne Richards or Edith Ramsbottom if you prefer, Jimmy Moss and his daughter Elizabeth.'

'Why them?' *But no Bellamy?*

'They were present when the officer was stabbed, and until we are satisfied they had nothing to do with it they will remain in custody.'

'But Elizabeth is only a kid.'

'She's eighteen, an adult, plus she's Jimmy Moss's daughter. We will get to the bottom of this.'

Did they arrest Bellamy? They must have known he was there. And Frobisher? Have the bastards being playing me?

Forty

**1pm. BBC regional news bulletin:
BREAKING NEWS. AT HALIFAX WEST RIDING MAGISTRATES COURT IN THE LAST HOUR, NICHOLAS NICKLEBY, ALSO KNOW AS NICHOLAS COLLINS, A BUSINESSMAN FROM SOWERBY BRIDGE WAS REMANDED IN CUSTODY FOR THE MURDER OF MRS GLORIA RODGERS IN BRIXTON, LONDON, IN AUGUST 1959. THE REMAND WAS TO POLICE CELLS PENDING INVESTIGATION ON FURTHER SERIOUS CHARGES. DETECTIVE SUPERINTENDENT RICHARD WALLACE WOULD ONLY SAY THAT THE INVESTIGATION WAS AT AN EARLY STAGE. HE DECLINED TO COMMENT ON WHAT THE FURTHER CHARGES MIGHT BE.**

COMMANDER JAMESON OF THE METROPOLITAN POLICE MAJOR CRIME UNIT SAID THEY WERE DELIGHTED AT THE NEWS AND WERE LIAISING CLOSELY WITH THEIR COLLEAGUES IN THE WEST RIDING. NO FURTHER COMMENT WOULD BE MADE AT THIS JUNCTURE.

'Did he say Nickleby?' Detective Inspector 'Linus' Bellamy slammed his foot on the brakes causing the vehicles behind to swerve and subjecting them to a fanfare. 'The bastards! I'm not having that.' He opened the door only to be grabbed by his passenger, Detective Chief Inspector Alex Frobisher.

'Never mind them. Get driving. I reckon we've thirty six hours to terminate Blake or we're fish food. It was Nickleby who got rid of Yvonne and that Aristocratic ponce she was towing round; concrete boots off the German coast. 20K he got for that.'

'Well if he's been nicked he's out of the running.

'Linus, if he talks we're sunk ... where are we now?'

'That last sign said Middlestown. Then it's Huddersfield. But this bloody snow isn't making things any easier.'

'Just don't prang the bloody car.'

DETECTIVE CHIEF SUPERINTENDENT Paul Yelland was angry; this had the stench of Harry Field. *I'm not having those bloody rhubarb pullers in the bloody West Riding making us look like fucking amateurs. I want everything there is on Nickleby. I want to know the details of every copper who has had anything to do with Nickleby and Field, whatever the rank. Document production. CRO. The archive. Fingerprints and Studio. Traffic, Everything. If any police records have been destroyed I want to know what and by whom, when and why. Hospital records. Coroner's officer, and a copy of the coroner's file. Undertakers records and everyone involved. And, I want it yesterday! Do-I-make-myself-clear!!*

Everyone had been read the Riot Act.

RAYMOND BARTON SMILED. 'You want Blake on this enquiry? You don't have enough men?'

'It's not the numbers, sir, it's the quality. We saw the quality of his thinking during the last big job.'

'That wasn't a one off ... Very well, but I'm not making him acting or temporary inspector. He hasn't held this rank long enough.'

'I understand, sir. I don't intend to interview Nickleby until I get the results back from Nottingham re the shotgun. But I will use him with DI Cartwright to interview Grogan.'

'Won't that put a few noses out of joint?'

'Perhaps, but we're not overburdened with good DS's and there is plenty for DS Greatorix to do. But I will have words with him.'

Ray Barton looked diagonally to his left. 'Mr Mithering?'

'I'll speak with Mr Cartwright, sir, smooth his feathers. He was saying only yesterday that Blake would become the rope in a tug-of-war.'

Forty-One

Harry Field stared at the television screen. 'What the ...' He drained the whisky before slamming the Waterford Crystal none too gently on the side table. He grabbed the telephone and dialled.

'Hello, who's that?'

'Don't recognise my voice, Charley?'

'Harry?' Charley Wilson, retired detective inspector from the Met knew a threat from Harry Field when he heard one. 'You sound pissed, what's up?'

'Pissed? Have you heard the news?'

'No, just this minute got in. Been swimming.'

'Remind me, Charley, how much did I pay you to get rid of anything that referred to Nickleby?'

'10K, Why, what's happened?'

'He's been nicked; they know that Nickleby and Collins are the same. How did that fucking happen?'

'Beats me, Harry. I did everything that you asked. Incinerated the lot.'

'So, how did they find out?'

'Beats me.'

'Find out. Get into New Scotland Yard and yank a few chains. I want to know and soon.'

'Harry, I'm retired. With this new security system I wouldn't get passed the front door.'

'Well, get somebody that's inside, out. Find out. I thought you were a bloody DI.' He slammed the phone down took a deep breath and re-dialled.'

'Jacob,' he said straining to impart a sense of bonhomie into his voice. 'It's Harry Field, how's the wife and kids.'

Jacob Montague, Harry Field's investment manager, had heard enough businessmen worried about the future to recognise stress when he heard it. Field sounded rattled. 'They're fine Mr Field. Now, what can I do for you?'

Harry's bank accounts were solid; The investments set up by Kenny Summers were his responsibility. 'Your investments are healthy, Mr Field. The total value two days ago was, one point nine million.'

'Excellent. I was considering retiring. Moving to somewhere with more sun.'

'Your villa in Curaçao, Mr Field?'

'Yes, It's a lovely spot. Would I have to cash everything in?'

'No, that won't be necessary. We can simply transfer you account. Save on fees,'

Field was impressed. It wasn't often there was somebody who didn't want to get their hands into his pockets. 'Thanks, Jacob.'

'Do you have a date in mind? I could then begin to make the necessary arrangements.'

'I was thinking next Monday.'

'Thank you, that is in my diary. Have a safe journey. When you arrive everything will be ready.'

Jacob Montague redialled. 'Harry Field says he is retiring. He flies out to Curaçao next Monday.'

'Thank you, Jacob. All will be ready'

'I'm sure it will.'

Forty-Two

Snowflakes were drifting in the gentle breeze. The sun trying to break through. Stray beams striking the massive doors of Leeds Prison. The two police officers stamping their feet, trying to revive their circulation.

Detective Inspector Peter Cartwright gazed around. 'Like old times, Brian.'

'It is, sir. It's not often there's sun and snow at the same time ... Here he comes.' Chris Grogan stepped into the watery sun. For a second he looked up at the sun, rubbed his eyes, bent down picking up a double handful of snow fashioning a snowball and flinging it across the car park.

The three that followed Grogan shook hands and hugged their welcome-out parties before making their escape in whatever vehicle presented itself. Grogan stood looking around as if waiting.

'Someone supposed to pick him up?'

'Could be Collins, sir.'

'It could indeed. Chris, Chris Grogan,' DI Cartwright called and waved. Grogan, in no hurry wandered across.

'You coppers?'

'How did you guess,'

'I've been in there for months. I've done nowt. Waitin' for Mr Collins. He said he'll pick me up.'

'He's tied up. We told him we'd pick you up. Beside there's some questions we would like to ask you.'

'Fittin' me up already.'

‘Not at all, Chris,’ I said. ‘We need some help in sorting something out.’ I said.

He stared at me. ‘You’re the sergeant that hit me. Where the chuffin’ ’ell did you learn to hit like that.’

‘Okinawa,’

‘Where’s that?’

‘An island south of Japan.’

He looked puzzled. ‘If you say so.’

‘Come on.’ I said and smiled. ‘Well get you a coffee.’

He grinned. ‘Rather ‘ave a pint.’

‘I’m sure you would. Coffee only this morning. Come on.’

Forty-Three

'I didn't think we'd bloody end up here.' Grogan said as we stopped outside Brighouse police station.

'Different station this time, Chris,' I said. 'And, we're going in the front door.'

'Still a cop 'ole.'

'Can't argue with that.'

John Bradbury, my old friend from Pannal appeared,. 'Bloody hell, Sergeant Blake. Making a takeover bid, Brian?'

We shook hands. 'I'll fill you in as far as I can, later, yes?'

Grogan safely ensconced in an interview room I contributed to their tea fund and acquired a packet of biscuits.

'Bloody 'ell, biscuits as well,' Grogan said as I entered. He helped himself. It was a small price to pay.

DI Cartwright entered, closed the door and sat. 'I've spoken with Inspector Royston and put him in the picture ... Now, before we begin, Chris, to be fair I have to tell you that you're not obliged to say anything if you don't want but whatever you say may be used in evidence. Do you understand?

Grogan sat back and stared at us, hard. 'I thought you said it were just a few questions to sort things out.'

'It is,' said the DI. 'We're not trying to trap you into anything. Just being fair.'

Grogan shrugged. 'OK, what do want to know.'

'I was having a coffee with your Grandad after you got sent down,' I said. 'He told me you'd been working for Mr Collins for a few years. How many?'

'You had a coffee with me Grandad? Bloody 'ell. When he were fit he left you lot for dead.'

'I know,' I laughed. 'He told me. 'Said you slipped him a few quid from time to time.'

'Aye, if I'd owt spare.'

'That was good of you.'

'Got to 'elp 'im out.'

'Now, how many years have you worked for the man you know as Collins?'

'Three 'appen four.'

'How did you meet?'

'In the Fox, 'aving a pint.'

'That's the Flying Fox pub?'

'Aye.'

'I presume he asked if you wanted to earn some cash?'

He nodded. 'Aye, and bought me a pint.'

'Just what did you do for him. We know you've got a heavy good vehicle licence.'

'Whatever he wanted. Going to his suppliers. Fetchin' an' carrying. Digging his garden. Anything.'

'How did you get paid?'

'Out of his back pocket. He were generous; that's how I could afford to slip grandad a few quid.'

'Ever hear him mention the name Harry?'

''arry? Sometimes on't phone. Kicked me out when that 'appened.'

'Who rang who?'

'This 'arry bloke rang 'im. Why what's up?'

'So you don't know what was said.'

He shook his head. 'Nah.'

'Chris.' the DI said. 'Did you know that Collins was not his real name?'

He laughed. 'Don't talk daft, course it were. Allus known 'im as Mr Collins. Everybody did.'

'That's as maybe, but it's true; his real name is Nicholas Nickleby.'

He laughed again. 'That's plain daft. Why would 'e do that? Change his bloody name.'

'Chris, listen carefully. Nickleby, or Collins, is in custody for murder.'

The blood drained from Grogan's face. 'That were nowt to do wi' me. You're not pinning that on me.'

'Chris, we're not pinning anything on anybody. But what did you mean? What was nothing to do with you?'

Grogan was beginning to hyperventilate and stuttered as he spoke. 'Them three in the car ...I I didn't shoot anybody; that were Mr Collins.'

I was round the table in a flash; I put my left hand on Grogan's right shoulder;. We needed to get his story. 'Chris, take a deep breath. Slow your breathing down. Trust me. We don't believe you shot anybody. Try and relax. Slow your breathing down ... good.

Whilst I was calming Grogan the DI headed for the Inspector's office. 'Mr Reynolds, do you have a typist we can borrow.'

'We could do with one but the answer is no.'

He picked up the phone and dialled. 'Wallace.'

'Sir, we need a typist. Grogan has volunteered the information that Collins shot the three in the car. I want to get his statement verbatim ... Yes, sir.' He replaced the phone, 'An hour.'

'Grogan coughed?'

Detective Inspector Cartwright smiled. 'Sorry, don't know what you mean.'

Inspector Reynolds grinned in return. 'Fair enough, that stays in this office.'

Detective Inspector Cartwright frowned. 'What stays in this office?'

Forty-Four

PC Johnstone, the office clerk, almost leapt to his feet as Assistant Chief Constable Mithering entered, preceded by a young woman.

'Good morning, sir. Inspector Royston is in his office.'

'Thanks, and DI Cartwright?'

'Interview room, sir.'

'Mrs Watson, take a seat. Two shakes.'

'Sir,' she said and sat.

PC Johnstone, smiled at her. 'Cold out today.'

'Bitter, she replied and half-smiled. 'We came by traffic car, a bit quick.'

PC Johnstone laughed. 'It's a habit of theirs.'

Mrs Watson stood as the ACC and Inspector Reynolds exited his office. 'Can I get you some tea or coffee, sir.'

The ACC looked at his watch. 'Tea, please, what about you Mrs Watson?'

'Not for me, sir, but the ladies room?'

'Down here Mrs Watson.' She followed the Inspector.

'The lads outside?'

'Tell them to stay in the canteen.' He put his hand in his pocket and handed Pc Johnstone a 50p coin. 'Put that in your tea fund.'

After a two minute chat with the ACC. 'Well done both of you. Let's hope for a positive result from forensic. Right where are my drivers.'

AS WE ENTERED THE INTERVIEW room I introduced the secretary. 'Mrs Watson. I am Sergeant 547 Blake. This is DI Cartwright and the gentleman behind the table is Cristopher Grogan.'

'Who's she?' said Grogan. 'She doesn't look like a copper.'

'She isn't, she takes shorthand, Chris,' I said as Mrs Watson sat adjacent to the door and began to write. 'She is recording our conversation, so that it's accurate.'

'Can I see what she's writing?'

'I don't think it will make any sense to you,' she said and handed me her pad. I showed it to Grogan.

'This isn't writing, it's squiggles.'

'Yes, it is,' I said. 'From this she'll type out a statement. 'We will include her notes so that any other shorthand writer can ensure what you say hasn't been tampered with. I told you earlier we're not trying to fit you up with anything. Ok?'

'Suppose,' he said.

'Right, this is what we had talked about before Mrs Watson arrived ... *Trust me. We don't believe that you shot anybody.* Do you agree?'

'Aye, that's about right.'

'Mrs Watson, will you read out what you've written since you arrived.'

'From the beginning?'

'If you please'

'*She isn't. She takes shorthand ... Trust me. We don't believe that you shot anybody.* That's all, sir.'

'You're happy with that,, Chris?' I said.

'Aye,'

'Let's go back. This shooting occurred on Tuesday 19th of September. Talk us through what happened when Mr Collins contacted you about it?'

'He didn't tell me 'e were going to shoot anybody. Just said there was something he had to do for 'Arry, early Tuesday.'

'He definitely said it was for Harry?'

'Aye.'

'Did he call at your home, or telephone?'

'We don't 'ave a phone. 'E called about half nine. Said 'e'd pick me up at half four.'

'And he did?'

'Aye, on the dot.'

'What sort of car was it?'

'A beat-up Zephyr 4, you know, like a cop car but it were a real banger.'

'Black.'

'Aye.'

'He definitely said it was *for Harry*?'

Grogan nodded. 'Just as I said, *for 'Arry*.'

'What happened after he picked you up?'

'We drove out towards Brighouse an' stopped in a side road, 'e told me to get out and opened the boot. It were full of gear: police signs, cones and a couple of police uniforms.'

I laughed. 'Did he find one big enough for you?'

He reciprocated. 'A bit tight, but it were ok. Helmet were a bit small.'

'Was there anything else in the boot?'

'Aye, brand new shot gun, pump action. Told me it were the first in the country.'

'He'd be proud of it, then.'

He laughed. 'Like a bairn with a giant bar o' chocolate on its birthday. Fair made up 'e was.'

'Then?'

'We drove through Brighouse to where he shot those three. Turned the car round and parked ont' verge. 'e put some cobbled up blue light on top; battery operated it were. Then we put the cones and signs out and waited.'

'What about the shotgun.'

''e loaded it in't car. I asked 'im if it were necessary.'

'How did he react?'

'Told me to ... ' He looked up at Mrs Watson. 'I don't like in front of ...'

'That's all right, Mr Grogan. I've heard it all before.'

'Still don't like ... he said. *Shut the fuck up and do as you're bloody told.*'

'He was angry?'

Grogan nodded. 'Aye, you could be all mates, but next second he's blazing mad, a few seconds later you're all mates again. Just as if nowt 'ad 'appened.'

'How long were you waiting before the car arrived?'

'Five or ten minutes.'

'How did you know which car it would be?'

'It were goin' like the clappers. 'e said it would be the one.'

'You knew what to do?'

'Aye, when 'e raised 'is hand I 'ad to rip the plates off.'

'So, you were where?'

''e stood in the road. I waited on the grass. 'E stopped the car; the driver had the window down an' waved his card. I didn't hear everythin'. I'll never forget that morning. 'e said summat like: *Accident, officer*? As if 'e were askin' a question. Mr Collins replied: *Not exactly but we didn't have any signs that said*, then he raised his hand. I got crackin' with the front plate. I 'eard 'im say the name *Kenny Summers*. Then the shots. I nearly shit mi self. I got the front plate off and reached the back when I 'eard him say: *Say 'ello to God*. 'e fired. All I saw were Kenny Summers' 'ead explode. The back window shattered, I got covered an' threw up. I'd got the plate 'alf off when I 'eard a car comin' down'ill, it were a Morris. 'e fired twice an' missed the driver. Then 'e got a bit panicky, picked the cartridge cases up, threw the blue light on the deck. I slung the plates in the boot and we set off after the Morris. 'e wanted me to shoot the driver but I wouldn't. So 'e rested the barrel on the door frame and fired as we drove past.'

Grogan's head dropped onto his chest. I saw the tears start to roll down his cheeks and glanced at the DI. He nodded.

'I think we'll take a break. Are you all right, Chris?'

He nodded. 'I'll be okay ... You're not going to let me go 'ome, are you?'

'Not today, Chris,' said the DI. 'Brian, take Mrs Watson through and get her some tea. Then fetch Chris a pot. Milk and sugar?'

He nodded. 'Two please.'

Forty-Five

Mrs Watson looked up. 'How do you do it?'

'It's not all like this. You blank it out. Leave it at the gate. I've got Lucy and a livewire called Claire; she's three. Plus identical twin boys just a few weeks old, a very big garden, and I teach karate. Burn off the aggression. That's why houses have gates ... But isn't your husband in the job.'

She nodded. 'Yes, he's on Wakefield traffic. He doesn't talk about the job either. I only find out by talking to other wives or if it's reported in the Express.'

The kettle began to boil. 'I'll take these and send Peter through. Help yourself to milk and sugar.'

PC Johnstone poked his head round the door frame. 'Now the sergeant's out of the way, Mrs Watson, what can you tell us?'

'We're working.'

'Yes, but what's Grogan saying.'

'You know I can't say anything. I like my job and like you I've signed the Official Secrets Act.'

Pc Johnstone jumped at the sound of the DI's voice. 'Not interfering in a murder investigation by any chance?'

'No, sir. Wouldn't dream of it.'

'Go on, hop it.'

'Sir,'

'Professional curiosity?

'Nosey buggers. Grogan is a local and a bit of a handful, he's only come out of prison today after six months for riot.'

'A colourful character?'

'One way of putting it.'

'HERE YOU ARE CHRIS. Tea with two.'

'Ta,' he said and took a drink. 'What will 'appen to me.'

'These are very serious offences, but I'm a sergeant and it's not my decision to make. All I can say is that you must keep telling the truth. The others will be back in a few minutes so can we leave it until Mrs Watson can get things down.

He looked at me and grinned. 'Better not say knickers 'ad I?'

I smiled. 'No, you bloody hadn't. Besides her husband is in the police; road traffic.'

'Bloody 'ell. Can't avoid you lot.'

Mrs Watson and the DI returned. 'Chris, you appreciate you're still under caution?'

'Aye, let's crack on.'

'I'll tell you now it was Sergeant Blake that arrested Nickleby for the murder of a woman in London in 1959. He was thought to have been killed in a road accident whilst being pursued by the Metropolitan Police. That's when he changed his name from Nickleby to Collins and moved north. This man is evil and will stop at nothing to get what he wants. Just keep telling us the truth. You owe him nothing.'

Grogan looked at me. 'That right? He killed another woman.'

'Yes, he strangled her.'

He paused and frowned. 'Will 'e ever get out?'

'Of Prison? Five murders that we know of. Four with firearms including two police officers? He will almost certainly die in prison.'

'Doesn't like people who grass 'im up. They get 'urt, some 'ave disappeared.'

'Can we talk about that later?'

'Okay, what do you want to know?'

'After Nickleby shot the driver of the Morris how did you get rid of the car?'

'Straight in the crusher at Tod. Uniforms and plates in the boot. Then in 'is car back 'ome.'

'Where was his car?'

'In't yard, manager were there early.'

'Just a sec,' said the DI and headed for the Inspector's office. He pointed at the phone.

'Help yourself.'

He picked the handset up and dialled. 'Colin?'

'Sir?'

'Where's the nearest magistrate?'

'Five minute drive, sir.'

'Get a search warrant for Tod scrap yard. That's where Nickleby disposed of the car, had the manager come in early. Collected the car and left his own out of sight. Arrest all the staff as accessories. We'll sort the sheep from the goats later. But first thing..'

'Yes, get control of the phone. I'll ring Inspector Fowler; he's been waiting for an opportunity like this for long enough.'

He put the phone down. 'Progress?'

'A start. Grogan's been a nuisance but he didn't sign up for what he witnessed ... I haven't said that.'

'Noted.'

The DI entered the Interview Room view with an apologetic smile. 'Sorry about that, just needed a quick word with DS Greatorix. Shall we continue, Brian?'

'Chris, after you left the scrapyard, then what?'

'E dropped me off at 'ome. Stuck some cash in me pocket and told me to take the day off. And not to get smashed and shoot me mouth off.'

'So what did you do?'

'Stayed in and watched TV.'

'All day?'

'Aye. Didn't see him until about ten next day. He was a bit rattled. Asked if I'd been out on the piss shouting me mouth off. I told 'im I 'adn't 'ad a drink but I was going to that night.'

'You say he was rattled. Any reason?'

'Sometimes if 'arry had chewed 'im off 'e was like that. But I don't' know.'

'You say he put cash in your pocket. How much?'

'An 'undred and fifty quid.'

'In notes?'

'Aye. That's all 'e ever carried.'

'Did he ever say anything about the shootings after that.'

'Not to me. But you could tell when 'arry 'ad rung.'

'He was rattled?'

'Aye. I know he got onto that copper, works 'ere, for summat.'

'Do you know who?'

'Lassi, summat like that.'

'Lassiter?'

'Aye, that's it, Lassiter.' He laughed. 'Josie's gonna be pissed.'

'Josie, who's she.'

'Nice looking lass. Drinks at the Bat.'

'Bat? Flying Fox?'

'Aye. 'Es planning to sell 'er?'

'Sell, sell who?'

'Josie. She told me 'e gives 'er ten quid a time.'

'For sex?'

Grogan laughed. 'Course it's sex, they don't play bloody dominoes. 'E as her doing all kinds of weird stuff, twice a week. She loves it. When 'e thinks she's ready 'e'll talk 'er into going to London and working for 'arry. 'E's done it before.'

'And Harry pays.'

'Too bloody true.'

'And she knows this?'

'Nah. It's a long time ago I overheard 'im on t'phone talking to 'arry saying 'e had another one ready. There's been a few since then.'

'Married or single.'

'Both. It's 'ow he got the car dealership.'

'Honey trap?'

'Aye, that were it, Angela it were, She were a cracker. 'e 'as a hotel in 'alifax; the Woodpecker, wi' one room wi' cameras in. Last owner were a bit kinky. Mr Collins got the lot on film then delivered an envelope to the showroom and give it 'im. Threatened to send the photos all over the shop if he didn't sell.'

'What can you tell us about the scrap yard in Tod?'

''E didn't 'ave to do that. Old 'enry wasn't a well man. Refused to sell. I think 'e used a jack to topple that stack, but I'm not sure.'

'I think that's it for today, Chris,' said the DI. 'Now, there is an offence called being an accessory after the fact ...'

'What the 'ells that mean?'

'What that means is that you knew a crime had been committed, and these are some of the most serious crimes, and you didn't report it.'

There were no tears this time, simply a look of resignation. 'Will I go back to prison?'

'I'm afraid that's likely.'

'But if Mr Collins finds out I've grassed him up I'm dead. And 'es scared stiff of 'arry. If he finds out I 've 'elped ...'

'Yes, we know. We will do our best to keep it out of the papers and to make sure you're safe. But for now I've got to arrest you, so I'll caution you again ....'

His shoulders slumped and his head dropped. 'I think I've said enough .. Can I see mi grandad?'

'Not at the moment, Chris,' I said. 'I'll go and explain.'

'That'll 'ave to do'

I booked him in whilst the DI went to brief Inspector Royston. Hopefully stop the information leaking out. 'We needed to keep him safe from violence and wagging tongues.

The office clerk found me in the cells. 'Sergeant Blake, this has arrived from Inspector Marshall, it's marked urgent.' He handed me an envelope.

Forty-Six

Back in the interview room I spread the telex on the table:

FROM: CHIEF CONSTABLE BIRMINGHAM CITY POLICE

TO: CHIEF CONSTABLE WEST RIDING CONSTABULARY.

FOR THE URGENT ATTENTION OF PS547 BLAKE, SOWERBY BRIDGE, HALIFAX DIVISION.

DETECTIVE INSPECTOR D. RILEY, BIRMINGHAM CITY POLICE CRIMINAL INTELLIGENCE UNIT

REFERENCE YOUR ENQUIRY: BRYAN FORBES.

BRYAN PETER FORBES D.O.B. 17TH OCTOBER 1923 IS RECORDED AS HAVING BEEN THE PROPRIETOR OF ARROW COURIERS, OF BIRMINGHAM. HE SOLD THE BUSINESS ON MARCH 23rd THIS YEAR. STATED HIS INTENTION WAS TO RETURN TO HIS NATIVE YORKSHIRE.

FORBES IS DESCRIBED AS BEING CLEAN SHAVEN, FIVE FEET TEN INCHES TALL, OF MEDIUM BUILD WITH BROWN EYES AND RECEDING DARK BROWN HAIR, WEARS A SIGNET RING ON THE THIRD FINGER OF HIS LEFT HAND

FORBES, A SINGLE MAN, LIVED WITH HIS WIDOWED SISTER MRS MARGARET PHILLIPS AGED APPROXIMATELY 40YEARS, BROWN PERMED HAIR AND OF SLIM BUILD.

MESSAGE ENDS.

This was what I needed but the last thing I wanted.

DI Cartwright read the telex, looked at me and smiled. 'You know what this means, Brian?'

'Yes, sir. I can't work two simultaneous murder cases, and this one,' I indicated the telex in the DI's hand, 'is in Sowerby Bridge.'

'Pity that. I persuaded Mr Wallace to ask for you specifically. Still, you've got your own murder case. Leave it with me, we'll speak tomorrow.'

Forty-Seven

DS Greatorix looked round at his party. Not many for this job. 'How many specials will be coming.'

'With a bit of luck, sarge, four. Arthur and Ted are here now. Not the youngest but keen.'

'This is likely to be a roughhouse. Let's hope they're up to it because we can't wait ... I'll go in with DC Weaver. The rest stay back and out of sight for thirty seconds, unless it kicks off. You know what to do. You two,' he indicated the Specials. 'Stay by the gate. Nobody leaves. All arrests for accessory to murder. Any punters just keep them inside. Stay safe. There's a double-manned traffic car and a dog en route, shouldn't be long. Who's got a watch with a second hand.'

The traffic car arrived, John Wilson and Will Kendrick exited. 'What's up, sarge,' said Wilson. 'Why the troops?'

'There's a link between this place and the triple shooting.'

Wilson and Kendrick shot a glance at each other. 'What!? Well, if it's Jacko you're after, he's not there. Saw him not two minutes ago round by the Town Hall.'

'Ok. You two go and find him. Accessory to murder,' Kendricks eyebrows raised. 'Cuff behind and take him to Sowerby. Keep force control updated.'

'Don't worry about that. C'mon Will.'

Inspector Fowler, silver-topped cane in hand, arrived. 'What's happening sergeant?'

'You've heard there's a link between Jackson, Collins and the triple shooting?'

'Yes, I heard. Traffic are looking for Jackson?'

'They are. We're to arrest all the workers for accessory to murder. My first task is the office phone. But once we start cuffing them anything could happen.'

Inspector Fowler raised his cane and laughed. 'Stood me in good stead over the years. Crack a few more skulls. You and Weaver going in first?'

'Yes, give me thirty seconds.'

'Right, you two are on the gate?' Inspector Fowler said to the specials.

'Yes, sir.'

'Good, Don't' try and stop speeding vehicles. That's not healthy. And this is a large scale on-going operation, so no chatting, not even to your wives. If I get word ...'

'We won't, sir.'

DS Greatorix stopped at the foot of the stairs leading to the office and

decamped.

'If you're looking for Jacko, he's out.'

'That's Ok, Frank,' DS Greatorix called back as he and DC Weaver climbed the stairs. 'Got a warrant,' he said and waved it.

'What the fuck 'ave you got a warrant for?' said Frank, catching up with them as they opened the door. 'I know Frank's done a few dodgy things but you need to talk to that weirdo Collins, he owns the place. I just work here.'

'Collins is in custody. And you, Frank, are under arrest as an accessory to murder. Turn round.'

'You must be friggin' jokin'. Murder? Our lass will piss herself. Can't stand the sight of blood. Can't even put traps down for soddin' mice ... Go on then if it makes you 'appy. Bang the cuffs on,' he said and turned around. 'Look, I worked 'ere for Stan afore 'e got crushed.

I stack vehicles because no bugger else can. I keep my nose out of Jacko's and Collins' business. I get paid and go 'ome. Owt to do wi' murder's nowt to do wi' me.'

'Not using cuffs, zipties.

Apart from protestations there was no trouble. How many were feigning innocence remains to be seen.

Forty-Eight

The atmosphere in the interview room was strained. Phillip 'Jacko' Jackson seated opposite DS Greatorix and me. 'How long have you worked for Nicholas Nickleby.' I said and sat back in the chair.

'Who the hell is Nicholas Nickleby?'

'You may know him as Nicholas, or Nick Collins.'

'Why didn't you say so? In that case ten years, maybe twelve.'

'That's as far back as 1955?'

'About right.'

'In what capacity? Odd jobs. Driving. Fetching and carrying?

'Nothing so menial. I've run businesses for him until he put someone else in and moved onto something new.'

'Any scrapyards?' Offered DS Greatorix.

'One, just outside Staines.'

'And he put you in as manager.'

'Yes.'

'For how long?'

'A couple of years and sold it. Then somewhere else.'

'So,' I said, 'you've known Collins since 1955 and worked in managerial positions since then?'

'Yes. Problem?'

'You haven't asked why you're here.'

'True. Some rubbish about accessory to murder. You'll get round to telling me eventually.'

'You're in deep trouble.' I cautioned him. 'Do you understand?'

'Course I do. I'm not stupid.'

'We'll see. Nicholas Collins' birth name is Nicholas Nickleby, not Collins. In 1959 when he was believed to have been killed in a road accident north of London, when being pursued by the Metropolitan Police for the murder of a prostitute on the 12th august 1959, that was how he was known. He only adopted the name Collins when he arrived in Yorkshire.'

'So would you like to amend your story in any way?'

'All right. But you're not pinning that murder on me.'

'We're not pinning anything on anybody. You knew when he gave you the job in Todmorden, he was wanted by the police in London, didn't you?'

'Yes, is that all?'

'Not quite. Nickleby is in custody for that murder. He'll be returned to the Metropolitan Police when our primary investigation is complete.'

'I'd heard you got him.'

'He's not going anywhere. And how you answer our questions will determine for how long you go to prison.'

'All right I admit that, but I've done nothing else.'

'Cast your mind back to Tuesday 18th September.'

'What about it?'

'On the A644 between Brighouse and Cooper Bridge,' I stopped when I saw the blood drain from Jackson's face. 'Something wrong?'

'That was nothing to do with me.'

'Three people were shot to death. Two of them police officers. Nickleby had you open the yard early. He left his car and drove off in an old banger of a black Ford saloon. Remember?'

There was no reply.

''Nothing? He and a lad called Grogan set up an ambush. Stopped a police car containing the three victims. Whilst Grogan was ripping the number plates from the car your boss blew their brains out using a pump-action shotgun at zero feet. Then drove back to the scrapyard managed by you. What did you do with the car?

There was no reply. Any resistance in Jackson's expression was fading fast.

'All right, Jacko,' said DS Greatorix. 'What did Nickleby tell you to do with the car?'

Again, no reply. Jackson's eyes were fixed on the table. Sometimes silence speaks louder than words.

'He told you to crush it, didn't he? ... But that wreck is your insurance policy.

You've stashed it. Just nod.'

He did.

'Do you understand the trouble you're in?'

'Do you understand the danger I'm in talking to you?'

'We do. Did you or anyone else look in the boot?'

No response.

'Did you or anyone else look in the boot?

'Yes, I did. After he left with that halfwit Grogan. Police uniforms, road signs and a couple of number plates. And before you ask, they're still there.'

'Did you touch anything?'

'I drove the car to the back of the compound; I'm surprised he managed to get back here. Totally clapped out. In the boot I only touched the uniforms and not the buttons.'

'Is Frank the only one who stacked the cars before they're crushed?' said DS Greatorix

'Yep, does as he's told. Keeps his nose out.'

'And the car is a black ford saloon??

'He nodded. 'Black Zephyr 4.'

'Ok, back in a minute.' DS Greatorix left the room.

'Everybody's frightened of Nickleby?'

'Too bloody true. When he loses it, he's batshit crazy. A fucking loon.'

'He does his own dirty work?'

'There's a couple of my lads earn a few quid by getting their hands dirty.'

'Care to name names?'

He sighed. 'Terry Proctor. Martin Crapper ..When I heard about the shooting on the news ... He's done some bloody crazy things in the past, but this ... there is a limit. How long's he going down for?'

'He should never get out.'

'Should? Harry Field has deep pockets and long arms; and I've a wife and a couple of kids.'

DS Greatorix re-entered the room. 'I've spoken with Inspector Fowler; he's taking Frank back to the yard to identify the Zephyr. Studio were already there and forensic en route.

'That's all for tonight, Jacko,' said DS Greatorix. 'We will require a full statement from you in due course.

'Not looking forward to that.'

'Consider this. You can bet that Nickleby will move heaven and earth to shift the blame, and you run his scrapyard, nevertheless he will try,' I said. 'There is one more thing. As soon as news gets back to Field's cronies you will get an offer of support from some big London Solicitor at their expense. He will turn up out of the blue and demand to see his client. They will want to make sure that you do not give evidence, or that allegations are made that the police applied undue pressure for you to make a statement and say what we wanted you to say. Anything to muddy the waters.

'You need your own solicitor. One I can recommend, Dermot Reeve from Dewsbury. He's the one I would go to if I were in trouble. He's straight. But it's up to you. You need some professional help. Let the detention officer know when he books you in.'

'Good point, Brian,' said DS Greatorix. 'I'll sort it.'

Forty-Nine

Linus Bellamy looked up at the clouds and shuddered. 'Snow at this time of year. They can stuff that.'

'Never mind the bloody snow, Blake's house is empty by the look of it, and we have a job to do. Try next door.'

'For all the good that's likely to do.'

'Stop bitching.'

In answer to three hefty knocks the door opened cautiously. 'Good evening, madam, I'm Detective Chief Inspector Webster from New Scotland Yard and my colleague is Detective Inspector Beamish. We're trying to contact Sergeant Blake as a matter of urgency. Can you help us?'

'Terry Blake?'

'Yes, he's the one.'

'Sorry, we can't. They've been away for a few days, visiting some friends; a Duke and Duchess.'

'Duke and Duchess, eh?' He said, tone disbelieving. 'That's nice. Do you know when they will be back?'

'Sorry I don't. Goodnight,' she stepped back and closed the door.

As the latch dropped they looked at each other and laughed. 'Bloody Duke and Duchess. The old dear's senile ... right, one more job providing this fucking snow doesn't get in the way.'

'Know the way?'

'Yeah. I've got the directions that Nickleby gave to Harry, plus a copy of his house plans. Get this job out of the way. Then tomorrow, once I've checked out the cellar and made sure it's clear, cancel Blake and we're done. From there it's about twenty-five miles to Yeadon airport; the flight to Malaga is at 11.15. By the time they find the body we'll be on the Costa; no risk of extradition. Come on.

'WHY DID YOU SAY BRIAN'S name was Terry?'

'Don't you remember what he told us. *If any strangers come asking for me, they should always know my name. If they don't let me know*. So, I changed it and they didn't know his first name.'

'You are crafty.'

'Because I mentioned a Duke and Duchess, they probably thought I was doolally as well.'

He picked the phone up and listened. 'Phone's still dead. I'd better go down to the Gate and try theirs'

'Well don't have more than a half. With your bladder you'll be up all night.'.

He grinned. 'Chance would be a fine thing.'

She hit him lovingly on the arm. 'Go on you old fool. Remember you're not forty anymore.'

'That's true,' he said. 'But there's nothing wrong with my memory, and from the look on your face with yours either, lass.'

She gave him a peck on the cheek. 'Mind your feet in this snow and remember, just a half.'

'Right you are, lass. Half a quart.'

She watched him out of the gate, smiled, closed the door and returned to her latest knitted offerings for the twins, and Radio Luxemburg – Lem and Doc. Journey

into Space.

Fifty

'Say goodnight to your brothers, Claire,' said Lucy. 'And quietly. I don't want you to wake them up.'

'Night night.' she whispered as I scooped her up. 'Can we play horsey now, Daddy?'

'Quietly,' I hissed.

'Oops, sorry.'

'Come on, it's time you joined your brothers in the land of nod.'

'Do I have to?'

'Yes, otherwise you'll be like a grumpy old lady in the morning,'

'I will not!'

'Yes, you will,' I said and tickled her. There was the expected wriggle.

'Daddy. Stop it. That tickles.'

'Good. It's past your bedtime. Go and clean your teeth.'

'Aww.'

'Settled?'

I joined the others in the lounge. Clive was doing his homework in the library,

'Eventually,' I said.

'Tell us again,' said Jen. 'It seems so unfair. You reported the murders and arrested this Collins or Nickleby character. now you're being turfed off the enquiry.'

I took a deep breath and sighed. 'Jen, crimes are recorded in the subdivision where they occur. It just so happens that I was the one who came across it. It is also true that I arrested Collins who lived in Sowerby Bridge

> sub-division. That does not make it my crime; it's a CID job. Nevertheless I made the arrest.'

'But how did you know who to arrest?'

'That's evidence; I can't tell you. You'll find out when it comes to trial.'

'Secret squirrel again. Typical!'

'I'll bet you told Lucy.'

'No, he hasn't. Brian leaves the job at the garden gate.'

Jen's look said she didn't believe either of us.

'Meanwhile ... This other incident occurred in my sub-division. I introduced a young female probationer to sudden deaths. She submitted the report and I did some enquiries. It turns out that the death was unnatural, therefore I am the officer in the case. I can't be involved in two murder enquiries simultaneously, So ...'

'Isn't this a CID job as well,' Jen was nothing if not persistent.

'Under normal circumstances it would. But, if I'm right as to who did it?'

'And you're not going to enlighten us?'

'Certainly not,' I said. 'You'll find out in good time.'

Fifty-One

'Come on Arthur, time for bed.'

'Aww,' said Arthur wrinkling his nose

'Aww,' mimicked his smiling father. 'Bed!'

Book, one ruler-width from the window and his 6 six-sided pencils in perfect alignment he clambered into bed.

'See you in the morning, Good night, Arthur.'

'Night dad.'

How much time had elapsed before the sound of a car turning into the drive penetrated his sleep he neither knew nor cared, but the engine made a different noise. He was awake and out of bed in a flash. It was snowing hard. Two men wearing hats were getting out of a Humber Hawk Series V and walking towards the door. They knocked. The door opened, the hall light illuminating to front of the car and its number plate. All registered. Book and pencils in perfect symmetry he smiled as he climbed back into bed.

Seconds later his dad's voice. 'Hey, what are you doing. Stop pushing. Arthur,' he shouted, 'Hide!' There was the sound from the hall like a Little Demon on bonfire night; he didn't like those.

Footsteps on the stairs!

Hide! Must hide. He grabbed his notebook and a pencil. Looked around. Opened his wardrobe door, wriggled beneath the spare blankets and lay on his back; peeping at the door. His heart thumping. *What was that noise. Why was Dad angry; he was never angry. Why wasn't he coming to see him. What was happening?*

There was a soft click as his bedroom light came on. He shivered. Frightened. He couldn't see anything but heard footsteps moving slowly round the room, stopping occasionally. The wardrobe door began to open. The man was holding a gun in his right hand. He crouched and pulled the blankets away. He saw the man's face as he pointed the gun at him. Was this where the sound came from?

'Christ! I didn't sign up to murder kids.' The man tapped him on the head. 'You're all right,' he said. Arthur opened his eyes. The man stood put his left forefinger to his lips. 'Shhh,' He pointed the gun at the floor and pulled the trigger

The Little Demon! The crack terrified him. He put his hands over his ears and whimpered. 'Stay there and be quiet,' the man turned and left.

Arthur heard the front door close and crept out of bed, put his dressing gown on and peered out of the window. The car was reversing. When it reached the gate he turned and ran downstairs. *Where was Dad*?

Malcolm Truelove was lying in the hall at the foot of the stairs bleeding from a chest wound. A pool of blood gathering where he lay. 'Dad!' he said as he knelt beside his father. Malcolm Truelove's eyelids flickered. The fingers of his left hand moved. 'Dad! Dad! Are you all right?' There was no response. Arthur felt his father's hands. 'You're cold. I'll get you something.' He ran upstairs and grabbed a pillow and the eiderdown from his father's bed and ran back down. Put his father's head on the pillow and covered him with the eiderdown. Then ran into the kitchen, put the kettle on then ran back upstairs for his hot water bottle. It was still hot. The phone was disconnected. He had to find Brian. Brian would know what to do.

He knelt down by his father's head. 'Dad, I'm going to find Brian. I'll be as quick as I can.'

Long trousers, wellies, His warmest jumper, scarf, raincoat and gloves on he closed the door and patted his pocket to make sure his book was there. He pictured the map he saw where the policemen were sending cars to an accident. He had to turn left into the wind.

That was uphill passed Mr Collins' house. During the day time there had been a policeman at the bottom of the drive. He would have known what to do. But he wasn't there now.

Half an hour later the wind was driving the snow, now knee deep, into his face. His new woollen gloves were soaked and his fingers burned with the cold. He'd never been so cold or wet. And, still he hadn't reached the top of the hill. He was frightened but his book was safe.

Between gusts a light caught his eye. In front and above. As he drew near it was like a big square box; there was music playing and voices.

Fifty-Two

'Fifteen-two, fifteen-four, fifteen-six, fifteen-eight, twelves-twenty and one for his knob, and that gentleman, is up!' he moved his peg to the end of the cribbage board.'

'You jammy sod. That's three on the bounce,'

'Skill gentlemen. Pure skill.'

'That's bollocks.'

'Shut up! There's somebody outside.'

'In this weather?'

'He's right, listen.'

A faint knocking and even fainter shout galvanised them. 'That's a kids voice. Christ.'

'Careful opening the door.'

The door opened slowly as a sobbing Arthur sank into the snow. A pair of strong arms lifted him into the light and warmth.

'Onion, get some towels and a blanket from the locker. Bring him over to the heater and get those wet clothes off. Somebody put the kettle on.'

'No!' Arthur shouted as they removed his coat.

They stopped. 'What, son?'

'My book.'

He went through the pockets. 'This one?' He held it up.

'Yes,' said Arthur clutching it.

'Is it special?'

Arthur nodded.

'It's only a bloody notebook.'

'It's his, Terry. After what he's been through.'

Three minutes later sitting on a buffet, swathed in towels and a large blanket and clutching a cup of tea with a spoonful of rum added they lined up in front of him.

One of them crouched in front of him. 'My name is Peter, what's yours?'

'Arthur.'

'These others are, Zac, he's in charge/.'

'He'd like to think so.'

'All right, Tom, banter later. And the last one is Onion.'

'Onion isn't a name, it's a vegetable.'

'Quite right, Arthur. My name is Gerald O'nions, but these ignoramuses call me Onions.'

'You're Irish.'

'And you're very intelligent.'

'All right,' said Peter. 'Can we leave the mutual admiration for later? Arthur, why are you out in the terrible weather. You could have died.'

'I'm going to find Brian, he would know what to do.'

'Why is Brian so special?'

'He's a policeman, a sergeant. They shot my Dad.'

The was a chorus of gasps.

'Who did?'

They listened. Rapt. 'Two men in a Humber Hawk series V. They knocked at the door and Dad let them in. Then he shouted, *Stop pushing* and *Arthur hide.* I heard a bang like a firework and hid in the wardrobe under the blankets. A man came in and put the lights on. Then opened the wardrobe door and pulled the blankets away and pointed the gun at me. Then he said: *Christ! I didn't sign up to murder kids.* He put his finger to his lips and said, shh. Patted me on the head and fired at the floor. I don't like loud noises

I watched them leave and went downstairs. Dad was lying in the hall, bleeding from his chest.' He started sobbing.

'I'll get the Moke out,' said Tom. See if he can tell you where the house is.' He left the group and put on his all-weather gear.

'You're safe now Arthur,' said Peter. 'Can you tell us anything else. Did you see your father move.'

He nodded, sniffed and wiped his nose. 'He opened his eyes and wiggled his fingers. I covered him up and put his head on a pillow and gave him my hot water bottle before I left. He said and sniffed.

'Arthur, look at this map. We're here,' he said touching the map. 'This is where we are building the new motorway. Can you show me where your house is?'

Arthur glanced at the map and pointed. 'It's there, on the right. A Mr Collins lives opposite. Brian took him away in handcuffs. I was watching from my bedroom window.'

Fifty-Three

'Could you tell me which police station this is?'

'Sowerby Bridge.'

'Good. My name is Zac Prentice. I'm the supervisor of security up at Ainley Top. Five minutes ago we pulled a young lad, name of Arthur, out of the snow. He was soaked to the skin, Says two men came to their house. One shot his father in the chest. The other pointed a gun at him but fired into the floor.'

'What?'

'What he says. Lives opposite a man called Collins. He's looking for a Sergeant Brian. Two of my lads are en route in a Moke.'

'That will be the Trueloves and Sergeant Blake. Ok, hold the line.'

He pressed the talk key. 'Sergeant Chalkley, over.'

'Go ahead, Mike.'

'Report of Malcolm Truelove being shot in the chest. Ambulance is en route. I've called force control, DS Greatorix and Inspector Marshall.'

'Ok, I'm en route. What about the boy?'

'Someone pointed a gun at him but fired at the floor. He's traipsed through this blizzard up to Ainley Top, apparently looking for Sergeant Blake. Their security supervisor called it in. Oh, they've sent a Moke to check it out.'

'Ok, but why didn't the lad telephone. Never mind. Give Fell Rescue a shout. Ainley Top will be in touch with the Moke by radio, tell them not to go wandering. Get a fresh Message Book and keep a log.

'Will do.'

Radio off he picked up the telephone handset. 'Still there Mr Prentice?'

'Still here, I heard what you said and the Moke crew are aware.'

'Thanks. Can I have a word with Arthur.'

'Hello?'

'Hello Arthur, it's PC Mike. There's an ambulance coming to help your Dad and lots of policemen.'

'Sergeant Brian?'

'He's off duty but I'll make sure he knows. Now, are you hurt at all?'

'I didn't like the noise when he fired the gun at the floor, he said he hadn't signed up to murder kids.'

'Good. But you're not hurt?'

'Frightened.'

'It was a very brave thing you did. Your dad will be proud of you. Now, can I speak to Mr Prentice, please?'

''Yes officer.'

'You probably heard, ambulance, CID and supervision are en route to the Truelove's house. Give me your phone number. I'll keep you posted.'

Fifty-Four

'Moke over.'

'Go ahead, Terry.'

'Tell Arthur his Dad opened his eyes.' *Although looking where the bullet hole is he should be dead.* 'Hang on, blue lights.'

'They're coming from all directions.'

'Sergeant,' acknowledged Terry as the sergeant exited his car.

'Sergeant Chalkley. I take it this is genuine.'

'It is, although he should be dead. The bullet should have gone through his heart.'

'Ok, but let the medics worry about that. Is there a problem with their phone?'

'Yep, the wires have been ripped out.'

'That explains it. Let's get inside.'

The snowfall eased as Inspector Marshall arrived, closely followed by DS Greatorix who knelt beside Malcolm Truelove. 'Mr Truelove?' He opened his eyes. 'Don't try to speak. I'm going to ask you some questions. If the answer is yes, blink your eyes once. If the answer is no, blink them twice. Do you understand?'

One blink. 'Good ... you know Arthur is safe?'

One blink. 'I understand he was wet through. I'll have some dry clothes taken to him.'

Tears appeared in Malcolm Truelove's eyes and trickled across his face. The sergeant took a dry handkerchief from his pocket and carefully wiped them away. 'Mr Truelove, did you recognise either of these men?'

Two blinks. 'Last question for now. Were both these men carrying revolvers?'

One blink. 'Thank you. Is it all right to go upstairs and get Arthur some dry clothes?'

One blink. 'Thank you. The ambulance is on its way.'

'Sergeant Chalkley, over.'

'Go ahead.

'Just had a message from force control, Salterhebble and the Halifax – Huddersfield roads are impassable. The ambulance is enroute from Huddersfield and will have to return the same way. It has a traffic escort. It should be with you within fifteen minutes. Mr Cartwright and Detective Superintendent Wallace in five minutes'

'All received,' he said. 'Fifteen minutes? *My god that's pushing it.*'

Detective Inspector Cartwright and Detective Superintendent Wallace arrived.

'I want someone on this door 24/7 keeping a record of everyone with entry and exit times. No-one except fingerprints, studio, forensic and CID for now. Cancel someone's day off if necessary; my authority,'

'On the run-up to Christmas? That will go down well.'

Arrange meal reliefs. Gives them a chance to get warm. That window,' he said pointing at the house. 'Looks like a toilet. Calls of nature permitted but no wandering ... Right let's go and have a look.'

A man in all-weather gear stood in the doorway. 'I'm Terry Siddon. With the security unit up at Ainley Top. I'm a first-aider but Malcolm's injuries are way beyond me. Just keep him warm and talk to him. He can open his eyes and move his fingers and, he can hear. Other than that? Do you know how long the ambulance will be?'

'Perhaps another ten minutes.'

'I don't know how much longer he can last,' he said quietly.

Flashing blue lights signalling their arrival. 'They're here now.'

'Thank God for that.' Terry crouched. 'The ambulance is here Malcolm, soon have you in hospital.'

Doctor, nurse and ambulance crew decamped. 'Doctor Widdop and Nurse Metcalfe,' he said. 'Where's the patient?'

'In the hall, Doctor,' said Sergeant Chalkley turning back into the house. The ambulance crew carrying a large case and a metal stand followed.

'Excuse me, gentlemen,' said the Doctor. 'Let the dog see the rabbit.'

Terry stood. 'I'm a first-aider from the motorway site. Malcolm can hear, open his eyes and move his fingers. But,' he leaned towards the Doctor, 'From where the bullet penetrated he should be dead. But the bullet did go all the way through.'

'Really? Thank you,' he knelt as the nurse opened the case and suspended a bag of blood from the stand. 'Hello, Malcolm. I'm Dr Widdop, I'm just going to give you a quick examination. Patch up your wounds and give you some blood. Then get you to hospital.' He looked up. 'Move back please, so the ambulance crew can do their work.'

Five minutes later, Malcolm Truelove on the stretcher and accompanied by Doctor Widdop and Nuse Metcalfe they left the house.

'According to Doctor Widdop and Terry,' said the Superintendent, the bullet passed straight through Mr Truelove. Somewhere there is a hole.'

The Traffic driver called across. 'Sir, the Huddersfield to Bradford road is now clear. We can take the road from Brighouse. That should save us a good twenty minutes.'

Blue lights working overtime the ambulance set off.

'Sir, it stands to reason that Malcolm Truelove would be facing the door,' said DS Greatorix. 'Therefore the bullet should be lodged either in the kitchen or near to the door.'

'It's there, sir,' said Inspector Marshall, 'There's a chunk missing to the right of the door frame.'

'Well spotted. Leave it for forensic.'

The Fell Rescue Team arrived and exited. 'Everything under control?' asked the driver.

'Please,' said the detective superintendent. 'Mr Truelove's son is up at the M62 construction site. I'm going to take him to the hospital to see his father, Can you give me a lift?'

Fifty-Five

'Arthur, do you remember that you asked if you could have another ride in a big police car?'

'Yes,' he said and nodded.

'Well, these two gentlemen are going to take us to the hospital, so you can see your father.'

'Are you going with me?' Arthur said, his eyes bright.

'I am. The ambulance is going to take longer because of the snow; they have to go the long way round. Now, say goodbye to Zac and Peter then we can leave.'

'Thank you for the dry clothes and the tea. It did taste funny.'

'Ah,' said Zac, smiling. 'We put something special in it to make you feel better. And you're welcome. Come and see us when your father is better.' He held his hand out and shook hands as did Peter.

'It's been a pleasure,' said Peter. 'Good luck.'

'Thank you gentlemen for all you've done; you've probably saved Arthur's father's life.'

'You're welcome. But without Arthur setting off to find his friend we would never have known. Now I've got to write a report. Could I have your name please or my Boss won't believe me.'

'Certainly, it's Detective Superintendent Richard Wallace,' he looked at the startled security team and smiled. 'Come on Arthur, it's time to go.'

They watched them climb into the police car and drive carefully back to the road. 'Young Arthur has some funny friends'

Fifty-Six

Arthur stood looking over the observer's shoulder. 'Wow! This is a Mk II Austin Westminster 110,' he said, '4 speed manual gearbox. Maximum speed 102 mph. 0-60mph in 13.3 seconds. Standing quarter mile 19.4 seconds. Develops 120 brake horsepower at 4750 rpm.'

Driver and observer laughed. 'Where on earth did you learn that?'

'In a magazine,' Arthur replied. 'I saw one in your garage at Wakefield. It had the bonnet up.'

'You were at Headquarters?' said the driver.

'Yes, we were,' said the superintendent. 'He had some information that might prove very useful. '

'Then they took me to the control room. There was an RTA on the A639 at Barnsdale. Fire brigade and ambulance were attending; so we had to leave. What does RTA mean.'

'Road traffic accident,' said the driver.

'Arthur, do you have your little book.'

'Yes.'

'Did you see the number of the car.'

He nodded. 'It's the last one.'

'Can I see it, please? The last page.'

'It's all wet,' said a disconsolate Arthur, 'The pages are stuck and the numbers smudged.'

The superintendent pointed to the last number. 'Is this the car you saw earlier this evening?'

'Mmm.'

'I know it's difficult, Arthur, but do you remember the registration number?'

'I'll try,' he said and thought about the picture in his mind from last night. 'It was B-U-L something F; Not sure about the numbers.'

'That's great, Arthur, thank you. That will do.'

The observer flicked through his police diary. 'BUL is a London number, sir.'

'London? Thanks'

'I'll get your book dried for you. Do you remember the make?'

'Oh, that's easy. A Humber Hawk series V. Light at the top and dark at the bottom.'

The observer and driver glanced at each other. 'Sir,' said the observer. 'Do you want those details circulating?'

He thought for a moment. 'Yes. I'll write it out for you.' Two minutes later he handed the observer a note.

'Control from Whisky 114. Urgent broadcast from Detective Superintendent Wallace.'

'Whisky 114, Standby one ... All cars Channel A and all cars channel B. Urgent broadcast. Whisky 114 go ahead.

'Whiskey 114. urgent observation request from Detective Superintendent Wallace. With reference to this evening's incident. The vehicle in question is a Humber Hawk five series, Two-tone. Light top and dark bottom. Registration mark believed to be Bravo Uniform Lima with Foxtrot suffix. This is a London registration mark. Likely to contain two male occupants, both armed and highly dangerous. Extreme caution to be observed at all time. Observations only. Message ends.'

'Whisky 114. The message will be circulated to all divisions.'

'Whisky 114, all received.'

'It was a one. BUL1F,' declared Arthur with a beaming smile.

'Just a single digit, number?'

'Yes, certain.'

'Whisky 114 Further ...' The pips recommenced. 'Complete registration mark is bravo uniform lima one foxtrot, over'

'All received control to standby.'

'Thank you,. and if anyone should ask, your only passenger tonight is me. You will not, under any circumstances, mention Arthur Truelove, understood?'

'Yes, sir.'

'Should anyone become awkward refer them to me and make sure it's in your pocket book.'

'May I ask you a question?'

'Of course, Arthur, what would you like to know?'

'Why did you say Bravo uniform lima, instead of BUL?'

'Good question. Because the letters D, P, T and V sound like B. and if there is interference with the radio it could be confused. Look,' he handed Arthur his diary open at the page. 'We call it the NATO phonetic alphabet. You can remember it.'

Detective Superintendent Wallace and Arthur were safely delivered to Huddersfield Royal Infirmary. 'Control, Whisky 114 resuming, transport complete.'

'Whisky 114, all received.'

'What do you think that last bit was about. It sounded as if he thought coppers were involved.'

'Possibility. Remember those three in the car. Two of them were coppers and the guy in the rear seat was cuffed. So who knows?'

Fifty-Seven

Huddersfield Royal Infirmary Accident and Emergency was busy. Detective Superintendent Wallace stopped a passing nurse and showed his warrant card. 'Where can I find the Almoner, please?'

'Down that corridor,' she said pointing to her right.

'Thank you. Oh, and her full name?

She frowned. 'Marjorie Dawson. That's Mrs.'

'Thank you again. Come on Arthur, let's go and see Marjorie.'

Marjorie Dawson was aghast. The superintendent standing in front of her with his arm round the boy's shoulders. 'And what do you want of me superintendent.'

'I need someone to look after Arthur for half an hour or so whilst I make arrangement to keep him safe.'

'And you want to use my phone?'

'Please. Oh,' he said and smiled. 'We only use first names, don't we Arthur.'

He smiled and nodded.

'Arthur,' said Marjorie, 'do you like biscuits?'

'Can I see my dad?'

'We'll go and find out, shall we? Then we can have a drink and some biscuits or a piece of cake. How's that?'

He frowned and looked at the superintendent. 'Is this my fault?'

Superintendent Wallace turned to face him. 'None of this is your fault, Arthur. This is connected to the Mr Collins across the road. Why, we're not sure. But none of it is your fault. And what you did after the two men left saved your father's life. You risked your life to save your father and that was a very brave thing to do. Now go with Marjorie, she will look after you. Your father was seriously injured. So they may not let you see him at the moment.'

'Is he going to die?'

'Honestly, Arthur? I don't know. But they will do their best. Now go with Marjorie.'

Fifty-Eight

'Why does someone ring when there's something good on the telly,' said Joe.

'I'll go,' said Clive getting out his chair. 'You oldies need your rest.'

'Cheeky.'

'Not you, Mum. Brian and Lucy.'

'Very funny.'

'Hello, Clive Mountain ... Just a moment. Brian, there's a Detective Superintendent Wallace for you, says it's urgent.'

'Yes, sir.'

The detective superintendent explained what had happened to Arthur and his father. 'Malcolm Truelove is in a critical condition in Huddersfield Royal Infirmary. We need to find a secure-safe place for Arthur ...'

'And he trusts me.'

'He docs. I know what you will have on your plate tomorrow with the Hathersage case, but?'

'Of course, sir. We will see you in fifteen to twenty minutes.'

'What was all that about,' said Jen as I entered the lounge. 'Or are you playing secret squirrel, again?'

'Not this time. We're going to have a visitor for a few days. A young lad by the name of Arthur Truelove ...

The only sound was Mum blowing her nose. Tears do that.

'Are we at risk?' asked Clive.

'No, we're not. The gunman who shot Malcolm Truelove thinks that he's dead, otherwise he would have shot him again to make sure.

The gunman upstairs heard the first shot. However the first gunman doesn't realise the other discharged his weapon into the floor. They both believe Malcolm Truelove is dead. As for Arthur ...'

'And he was trying to get to your house in that blizzard?' said an incredulous Joe.

'Apparently so.'

'Let's do it.' said Clive.

That galvanised us. 'Lucy, I want you to come with me.'

'For when you're not here?'

'Yup.'

'I'll come as well,' said a grinning Clive. 'Add a bit of intelligence. Besides a family group will look more natural.'

'If you say so,' I said,

'What about clothes?' said Mum. Has he any spare?'

'Yes, Superintendent Wallace took him some.'

Fifty-Nine

We found Arthur and Mr Wallace in the medical social worker's office. Marjorie Dawson, the name on the door.

'Hello, sir,' I said and smiled at Arthur. 'You were very brave, Arthur. How are you now?'

I received a weary smile. 'Tired.'

I grinned at him. 'I'm not surprised. I promise you we will catch those men; they're not coming back. Now, you will be staying with us until your dad is fit to leave hospital? Are you happy with that?'

He nodded.

'Good, let me introduce everybody. This is Lucy, my wife.'

'Hello, Arthur. Brian tells me that you live alone with your father.'

He nodded again and yawned. 'Just us two.'

'You will find our house is very busy; Brian and I have three children: Claire is three and the twins are a few weeks old; in fact the younger twin's name is Arthur.'

Arthur's eyes lit up. 'I haven't met anyone called Arthur before.'

'And I'm Clive,' he volunteered. 'Brian's little brother. My sister Jennifer might be there with her son Mervyn; he will be in bed. Norman might be there, Mervyn's dad.'

'That's a lot.'

'Noisy as well,' added Clive

'Brian, they won't let me see my Dad,'

'What is the problem, Mrs Dawson?' said Mr Wallace.

'We need to contact someone who can act in loco parentis.'

'Arthur says he hasn't any relatives other than his father. But, there must be someone.'

'Why,' I said. 'It's not unknown for people to have no living relatives. But if you need someone, I'm quite amenable to act in that capacity. I take you have heard his story?'

'It was heart rending.'

'And if he had been injured today you would have begun treatment without contacting a relative.'

'Of course.'

'So, as a police officer, and someone he trusts, can I take him to see his father?

Sixty

Kevin Spencer FRCS smiled benignly at Arthur. 'Can I hold my Dad's hand.'

'Of course you can. And talk to him,' he said. 'He's asleep but he may be able to hear you.'

Arthur hadn't batted an eyelid when he saw the ECG and the saline drip. He ran across and grasped his father's left hand. 'Dad, it's me, Arthur. I'm all right and you're in hospital,'

Lucy and Clive stood to one side with Arthur happily chatting to his father, Messrs Spencer, Wallace and I were observing and talking. 'Your name is Blake?' said Mr Spencer.

'It is. Is there a problem?'

'No, but does the name of Vivienne McKeen mean anything to you.'

'Yes. Could I ask why the interest?'

'She was the daughter of my wife's youngest sister. That was a terrible shock.'

'I'm so sorry. It was a bad case.'

'I understand, but thank you for what you did.' He held his hand out for me to shake.

'Could you tell me why Arthur's father is still alive?'

'If I remember rightly you have a degree in exercise physiology; what do you make of it.'

'Thanks. If it hadn't been for the apparent lack of other problems I might have thought it was dextrocardia.'

He nodded. 'It's called Isolated Dextrocardia. The heart is to the right instead of the left; no other organs are affected; 1/12,000 births.'

'And the bullet missed the vital organs *and* major blood vessels?' said Mr Wallace.

'It did, superintendent. An inch either way, and ...'

'A bit too close. But, can I ask you a question?'

'Fire away.'

'Do you know what happened earlier today?'

'Only in as far as Malcom Truelove is concerned.'

'As we understand it ... ... do you think Arthur should be seen by a psychiatrist?'

'There is a large body of people that do not accept Autism is genuine. But I do. Where will he be staying?'

'With my parents until his father is fit to leave. In the meantime I think I know someone who could help.'

'I will contact one of my colleagues about Arthur.

'Brian!' Arthur's delighted shout. 'Dad's opened his eyes and moving his fingers.'

One pace and I was there. 'Malcolm! Brian Blake. You're in Huddersfield Royal Infirmary and Arthur is safe. He's going to stay with my parents a few miles away and they will fetch him down to see you, every day.'

Tears began to run down Malcolm Truelove's cheeks. Arthur turned to me. 'Why is Dad crying?'

'It's what parents do when they thought their children were in danger and are safe.'

'I'm afraid you will have to leave now,' said Mr Spencer. 'But you can come back tomorrow; after ten thirty.'

I'll see you tomorrow, Dad. I promise.' After kissing his father on the cheek he stopped at the door, turned and waved. 'Good night.'

There was a small answering wave.

Sixty-One

The journey home was peppered by Arthur's questions about everything from Greenhead Park; I took Park Drive which follows the park boundary, to the Salendine Nook school complex. No doubt he would be able to construct a tourist guide in due course.

What was going through Arthur's mind as we entered the lounge I had no idea. What he had endured in the past few hours would have been enough to flatten an adult. I kept my arm round his shoulders for that extra support. 'Hello everybody. This is Arthur. He will be staying with us for a few days.'

I needn't have worried. 'My Dad's woken up,' he said with a beaming smile. 'That man shot him but he's all right.'

The silence broken by Mum. 'That is good. Are you hurt?'

'No, he fired the gun at the floor, not at me.'

I thought Mum and Jen were going to start crying. Joe and Norman looked shellshocked. 'Right,' I said. 'Introductions. This lady on my left is my mother.'

'Hello Arthur,' she said. 'I understand you only use first names. Is that right.'

He nodded.

'Call me Dorothy.'

'Dorothy.'

'I'm Brian's step-father, Joe.'

'Joe.'

'The lady over there is my sister, Jennifer, but she prefers to be called Jen.'

'Jen.'

'And this is my husband, Norman.'

'Norman.'

'Hi, he said, smiled and waved.'

Arthur began to yawn. 'Look at the clock,' said Lucy. 'Are you ready for bed.'

He yawned again and nodded.'

'Come on then,' she looked at Mum. 'Frankie's?'

To a chorus of goodnights we took him upstairs. How he would sleep after the earlier events was anybody's guess.

Sixty-Two

The road to the Calder Valley still wasn't clear. So it had been the long way round via Cooper Bridge. It was turned 8.30am when I arrived.

I closed the door behind me to keep the cold out. Neil Farrar was the Office Clerk. 'Sergeant Blake, how the hell are you?'

'Cold. Just passing through, Neil. How did it go on Wednesday?'

'It was a good session, beginning to get the hang of it now. I should have started when the kids did. Help keep them under control.'

'Don't bank on it, Neil,' I said and laughed.

'Oh before you disappear there are a couple of Met officers in the canteen; gave 'em a cuppa. A DCI Webster and a DI Beamish; sent by a Commander Jameson. Specifically asked for you.'

I frowned. 'Not expecting anybody. Canteen?'

He nodded.

'Ok. Book me a radio.'

They were standing with their back to the door. Two half-empty mugs of tea on the table. Perhaps they didn't like Yorkshire tea.

'DCI Webster, DI Beamish?' they spun round and smiled.

'DCI Webster. Sergeant Blake, nice to meet you.' Each shook my hand.'

'Tea not your drink?'

'Not that strong,' said the DI.'

That forced a grin. 'My Gran used to say that if you couldn't stand the spoon up in the mug it wasn't strong enough. Probably why I prefer coffee.'

'I don't blame you.'

'Right, what can I do for you?'

'We were up here doing a job for Commander Jameson, who thinks highly of you.' *I wonder why he said that? I've never met the man.* 'He wanted us to take a look at Nickleby's house. That snow yesterday caught us out. We don't know where it is and thought you might spare us a half hour.'

'Anything in particular? I have a tight schedule today.'

'Yes, if Nickleby runs true to form he will have some kind of hidden room. Just a quick look round shouldn't take long.'

Hidden room? But Nickleby's supposed to have died in 1959; why didn't the Met ring? Only one way to find out. 'Ok, but it will have to be quick.'

'Great, we can use my car.'

'Hang fire, gentlemen, won't be a minute.' I tore a sheet from the pad on my desk and scribbled a note, folded it in half and handed it to Neil Farrar. 'Give that wally Mithering at HQ a bell, yank his chain.'

'Ok, sarge, will do.'

'What was all that about?' said the DCI.

'Got the keys,' I said wafting the keyring. 'HQ timewasters. Some stuff that

was promised for two days ago.'

'We've all got those. Here, this car is mine.'

'Nice,' I said. Humber Hawk. Light top and dark base. 'Only take ten to fifteen minutes.'

Neil Farrar opened the note: *'Something odd about these two. DCI Webster and DI Beamish. Call Mr Wallace or failing that ACC Mithering.*

BB Ps547

Sixty-Three

Commander Richard Jameson was blazing as he took the stairs two at a time. *How the Hell did this happen?* His phone began to ring as he unlocked his door.

'Jameson,' he said as he sat down.

'Good morning, sir, DI Wetherby. Can I have the authority for DCI Frobisher and DI Bellamy, please.'

His stomach started to twist. 'For what?'

'To carry.'

'I haven't authorised anything. Talk me through it.'

'PAUL?'

'Sir?' It was only a single word but Detective Chief Superintendent Paul Yelland had never heard the Commander this angry.

'The security on Frobisher and Bellamy was supposed to be airtight. I found out less than five minutes ago they slipped the net, drawn weapons and six rounds each.'

'What!?' If that hadn't come from the Commander he wouldn't have believed it.

'When they were signing them out they joked about *never having had a*

Yorkshire Pudding before. It's quite possible they've gone after a Sergeant Blake, Nickleby's arresting officer.'

'Christ! Coppers hunting coppers? How much is Field paying them?'

'£41,000.'

'What!? They're going to disappear?'

'Try to, Chief Superintendent,' he said and smiled. 'Last night there were a couple of shootings. Neighbours of Nickleby's, including the neighbour's eleven year old son who had a collection of car registration numbers of Nickleby's visitors ...Are Field and Co. still in custody?'

'Yes they are. I'll get an All Ports out. You're from Yorkshire, where's the nearest regional airport?

'That would be Leeds-Bradford, Yeadon. Twenty to twenty five miles.'

'You can leave that to me. I'll also have an intimate chat with those on security.'

'Good,' he said and replaced the phone. *First Wakefield. Then the Commissioner.'*

Sixty-Four

'Mithering.'

The last thing Jeff Farrar had expected was to call the ACC crime; a man noted for being prickly. 'Good morning, sir. PC Farrar, Sowerby Bridge. I have a message from Sergeant Blake. We have two officers from the Met, a DCI Webster and a DI Beamish. He thinks they're a bit odd and says to call Mr Wallace or you.'

'Mr Wallace was not available?'

'No, sir. Sergeant Blake and the two Met officers have left and gone to Collins' house.'

'Do you know why?'

'No sir, I overheard the DCI mention it.'

'You're in radio contact with the officers at the Truelove's house.'

'Yes, sir.'

'Get hold of the senior officer present and pass Blake's message on; I want to know why Sergeant Blake has seen fit to interrupt my morning coffee. Well done.' The line went dead.

Jeff Farrar looked at the handset. 'Yes, sir,' he said to himself and flicked the talk key on the radio. 'DI Cartwright, over.'

'Go ahead.'

'Sergeant Blake left the office heading for Collins' house with a couple of Met officers. A DCI Webster and a DI Beamish. He left me a note saying there was something a bit odd and to call either Mr Wallace or ACC Mithering. The ACC told me to contact you.'

'OK. Any idea why Sergeant Blake felt like this.'

'Nothing, except he referred to the ACC in disparaging tones, as if it were serious.' Nothing that I could put my finger on.'

Sixty-Five

We were passing Truelove's house, eighty yards shy of Nickleby's. Several police vehicles parked on the nearside, a couple with blue lights on. Several police officers milling about, including Keith Fleming.

DCI Webster caught my eye in the rear-view mirror. 'What's all this about.'

'Not sure. I finished at four yesterday; get ready for today. Some burglary that went wrong I heard. Don't know any details.' I grinned in return. 'You hi-jacked me before I could get up to date.'

I looked to my left making eye-contact with Keith Fleming.

'When you say, *went wrong*, firearms involved?'

'So I heard. No details though.' There was a quick glance between the DCI and the DI. *Why? Was I riding with my head in the tiger's mouth?'*

'Now then, this job we're holding you from. Anything important?'

'Suspicious death. Local businessman with an incurable medical condition died too early.'

'Possible murder?'

'Almost certainly.'

'You're not dealing with it?'

'Why not? I've a DS and a DI watching over me.'

'What service you got in?'

'Four, just.'

'Any CID?'

'Twelve months or so.'

The looks that passed between them as we turned into Nickleby's drive said they weren't impressed.

PC FLEMING RAN INTO the hallway of the Truelove's house. 'Mr Cartwright?'

'What is it?'

'I've seen Sergeant Blake in a car with two other men, turned into Collins's drive. The car was a Humber Hawk two tone. Answers the description of the car wanted for the shooting yesterday evening.'

'Streuth. Where's that traffic man?'

'In his car, sir, just going.'

A couple of slaps on the patrol car roof brought it to a halt. 'Sir?'

'I need a secure chat with the duty officer.'

'Come and sit inside ... Whisky 97 Urgent.'

'All cars standby. Whisky 97 go ahead.'

'Pips and duty officer, please.'

The pips began. 'Inspector Helliwell.'

'D.I. Cartwright. Norland. We have a potential firearms incident at the Collins house eighty yards from the scene of last night's shooting. The vehicle concerned is described as identical to the one circulated. Sergeant Blake is in the vehicle. How many firearms officers are available? Over.'

'Inspector Helliwell. Leave that with us. Can you keep obs on the house, safely. I'll get the ball rolling ... Whisky 97 act as comms.'

'All received.'

Sixty-Six

I opened the door, pocketed the key and walked through the kitchen into the hallway. 'Right, what do you want?'

'I'll check the cellar,' said DCI Webster. He turned and walked away.

How the hell does he know where the cellar is? They've never been here before. I saw the look on DI Beamish's face and his right hand disappear inside his jacket. 'ALEX!' he called.

This was not playtime. My yokogeri caught him on the point of his jaw, his hand, holding a revolver appeared. His head smashed into the door frame as the revolver flew from his grasp when he bounced back. The mawashi geri caught him across his jawline propelling him into the opposite side of the doorframe with a sickening crack. He collapsed in a heap.

Perhaps because of the adrenaline and the fact that I was still rotating I felt the bullet more than heard the shot. It hit me somewhere towards the right outer edge of my ribs. Low down. Nevertheless I was lying on my back trying to shut out the pain. My right forearm beneath me. *Would the next shot be the end?*

DCI Webster strode passed me, crouched and looked at his colleague. 'Linus?' he said shaking him. 'Linus? ... if you've killed him?' He didn't turn his head.

I wasn't feeling too well disposed towards either of them. 'He was drawing a weapon and you've just shot me in the back. Don't expect an apology.'

He stood slowly, turned and looked down and raised the revolver. The hammer was down. His hand was shaking. So was

I: Senior detectives. Collins house. Harry Field? It was a natural progression. So was his pulling the trigger.

Eighty yards away were at least a half dozen coppers and a traffic car. This isn't the kids matinee at the cinema. The cavalry are not coming over the hill.

FLEMING PARKED THE Panda, blocking the drive and crouched behind the wall when he heard the shot. He pressed the talk button. '1708, shot fired. And I can confirm that the registration mark is bravo uniform lima one foxtrot. Over"

'Talk thro is on. DI Cartwright did you get that?'

'I heard. 1708, Any sign of movement?'

'Nothing since they went in, sir. I've blocked the drive with the Panda.'

'Force Control have started the ball rolling. Obs only.'

But he didn't say stay put. Fleming edged up the drive, passed the door, ducked under the window to the corner of the house where he could see into the kitchen; and assumed the door was open. Nothing in sight. It took seconds to deflate both front tyres; they were going nowhere. Then voices.

'1708. I can hear voices. One of which sounds like Sergeant Blake.'

Sixty-Seven

'Yes, sir. I'll go straight to the house.' Detective Superintendent Wallace leapt into his car. The message from the Chief Constable of two rogue senior Metropolitan detectives alone with Blake. And now a shot having been fired; it didn't bear thinking about.

SOMETHING WAS STICKING in my lower back which didn't improve matters. Seconds later my fingers came into contact with the cylinder of the revolver that DI Beamish had dropped. My would-be assassin was looking frightened; that didn't help. 'What the fuck's this about? We're all coppers. How come you're pointing that bloody revolver at my face. For God's sake I'm married with a three year old daughter and twin boys just a few weeks old. Doesn't that mean anything to you? Look at your hands, they're shaking.' *I almost had the revolver by the grip,* 'We can sort this out. Protective custody.'

'You don't understand.' There were tears in his eyes. 'There is no safe place. I die if you live.'

I had the revolver by the grip. Moving hurt like hell but I managed to cock the hammer. 'How much is Field paying you?'

'What?

'Field, how much is he paying you?'

He looked non-plussed. '£40,000. But how?'

'How did we know? We're not stupid. We know Collins shot those two coppers and Kenny Summers. We have a witness; and it's not me. Collins identified Summers and this is Collins' house. You said you had never been here, yet you knew there was a cellar and where it was. And, we have your car number. It was you who attempted to assassinate Malcolm Truelove and his son last night.'

'They're dead. I shot the father. Linus, the lad.'

'Sorry, they're both alive which is why we have the car number.'

'Then you die.' He straightened his arm. His look changed. I rocked my head from side-to-side. Desperate measures. Make the target more difficult? He leaned forward; I had one chance. Clenching my teeth in an attempt to block the pain, I made a despairing lunge and grabbed the cylinder as he pulled the trigger. The cylinder stopped revolving. The hammer froze. The pain was horrendous. Sweat was pouring down my face as I pulled the other revolver out from under me and rammed it under his ribs.

'This one ... cocked. Let go.'

'I can't.'

'Let go ... cylinder ... can't turn ... gun won't cock ... Let go.'

Then the most welcome sound. 'Sergeant Blake?'

Breathing was painful. 'In here Keith .. Got ... cuffs? ... revolver.

Keith Fleming appeared tentatively round the door jamb. Staff in hand. 'Hold still, sarge.' He brought his staff down on my would be assassin's wrist twice before he let go.

I collapsed on the floor a revolver in each hand as Keith cuffed the DCI behind his back.

'You ok?'

I attempted a grin. 'One in back,' I gasped. 'He's yours.'

'I'm arresting you for the attempted murder of Sergeant Brian Blake. You're a DCI you know the caution.' He pressed the button on his radio. '1708, Sergeant Blake has been shot in the back,' he grinned at me, 'but he'll live. One in custody for attempted murder.'

The first two to arrive were DS Greatorix and the traffic man.

'You're the arresting officer.' DS Greatorix said to Keith Fleming.

'Sarge,' he acknowledged.

'You stay here with Sergeant Blake. We'll take care of chummy,' he said. 'But before we go,' he knelt at the side of DI Beamish and felt for his carotid pulse. He pursed his lips. 'Faint but it's there,' he said. Turned him in to a prone position and cuffed him behind his back. 'Whoever you are, you're nicked.'

I beckoned to Colin Greatorix. He knelt beside me. 'Ambulance on its way, Brian.'

'I nodded. 'Let Wallace know ... Field paid ... 40k to kill me.'

'Forty thousand?'

I pointed at Keith Fleming. 'Keith overheard.'

Colin Greatorix looked up. 'That's right, sarge. I was in the corridor trying to work out what to do next. I heard the conversation. When Sergeant Blake said he had hold of the cylinder.'

'So he couldn't cock the revolver.'

'Yep.'

'Well done,' he said and looked at me. 'I'll make sure Lucy knows.'

I nodded. 'Don't frighten her ... just hurt back.'

'Will do.' He took a couple of large envelopes from his pocket and placed a revolver in each; identifying each envelope. 'This would prove interesting when they print the rounds.' He stood and they left.

Peter Cartwright arrived with Mr Wallace, a doctor, nurse and two ambulancemen.

'I got the message about the money. I'll let Commander Jameson know when I'm back to the station,'

I nodded acknowledgment before the doctor shooed everyone out of the room.

'Who did this?' he pointed at the unconscious, handcuffed DI.

'I did,' I said. 'Tried to shoot me .. other... succeeded.'

'I see,' he felt for the carotid. 'He's alive and not going anywhere. Now, let's have a look at you.

Sixty-Eight

I was lucky. If you can call being shot in the back lucky. The bullet passed through the ninth intercostal space, more painful than dangerous in that my ribs were intact and my right lung unaffected; although how it would affect my karate remained to be seen. Where the bullet lodged was not my concern,

The only compensation to being in the Royal Halifax Infirmary, I had my own sideward.

After a procession of senior officers, including Cousin Raymond, the only one I wanted to see was a Claire-carrying Lucy accompanied by Mum.

4pm. There they were. 'The last time we were like this I was carrying Claire,'

'Seven months if I recall.'

'Can I go to daddy?'

'You do not climb on the bed and bounce; daddy has been injured.'

'I can rub it better.'

'Not this time, Claire,' I said. 'I have to rest.'

'Not fair.' Claire was having a sulk. She would be an Olympic finalist at bed-bouncing.

'Well, fair or not you do not climb on the bed.'

'Aww.'

'Is your left side all right?' said Mum. 'Just for a hug.'

'Possibly.'

'Come on, Claire. Round the other side. Just for a hug. But no bouncing.'

A plea for just one bounce rejected, Mum took Claire to the cafeteria.

Lucy pulled her chair forward, held my hand and we shared a peck. 'How are you? or is that a silly question.'

'Sore. How much do you know?'

'I got a call from Colin Greatorix to say you had been hurt; but no details. Then cousin Raymond that you had been shot, but it was a minor injury and you were in no danger.'

'That's true. It's just painful.'

'And policemen?'

Time to be careful. 'Yes. But I can't give you any details. Both are in custody.'

'Thanks to you.'

'Not just me.'

'It's just that I worry, and I don't want to be a policeman's widow.'

'Lucy, I don't want that either. But who would have suspected two senior detectives?'

'I know. And I suppose the chances are infinitesimal that it might happen again.'

The next morning things had improved and I was told I should be able to go home in a week. A week?

Sixty-Nine

Peter Cartwright arrived to take my statement. Later, Peter told me about the message from my neighbours, concerning the two mysterious visitors had somehow ended under my desk. And the note giving the description of the car outside the Truelove's home was in my IN tray. Had I read the note and seen the car, Frobisher and Bellamy would have been arrested before any further harm had been done. Such is life.

Peter brought me up to speed regarding Jackson and the Scrapyard. As predicted, at 3pm the following day, a smartly dressed London solicitor arrived and demanded to see his client only to be introduced to Dermot Reeve. It was a *gentlemanly exchange*. Business cards changed hands with Dermot Reeve stating hr would take a dim view of the matter should any pressure be applied for him to step aside.

Identified by Frank, the Zephyr 4 was seized and the property documented and sent for forensic and fingerprint examination.

A half hour later the Chief put in another appearance. This time accompanied by a smartly dressed gentleman.

'Blake, this is Commander Jameson.'

He stepped forward, right hand outstretched. 'Sergeant, I wanted to apologise and to congratulate you for what you did.'

I held my left hand out. 'Other hand, sir, please.'

His brow furrowed. 'What? Oh yes, sorry. It's a flesh wound?'

'Between the ribs and missed my right lung. Just unpleasant, but that's transient.'

'Quite. I'm not certain how you dealt with DI Bellamy. He was a bare-knuckle fighter. I've never heard of anyone besting him.'

I told him about the two notes I'd missed. 'There were a couple of minor things at the station. The DCI told me they were doing a job for you, and that you thought highly of me. I thought that was odd because I don't think we've met.'

'You're correct. I had heard of you after your incident at Tadcaster. However, I've never discussed you with either of them.'

'Then he talked about Nickleby having a hidden room somewhere. But he was supposed to have died in 1959 ... It seemed odd. I left a note for the office clerk to contact either Mr Wallace or Mr Mithering. Then as we passed the Truelove's house the DCI made reference to the police activity. I told them I'd heard it was a burglary that went wrong. He made the assumption that it was firearms.'

'And it could have been anything.'

'Yes, sir. And there was a look between them. Once in the house I asked what they wanted to see. The DCI said, "I'll just go and check the cellar".'

'Even though they didn't know if there was one, or how to get there.'

'Yes,. DI Bellamy saw the look on my face. Shouted Alex! and thrust his right hand inside his jacket. I didn't wait and planted a yokogeri on the point of his chin. That's a ...'

'I understand, Sergeant,' he said smiling. 'I did a spot of karate in my youth.'

'He was well built. I knew he would bounce off the wall and rotated 'into a mawashi geri, landing it along his jawline. He hit the doorframe and collapsed as I felt the shot in my back.'

The door opened and Keith Fleming walked in. He took one look at the chief. 'Sorry, sir. I can come back later.'

'No, we were just leaving.'

'You're a friend of Sergeant Blake's?' said the Commander.

'This is PC Keith Fleming, sir,' I said.

'Ah, you're the one who went into the house unarmed and secured the arrest.'

'Yes, sir,' he said with a grin. 'You know what it's like with these enthusiastic young sergeants. Need someone with a bit of wool on their back to keep an eye on them.'

To be fair they both laughed. 'Commander Jameson,' he said and held his hand out. 'I look forward to reading your statements. That took guts, Fleming. Well done. It showed true loyalty.'

As the door closed Keith looked at me and grimaced. 'Commander?' he mouthed. 'I won't wash my hands for a month.'

'YOU HAVE SOME GOOD men, Raymond. We knew about Blake following that incident during his initial training. He's making good progress.'

'You're aiming to get your claws into him?'

'Not beyond the bounds of possibility. And Fleming? He seems a good solid officer.'

'He is; and since Blake was sent to Sowerby Bridge has shown real progress.'

'Perhaps Fleming hit the nail on the head: young enthusiastic sergeants.'

'Always providing they can do the job. And Blake hasn't been to Bramshill.'

Seventy

The officer on the interview room door rapped once and stepped back. Detective Superintendent Wallace, Detective Chief Superintendent Yelland of the Metropolitan Police and Mrs Watson entered. Detective Superintendent Wallace nodded to the officer inside who left. Mrs Watson sat on a chair behind the door, opened her pad and prepared to take notes.

Both senior officers settled. 'I'm Detective Superintendent Wallace. I understand you and Detective Chief Superintendent Yelland are already acquainted.

'We certainly are.' The DCS said with a grim smile. Frobisher paled.

'For the benefit of the shorthand writer will you give your full name and rank?'

'What's her name?'

'That's no concern of yours,' snapped the DS. 'Now?'

He sighed. 'Alexander Martin Frobisher. detective chief inspector in the Metropolitan Police Major Crime Unit.'

'You know the caution, Mr Frobisher, however, you are not obliged to say anything unless you wish to do so but anything you say will be taken down in writing and may be given in evidence, Do you understand?'

Frobisher sighed. 'Yes, I understand.'

'Good.' DS Wallace ran his eyes over the heavy strapping. 'How is your wrist?'

'I'll live.'

Unable to contain himself DCS Yelland grinned. 'I take it, *DCI Webster*, you'll not be submitting an *injury on duty form?*'

If looks could have killed. 'No sir, I am not.'

DS Wallace smiled at his colleague before turning to the prisoner. 'You're in a spot of bother Mr Frobisher,' he said. 'According to Commander Jameson, you drew a revolver and six rounds of ammunition, as did Detective Inspector Bellamy yesterday morning falsely claiming it was on the authority of Commander Jameson. Why was this?'

'No comment.'

'Why did Detective Inspector Bellamy telephone the information room and enquire from the Duty Officer, Inspector Colin Jackson, the whereabouts of Sowerby Bridge?'

'No idea, you'll have to ask him.'

'A strange answer when you and Detective Inspector Bellamy are described as being joined at the hip. And, both you and Detective Inspector Bellamy travelled to Huddersfield, in your personal car, a Humber Hawk V series, registration mark BUL1F, where you paid cash for two nights board and lodging in the Morning View Guest House in Huddersfield; seven miles from Sowerby Bridge. Hiding your tracks?'

All Frobisher offered was a stoney look.

'A search warrant was executed in relation to the Morning View Guest House and your property is now in our safe-keeping. Enquiries are now being conducted in relation to your car, your house and the passports in both your possession; especially those in the names of Webster and Beamish; they're very good, but you already knew that.'

'Your car was deposited at Yeadon airport and kept under observation. It was collected less than two hours ago by an unidentified male. It is currently being shadowed south along the A1 ... Who will be the recipient?'

'No Comment.'

'That's a shame. Remember the oath you took on the day you joined? To our Sovereign Lady the Queen. How about making good on that oath? turn Queen's evidence.'

'No comment.'

'Mr Frobisher, you have no convictions. You are aware there are avenues through which we could arrange for your safe transport to another country and a new identity. Turn Queen's evidence.'

Frobisher glared at his interrogators. 'If you think I'm falling for that you must think I'm stupid. With what I'm facing? There's no way you wouldn't stick me in court. In any case, once the FBI became aware they would ship me straight back here. I'm saying nothing.'

'As you wish .. A search warrant in relation to your home address will be executed within the next hour.'

'No comment.'

An application has been made to a Judge in Chambers to gain access to your bank accounts; that should prove interesting.'

'No comment,' Frobisher said through gritted teeth.

'Are you prepared to tell us where you obtained the home address of Sergeant Blake?'

Frobisher was in deep shit and becoming deeper by the second. 'No comment.'

'Telephone records can be most enlightening. We know that they were obtained by Nickleby and passed to Field. Is that where you obtained them?'

Frobisher snorted a laugh. 'Another bent copper. What a surprise. Next.'

'A little matter of your meeting with Harry Field on the tube and £41,000.'

'What?'

'Come now. Let me refresh your memory. You boarded the Tube at North Acton. Field was in the seat adjacent to the door overlooking the platform, you sat next to him; although the compartment was half empty. Any comment?'

'I have no recollection of that.'

Both Wallace and Yelland laughed. 'Of course you don't,' said the DCS. 'To continue. You and Field get into a huddle. Field takes an envelope from his inside pocket and hands it to you, you put it in your inside pocket and tap your jacket pocket twice. As you stand waiting for the doors to open, Field says, "don't forget." Your reply, "The 6 dog, got it." You exit the Tube at East Acton ..'

'You have a fertile imagination, sir.'

'No Frobisher,' said the DCS. 'We have an eye witness.'

Frobisher pursed his lips and shrugged his shoulders. 'Nothing to do with me.'

The DCS leaned forward resting his forearms on the table. 'Listen lad, I know Field better than any man in the Met. Your mouth might be lying but your eyes aren't. The envelope? Seed money? And once you take the money, whether or not you know what the contract is, you are in. So, what was it? £1000 in used notes? You go to his bookies in Camden and place the money on the 6 dog in the last at Romford. And what was the length of the contract before you were liable? Your meeting was two weeks ago so I'm guessing it was a two-week contract to assassinate Police Sergeant 547 Blake. A young officer, married with a three-year-old daughter and infant twins. An officer invested by Her Majesty with the George Cross and the Conspicuous Gallantry Medal .. and what did you say when he was pleading for his life? "If you live, I die."'

'No comment.'

The DCS sighed. 'Let's make it simple. Put the building bricks in a column. You have a private meeting with Field on the Tube. He gives you an envelope containing, for the sake of argument, £1000 in used notes, to be bet on the 6 dog in the last race at Romford that night.

You discuss this with Bellamy who calls the information room because neither of you know where Sowerby Bridge is. But *you* go to Romford, where we have your every move photographed. You put £100 of your own money on the 6 dog and loses. The £1000 is in the hands of Bellamy who places, and I quote, "A grand on the 6 dog at Romford". A bet accepted by Jimmy Moss and confirmed by daughter Elizabeth.

'DC Robert Green of the surveillance team was under cover in The Betting Field. Also there are Carl Edwards, one of Fields heavies and Edith Ramsbottom, one of Field's Toms. Green likes a flutter. He wins the last at Romford, making five and a five-fold. Naturally, makes a protest when Bellamy is paid out for his losing bet and receives a knife wound to his back from Edwards, so severe, it severs his renal artery. He makes it back to the car where he collapses and dies.

'As you know, Field hangs onto the money until Blake is dead. Now there's a price on your head. How much I don't know. But as things stand you're going to prison for a long time with the Sword of Damocles hanging over your head. A DCI arrested for the attempted murder of a serving officer. The TV companies and the Press will have a field day. If you'll pardon the expression.

'When I interview Field he'll tell me, Nickleby, you and Bellamy approached him and for £40,000 you would get rid of Sergeant Blake, Nickleby's arresting officer. If he refused you would grass him up.'

'I am not a grass.'

'So you say. But, Field's QC, Mansford Lawler would arrange with the Old Bailey Court Listing that because of his workload he couldn't possibly defend his client until much later. That means until after your trial.'

'I will repeat. I am not a grass.'

'You would be called and treated as a hostile witness. You understand?'

Frobisher glared at the DCS and spat the words out. 'You bastard.'

It was answered with a smile. 'True. And you are a corrupt police officer who would have murdered Sergeant Blake for the £40,000 if he hadn't the strength to do what he did with help from another unarmed police constable. Blake had recovered Bellamy's revolver and could have killed you, but didn't. Do not expect sympathy. Do what you are paid to do and I promise we will keep you alive as long as possible. Play hardball and you're on your own. I wouldn't give tuppence for your chances. Think about it.'

The simmering silence continued for almost five minutes. The one who breaks the silence loses the argument.

Frobisher broke eye contact and lowered his gaze to the table. 'What do you want to know?'

There was an abrupt release of tension from across the table. 'You were the detective constable who, along with Nickleby's mother, identified Nickleby as the one who died in the crash at Buckhurst Hill in '59. Yet, ten years later he is in custody, here in Yorkshire. So, who did you and his mother identify?'

'An absconder from an approved school, Alex Matthews. He went through the windscreen. So badly cut-up he was unrecognisable. Nickleby wore a belt with a buckle like a Roller; I switched them.'

The DCS frowned. 'And that was the sole means of identification?'

'It was accepted by the coroner. Mind you, that was Gatesby, and he's dead.'

'Nevertheless, I think with Nickleby in custody re-opening his inquest will be routine.'

There was a sharp rap at the door. Detective Superintendent Wallace stood. 'Yes, sergeant?' he said as he opened the door.'

'A message for DCS Yelland, sir,' the sergeant handed over a folded note. 'I was told it was urgent.'

'All right, thank you.'

He closed the door, handed the note over and sat.

'You haven't asked how Bellamy is,' said the DS.

Frobisher looked up. 'I thought Blake had killed him.'

'No, he's unconscious, but may yet stand trial. That must have given you a shock. A young lad like Sergeant Blake taking him out.'

'He was lucky, used his feet.'

'You were watching,' snapped the DCS. 'Luck had nothing to do with it. Then you shot him in the back. That will go down well in court .. And don't think that by cooperating you are going to just walk.'

'I wasn't.' *Co-operating was the best way at the moment of staying alive a little bit longer. Needs must!*

DCS Yelland held his hand up. 'This note,' he said wafting it. 'Is conformation that a Judge in chambers has granted access to your bank accounts. And whilst Field paid out in cash it will give us useful window into your life. It also states that Inspector Manners has taken an interest in your wife's jewellery. He describes it as being slightly out of your expected price range.'

All Frobisher could summon was a sickly grin. Manners was the son of an Antwerp based diamond dealer who'd chosen the police as a career instead of following in his father's footsteps. He was the last person Frobisher wanted poking into his affairs.

'Mr Frobisher,' said DS Wallace. 'Irrespective of any historic charges, this enquiry involves the murders of three police officers, Harry Field's Bookkeeper, the attempted murders of Sergeant Blake and Malcolm Truelove and, conspiracy to murder his eleven-year-old son, Arthur. You will be charged with the attempted murders of

Sergeant Blake, Malcom Truelove and Conspiracy to murder Arthur Truelove. An application will be made for you to be remanded to Police cells whilst further enquiries are carried out.'

Seventy-One

I don't know how they got passed Sister Spavin, not noted for her sense of humour and my sideward was almost full. Caroline, Wendy, Carol, Sally, Amy and Brenda trooped in, all in their GIs. Bearing cards and gifts of grapes, chocolate and a couple of bunches of flowers. Lucy, Claire, the twins and Liz close behind.

'So, this is what you get up to when Lucy isn't here,' said Liz smiling at the girls.

'We wanted a group photo,' said an embarrassed Caroline. The others agreed.

Right on cue Sister Spavin arrived. The conversation died. 'One photo you said. So please let's get it taken then my ward can return to sanity. Quickly now.'

The girls split three either side; all trying to get a seat on the bed. I looked at a miserable Claire. 'Come on, you as well. You can sit on my lap.' She didn't need inviting twice. She scrambled onto the bed and claimed her place, crossing my arms round her and wriggling back. We'd both missed this.

'Wait a minute,' said Lucy. 'There's two more.' Lucy deposited Douglas into Caroline's embrace. Liz, Arthur into Amy's. 'A good blackmail photo,' said Lucy.

'Are we ready now?' said Sister Spavin, raising the camera.

'Just a sec,' said Caroline. Sister Spavin sighed and lowered the camera. 'Mrs Blake, why don't you and your Mum join us.' Lucy on my left and Liz on the right, standing behind the girls. All was ready.

'All say, cheese ... Good ... One more ... Cheese .. Right can I have my ward back?'

The twins back in their pram, the girls waved as they left.

Seventy-Two

'Did you know they were coming?' said Lucy.

'Not until they arrived. I'm surprised the sister permitted it. The main thing is you're here.' Hugs and kisses all round and things were more or less normal.

'Claire,' said Lucy. 'This is just a flying visit. Give daddy a kiss.'

She stood on my thighs, flung her arms round my neck and planted a kiss on my cheek. 'I love you, daddy. When are you coming home?'

'I love you too. It won't be long. Just a few days.'

I heard the officer outside. 'Sir!' A warning of senior police officers.

'Who's this,' said Lucy as the door opened and Mr Wallace and another, this one unknown, walked in.

'Mrs Blake, sorry. I didn't realise you were here.'

'Flying visit, Mr Wallace. We were on the point of leaving.'

'Let me introduce you. This,' he indicated the tall thick-set man in the immaculate pin-striped suit, striped tie and highly-polished shoes. 'is Detective Chief Superintendent Yelland from the Metropolitan Police. Sergeant Blake. His wife Lucy and daughter Claire and the twins. I'm afraid I don't know the other lady.'

'My mother, Mrs Elizabeth Vernon.'

Introductions made and hands shaken

Mr Yelland hitched his trousers, crouched and smiled 'Now,' he indicated the twins. 'Are these your little brothers?'

Claire nodded. 'This is Douglas' she said pointing to the one on the left. 'And the other one is Arthur.'

'How on earth do you tell the difference?'

She shrugged. 'Don't know. I just do.'

'Come on Claire. Time to go and leave daddy to his new visitors.'

DCS Yelland stood. Claire turned and waved as the door closed. 'Bye daddy, I love you.' the door closed.

'Worth fighting for, sergeant.'

'Definitely, sir.'

'Your daughter, Claire. A bit of a livewire.'

'She's fearless ... On another point, can you tell me if me and my family, and the Trueloves, are still potential targets?'

The DCS took a deep breath and exhaled. 'No-one can ever make a one hundred percent guarantee. However, Field and his cohorts are on remand, and once we get round to interviewing them about the murders they will sing, especially Jimmy Moss; he dotes on his daughter. Moss runs one of Field's bookies, does the payouts. Frobisher and Bellamy failed to meet the terms of Field's contract; each now has a price on his head. Frobisher is offloading in the hope that we can keep him alive. As for Bellamy, he will have plenty of questions to answer once he comes round. If he ever does. The Doctors don't appear to know why he is still unconscious.

'Our biggest problem is the turf-war waiting in the wings, Nature abhors a vacuum. There will be trouble; but I don't think it will be heading your way. They have enough to think about without worrying about Field's failures. Does that settle your mind?'

'To some extent, sir; especially for Lucy and the children. At the moment they're stopping with my parents, along with Arthur Truelove .. I was also thinking about Arthur and his father; their house is quite isolated.'

There was a loaded silence broken by DS Wallace, 'If you're thinking what I think you are, I will clear it first with Mr Barton,' he said. 'If the answer to your query is in the affirmative I will contact their ACC.'

DCS Yelland was looking confused. 'This code? What I don't know I can't let slip?'

'Something like that,' said DS Wallace. 'Sergeant Blake has developed some special friends of late.'

'Well, they don't affect my enquiries, and you have statements from them both?'

'We do.'

He nodded in acknowledgement. 'I asked Mr Wallace to bring me because I wanted to meet you. I can't think of anyone else who might have survived Frobisher and Bellamy's attempt on their life, never mind two prisoners to show for it. So my congratulations.' He held his hand out.

I took the hand but didn't shake it.

'You take care of yourself, Blake and your wife and children.'

'I will, sir,' I said as he stood. In doing so bumped into the bedside drawers. The cards fell over something sliding from the top and floated to the floor.

DCS Yelland bent and picked it up. As he straightened I could see his eyebrows raise and he laughed. 'Hidden depths our sergeant,' he said as he handed the photograph to Mr Wallace who also laughed and handed it to me.

'It seems you have an admirer, Brian.'

I looked at it and gasped. 'What?' It had been a 6 x 4 colour photo but the top inch had been removed. Obviously female. Naked except for the sheerest lace panties; she was dark haired. Feet shoulder width apart and hands on hips. A great figure with pert breasts. But who? I had to laugh. 'Those cards are from my karate club; they arrived just before you did. How many have signed it?'

The DCS picked the cards up and opened them. 'About fifty. How many in your club?'

'About fifty. With around twenty that age and build. And they're all good looking lasses.'

'I don't suppose you recognise the underwear; what there is of it?' Said Mr Wallace, tongue in cheek.

'No, sir. I don't watch them change.'

'What are you going to do?'

'Give it to Lucy. She can go to the club and announce that somebody dropped something and ask if they would like it back.'

'She would be all right with that?' Said a puzzled DCS.

'Better than hiding it and risking it coming out at a later date having done nothing. Besides, she would probably see the funny side.'

'I don't know if my wife would have been so understanding,' said the DCS. 'But if that's what you want to do, good luck.'

He left with a smiling backward glance.

Thirty minutes later I was told I could go home; they wanted their room back.

Two hours later I was back at Salendine Nook. Letter for the doctor. A selection of pills and dressings and instructions to rest and not to do anything stupid.

In a quiet moment I handed the envelope and photo to Lucy and waited for the reaction.

'What!? Who?'

'No head.'

'I can see that, idiot,' she said. 'And those girls delivered it just before we arrived?'

'I think it was inside one of the cards, but not in an envelope.'

'The cheeky mares,' she said and laughed. 'Do you want to see me like that?' Well, it had been almost a week.

'Without a head?'

She laughed and slipped the catch on the bedroom door. Her clothes on the chair she turned. 'And I suppose because you have to take it easy I have to undress you as well.'

'That would be nice.'

'Close your eyes and relax. Remember my welcome to Capri?'

Holding my hands against her breasts she lowered herself and gasped. The feeling was superb. 'I hope I never get used to this,' she said and picked up the speed.

She sank onto my chest and put her right hand on my left shoulder. 'Welcome home, darling.'

Seventy-Three

The phone was answered on the third ring. 'Martin Beck.'

'Brian Blake.'

'Good heavens. Carol and I were only talking about you with the twins yesterday.'

'And now we have twins of our own.'

'That's wonderful,' Carol joined the conversation. 'You will have to call in.'

'Is this pleasure or business, Brian?' said Martin.

'Ah, I'll explain. At the moment only two people other than myself know what I'm going to ask. Detective Superintendent Wallace and Mr Barton, the Chief Constable. What I am going to tell you comes within the provisions of the Official Secrets Act'

'Sounds intriguing,' said Carol. 'You are quite safe; the boys aren't here.'

'Good, this isn't for children. A few months ago there was a story that hit the headlines. About the murder of three people, two of them police officers, shot to death in a car.'

'Yes,' said Martin. 'That was horrendous. You were involved?'

'Yes, It was my first day as a sergeant. I was on my way to work when I came across the scene.'

'Sergeant? You've only been in the job for two minutes,' said Martin.

'That's wonderful, congratulations,' said Carol

'Thanks. I was also the arresting officer of the gunman.'

'This gets better,' said Martin. 'I don't remember you being mentioned.'

'I wasn't. A major London criminal was involved and put two and two together, although he didn't know my name realised who I was, from information he had and put a contract out on me with two corrupt Metropolitan police officers.'

'Seriously?'

'Very. But this is not about me. It concerns a man and his son who live close to where the gunman lived. Arthur is eleven and was born with condition called autism; amongst other things he has a photographic memory and kept a written record of all vehicles seen in the area.'

'Including any seen near to where this shooter lives.'

'Exactly, Martin. One of the two shot the father in the chest, but survived owning to a rare genetic condition. The other refused to shoot Arthur, who is now staying with my parents.

'I was unaware of who they were, or the vehicle. The next morning. I walked into a trap, realising just in time. I knocked one of them out; he is still unconscious. The other shot me in the back, but it's a minor flesh wound. One of my colleagues had seen the car I was in and recognised it from the description. He arrived in time and the other was arrested and has since been charged with my attempted murder.'

'That is some story,' said Martin.

'My guess,' said Carol. 'Is that you are looking for somewhere this man and his son can recuperate.'

I took a deep breath and sighed. 'Yes. '

'What's the danger level?' said Martin.

'According to Detective Chief Superintendent Yelland of the Metropolitan Police, very low. The criminal, Harry Field and all his associates have been remanded in custody. And the attack on me and, Malcolm and Arthur Truelove is nothing to do with anyone else.'

'Does this Detective Chief Superintendent Yelland know about us?' Said Carol.

'No. Just the three. He knows we're thinking of somewhere, but nothing more. If you agree then Detective Superintendent Wallace will liaise with ACC Patrickson, and he with you.'

'In essence I have no problem. As we have done in the past, the staff will be made aware to look out for strangers hanging around.'

'Thanks. It will be one hell of a shock when they see the house. I'll call Mr Wallace. In the meantime I'll try and find out just how long before Malcolm Truelove will be discharged ... Now, how are the boys?'

'Large as life and twice as busy,' laughed Martin. 'There aren't enough hours in the day.'

Carol burst out laughing. 'That's true. Due in no small part to my husband teaching them to build castles in the sky.'

'True, but after the events of that evening it helped to occupy their minds. Give them something else.to concentrate on. And, they're closer than ever.

'Graeme has his next book on the shelf and his first Christmas Annual will be published this next week; in time for the festive season,'

'He's doing well.'

'If his first book was anything to go by, very promising.'

There was the sound of a raised voice. 'Sorry, I have to go. Visitor. Claire is three; she'll love your castles in the air.'

'We'll see you soon.'

Seventy-Four

'Yes sir,' I said. 'the force medical officer says it's all right providing there is no rolling round on the floor.'

'I see. How long do you anticipate it will take?'

'At the Hathersages? I would think twenty to thirty minutes. I just need the entire family to be present, plus gardener and housekeeper.'

'I understand. I will fill the Chief Superintendent in and make the arrangements. Next Wednesday 7pm.'

I WAS A UNIFORM SERGEANT in the early part of my twelve months probationary period, and as such not involved further in the Nickleby – Harry Field enquiry. Although I'd have given my eyeteeth to be so. Still ...

Analysis of Field's telephone accounts were invaluable. The Golden Cascade Amusement Arcade Blackpool, leading to several arrests and another opening to Field's business affairs.

Chris Grogan gave a comprehensive statement of the work he had done with, and for, Nickleby; including his prostitution and blackmail business.

Grogan was given a new identity and a twelve month sentence in an open prison in Somerset. His mother and grandfather died before his release. He was found work as a driver for a wildlife charity in the West Country where they had plenty of bats. He never returned to Yorkshire.

Seventy-Five

7 pm Wednesday. The Beeches, Wakefield Road, Bolton Brow. Detective Superintendent Wallace, Detective Sergeant Greatorix, Detective Constable Mark Foster and myself alighted from Mr Wallace's car. Chief Superintendent Cartwright was waiting. My surprise for Mrs Hathersage alighted from the Rover saloon behind us.

'How long will this take, sergeant?'

'Twenty to thirty minutes, sir.'

He nodded. 'I've discussed your evidence with Mr Wallace and I agree. Now, it's down to you.'

'Sir.' I mentally exhaled and crossed my metaphorical fingers. *Don't screw this up.*

I sidled up to my surprise. 'Sergeant Blake,' I said and offered my hand. 'Thank you for agreeing to come.'

'Not at all, sergeant. I'm intrigued.'

'If you would stay in the background until I introduce you.'

'Certainly.'

The door opened as we approached and ushered into the Drawing room where Mrs Marcia Hathersage, Mrs Phillips the Housekeeper and her gardener husband, John, were gathered. In addition, a group of three younger people which became four when the young woman who opened the door joined them.

'Chief Superintendent, a rather strange request but all my staff and my children are here. Let me introduce you ...'

A large man in his early thirties stepped forward, drew himself up to his full height and said curtly. 'I can manage this, Mother. I am

Hugo Hathersage, prospective conservative Member of Parliament for Old Hampton and Peakeshole. These are,' he wave expansively in the direction of the others who looked less than pleased. 'My siblings, Eleanor, Evadne and John. I hope this is not going to take long, chief superintendent. I am a busy man.'

The chief superintendent sounded irritated. 'We are all busy people Mr Hathersage, but this is a murder enquiry and it will take as long as it takes. Sergeant?'

I stepped forward.

Hugo Hathersage was not impressed. 'Sergeant? If this is a murder enquiry I expect nothing less than a detective inspector.'

'Hugo, do be quiet, said his male sibling. 'Let the police do their job.'

The chief superintendent began again. 'I am confident that Sergeant Blake is capable of doing what is necessary to bring this case to a satisfactory conclusion. Sergeant.'

'Sir. I should have been here three weeks ago. However, circumstances prevented that.'

'So,' Was there no way to shut this man up? 'we have been inconvenienced for your convenience.'

'No, Mr Hathersage,' Mr Wallace had had enough. 'Three weeks ago Sergeant Blake and one of his colleagues were in the process of arresting two murderers when Sergeant Blake was shot in the back. He has been in hospital and is only here now because of his insistence.'

The male sibling had had enough. 'Hugo, you're just a blowhard. For god's sake shut it ... Sorry sergeant, carry on please.'

I nodded. 'Before I continue, Mrs Hathersage I have two documents here from Verity.' I stepped across and handed one over. 'This is a letter of resignation, dated yesterday.'

She took the letter. 'You knew?'

'Yes, she wrote it in my presence.' I turned to face the others. 'When I received information from Mrs Hathersage of her husband's untimely death, I attended with a young policewoman: Weatherly, her first sudden death. Having spoken to Mrs Hathersage, where she gave me the death certificate ostensibly signed by a Doctor Olivier. I went with Verity, the maid, to the bedroom. She waited outside whilst I made a cursory examination which included feeling for Mr Hathersage's carotid pulse; it was absent. I raised his eyelids to check for reaction from light. There was none. However I noticed small red dots in the white of his eyes. These are called petechiae. Possible evidence that the death required further investigation.'

'Now I've heard everything,' said the loquacious Hugo. 'A doctor has issued a death certificate and you have the arrogance to question it?'

I ignored him and turned to Mrs Hathersage. 'Have you ever seen this gentleman before.' Doctor Olivier stepped forward.

'No,' she said after giving the doctor a cursory look. 'I've never seen him before.'

'Are you sure?'

'Positive. Why should I?'

There were shocked looks all round as I continued. 'This is the gentleman that you allege signed your husband's death certificate, and who both you and Verity described as looking like Steve McQueen.'

The Doctor laughed, 'You didn't tell me that, sergeant. But yes Mrs Hathersage, I am Doctor Olivier. I have never been to this house before and I knew nothing about the death of your husband until the police called the Practice. The only people who knew, at the time, that I was linked in any way to the Practice are employees, and patients who were informed by letter.

And for the benefit of Mr Hathersage and anyone else agreeing with his views, I will also confirm that the sergeant was correct. The appearance of petechiae would automatically be cause for serious concern and a death certificate should not have been issued, especially one bearing my name, whoever it was ... chief superintendent has there been a post mortem examination of the deceased?'

'Yes, Doctor,' said Detective Inspector Cartwright. 'The cause of death was suffocation. Fibres from his pillow were recovered from his mouth, nasal passages and bronchi.'

'Thank you. I hope that settles the matter.'

'Doctor,' I acknowledged. 'The discovery of the petechiae automatically brought this investigation closer to the family orbit.'

'Good God,' exploded Hugo. 'You're accusing us now.'

'For crying out loud, Hugo,' said the young woman who had opened the front door. 'Engage your brain for once in a while. If father was suffocated in his bedroom; just who has access to the house?' several pairs of eyes drifted to Marcia Hathersage. 'Of course we're suspects. And that includes you. You were the one who is going to inherit father's estate, or so you've told us on a regular basis. In my book that makes you the prime suspect. If I were you I should start to worry,'

Hugo's face clouded over. 'It, it wasn't me Evadne,'

Evadne looked at me and smiled. 'Sorry, sergeant but Hugo suffers from foot and mouth disease on a regular basis. I feel sorry for any constituents he may ultimately represent.'

I returned the smile. 'Thank you. Mrs Hathersage I notice that you haven't opened the letter.'

'Good god,' said Hugo Hathersage. 'You've told mother what's in the damned letter. Is it a crime not to read it.'

'I thought she might be curious. But if you continue to interrupt I will have you removed from the room.'

'You wouldn't dare.'

I made eye contact with Colin Greatorix. 'With pleasure Brian,' he said and took a step forward.

'All right,' Hugo said and took a step back.

'No, she doesn't have to read it; but bearing in mind the part Verity played in this investigation at the instigation of your mother, I thought it might be of interest ... I mentioned that Verity wrote two documents.' I unzipped my brief case extracting the second. 'This is a witness statement made voluntarily by Verity Meredith and signed in my presence yesterday.' I handed it to Detective Superintendent Wallace. 'In it she retracts much of what she told me about the day Duncan Hathersage died. The fact that you, Mrs Hathersage, sent her to the shops and instructed her not to return for an hour. When she returned you fed Verity a story of what she had to say when the police arrived, including the Doctor's name and his resemblance to the actor, Steve McQueen. The comparison between Verity's initial statement and yours, Mrs Hathersage, showed them to be too similar not to have come from the same source.'

'How dare you?'

Before I or anyone else could react, Marcia Hathersage said. 'Hugo, do be quiet. You are only making things worse.'

'But mother.'

'Be quiet!'

Mr Wallace passed the statement to the chief superintendent.

'Verity was also under the impression that if she did not comply with your instructions she would be dismissed without pay or references, and you would ensure that she would not gain employment anywhere in the town. I am pleased to tell you that she has found employment, and at a higher level of remuneration.'

Marcia Hathersage dropped her eyes and refused to comment.

'I will tell you now that you are not obliged to say anything but whatever you say may be taken down in writing and used in evidence.' There was no reply.

The atmosphere in the room was icy.

'To continue what I was saying. I had noticed the petechiae and instructed Policewoman Weatherly to sit with Verity and take brief notes regarding that day's regime, much of which has now been contradicted. In fact, I was admiring the plaster mouldings on the ceiling when I bumped into the bed. There was a clatter as a silver photo frame with photo fell to the floor. For some reason it had been pushed down the bed under the bedclothes. The reason eluded me for some time.' I fished a bundle of photos from my briefcase and handed one each to Chief Superintendent Cartwright and Detective Superintendent Wallace, kept one and handed the remainder to Colin Greatorix to distribute. Marcia Hathersage refused to take one; a point noticed by all her children.

'As you see the photo is of a group of four Royal Air Force dispatch riders dated 1943. I recognised the sergeant as your father. I also recognised the second left as being one Vivian Smedley who was known to me, although I did not make this known to your mother at the time. Smedley was on life licence having been sentenced for murder several years earlier. I arrested him for a crime of violence and he was returned to prison. He died in prison from TB a few weeks ago.

Your mother identified your father, Duncan Hathersage, and the others from left-to-right as Nicholas or 'Nick' Collins, who strangely enough. was now a businessman local to this area. They had known each other for over twenty five years, he would be my next call. I obtained permission to borrow the photo and frame, and to obtain copies. Your mother made it patently clear that she never liked Collins although she had known him with the rest of those in the photograph. However, one thing that she didn't mention, and I for one would like to know why, is why did she refer to him as Collins?'

'Perhaps because that was his name,' said Hugo, almost as a sneer.

I didn't comment. 'Until 1959 when he was reported to have been killed in a road accident to the north of London, the man we know as Nicholas Collins was called Nicholas Nickleby, as in the Dickensian character. Your mother knew him as Nickleby, not Collins. One of the things we shall want to know is why she didn't tell me at the time. We only became aware of this personation when Collins' fingerprints were checked for elimination purposes in an entirely different matter.'

The anger in the voice took everyone by surprise. 'Leave her alone for God's sake. She's innocent.' The man everyone knew as John, the gardener, walked across the room crouched at Marcia Hathersage's side and held her hands.

'What the hell?'

'Leave him be Mr Hathersage. This,' I indicated our new contributor. 'is the fourth motor cyclist in the photograph, Bryan Forbes. Still not wearing your signet ring, Bryan?'

Collin Greatorix opened the curtain. Three rotating blue lights appeared.

Forbes laughed. 'If that's for my benefit, sergeant, you'll never get me to court. Yes, I killed him. Duncan Hathersage was an evil bastard and I don't care who hears it.'

There were cries of outrage from the four children, but nothing from their mother.

'B-but he's a g-gardener,' spluttered Hugo.

'Not in 1943, Hugo,' said Evadne. 'Look at the photograph.'

'And not until he sold his motor cycle courier business in Birmingham this last March, in order to move back to his native Yorkshire.'

'You've done your homework, sergeant.'

I cautioned him. 'What makes you think you won't be going to court?'

'Because he's dying,' said Marcia Hathersage.

'Eight months ago, I was diagnosed with stage four lung cancer; given between three and six months to live. So ...' he said and smiled. 'I think you call them dying declarations. I want to explain why.'

I glanced at Mr Wallace who nodded.

'All right, go ahead.'

Forbes lifted Marcia's hands and kissed them. 'Your mother and I met at a NAAFI dance not long after that photo was taken and we got along really well. It became steady. Duncan Hathersage enjoyed getting his own way; in fact he always got his own way and decided he was the better man. Your mother disagreed. Duncan couldn't stand the rejection. Irrespective of what your father wanted, your mother and me got engaged. It was wartime. Things were different and we slept together.'

'I became pregnant,' said Marcia. 'But we didn't care, we were getting married.'

'Duncan Hathersage got his own back. He and Nickleby were up to their necks in the Black Market and other fiddles. He planted a stolen necklace in my locker. Then he reported *what he had heard.* Of course the MPs found it. I was charged and court martialled, and received six months in a military prison.'

'Duncan told me Bryan had been sentenced to five years. I was pregnant but Duncan didn't know so I agreed to marry him. By the time Bryan was released it was too late. It was not a happy marriage. Yes, I had plenty of money but he didn't love me; I was a prize in a rigged lucky dip. Duncan had a string of women and it didn't do to question him. After the war we moved back to his home in Halifax where he started his haulage business. He made friends in the right places ensuring him lucrative contracts. I didn't see Bryan for years.'

'After demob I had no idea what to do,. But a friend, whose father worked in the bullion trade asked me to courier a package for him. It was what we did during the war. Supply to customer direct. Faster. Cut out the risk of loss in transit. That was the start. It was good business. I found other former dispatch riders and took them on. A new client asked me to deliver a package long-distance: Duncan Hathersage Transport, Salterhebble, Halifax. I couldn't believe my luck.

It was Hathersage in person. I was wearing helmet and goggles. No conversation. Sign each other's dockets and away. Perfect. My business was doing about fifteen of these runs each week on top of other runs. I made sure I did the Yorkshire runs. One day I was leaving to return to Birmingham,' he stopped and smiled at Marcia. 'I bumped into you in the doorway.'

'I didn't recognise Bryan in his helmet.'

'But I recognised her. And spoke. It took a few seconds before the penny dropped. It was like a flash of light.'

'I hadn't felt as happy for years. He couldn't stop so I gave him my phone number for the next time. We'd meet up for a coffee. Later, when Duncan was having a golfing weekend, often in Scotland, Bryan and I would have a weekend away at Duncan's expense. Reparation for the damage he'd done.'

'Then Bryan told me about his cancer .. My housekeeper left, fed up with Duncan's tantrums so I offered the job to Margaret, Bryan's sister, and set Bryan on as gardener.'

'I nearly blew it talking to you when I got confused between Wallflowers and Antirrhinums,'

'Yes, I thought that odd. But you eventually confronted Duncan Hathersage, told him about Hugo being *your* son, two to three weeks before you killed him.'

'W-What?' Spluttered Hugo. 'How?'

'Never mind, Hugo,' said Mrs Hathersage, ' ... Because two weeks before Bryan smothered Duncan he changed his will.'

There were startled looks from the children.

I fished a copy of Duncan Hathersages new will, provided by Erskine and Co their family solicitor, out of my briefcase and handed it to Hugo's younger brother. 'Paragraph two.'

'Do you have to arrest Marcia and Margaret. When I smothered Duncan it was a snap decision. I knew he was going to die, but I would die before him. It was something I needed to do, pay back for all the hurt he'd caused. Something he richly deserved. They only knew when I told them.'

Chief Superintendent Cartwright interjected. 'That will be a matter for the Director of Public Prosecutions and the Coroner, Mr Forbes.'

'I understand, but I trust you.'

There was an explosion of laughter. 'Nothing? He gets nothing?' laughed Evadne.

'Not a bean,' said John.

'He's not going to like that.'

'I'm not going to like what?' said Hugo. 'Talk to me not about me.'

'Shall I?' said John.

'Go on,' said Eleanor. 'Put him out of his misery.'

John looked at me. 'Thank you, sergeant. In the circumstances this news in some way compensates for everything we've learned this evening. Hugo. This is a copy of *our* father's will, dated six weeks ago. Mother gets a life interest in the house plus a generous monthly allowance. The remainder of *our* father's estate, his business and other interests, all his investments and the content of his bank accounts will be divided equally between *my* children, or disposed of as *they* see fit.'

'So?'

'You don't get it, do you. You are not our father's biological son. You are the son of Bryan Forbes. You-do-not-get-a-penny. All these years of threats, bullying and cajoling that, as the eldest child, you inherit his entire estate is just smoke. You get nothing.'

'But I am the eldest child,' he protested.

'You are mother's eldest child, but this is *our* father's will and *you* are not *our* father's biological son. You are our half-brother. If you want clarification you need to see Mr Erskine as soon as possible.

Ignoring the conversation between the siblings Detective Superintendent Wallace tapped me on the shoulder. 'Time to wrap it up, Brian.'

'Sir.' Keith Fleming and Janet Weatherley had arrived and standing by my side. 'Keith, Forbes for murder.'

'Sarge. I'll get the Police Surgeon out in view of his medical condition.'

'Fair enough. PW Weatherly?'

'Sergeant?'

'Marcia Hathersage, suspicion of conspiracy to pervert the course of justice. Remember to caution.'

'Yes, sergeant.'

I turned the other way. 'Mark, Margaret Phillips.'

'Same? Suspicion to pervert?'

'Yup.'

Dr Olivier made himself known. 'Gentlemen, that was fascinating. Much more satisfying than reading a crime novel, which I like. You should start writing, sergeant. Add an air of authenticity to the story.'

I had to laugh. 'Three children and the job, not to mention my wife, Doctor. Only so many hours.'

'Ah well. Now I must leave you. good night. Oh? Will you require a statement?'

'Yes, Doctor, I will contact you tomorrow?'

'Well done, Blake,' said the chief super. 'Get the file in and take some leave, if only for a few days.'

'Sir.'

'Excuse us.' The *Hathersage children* were standing there.

'What can we do for you Mr Hathersage?' said Detective Superintendent Wallace.

'We feel Verity was badly treated and would like to make restitution. Are you at liberty to tell us where she is employed?'

'Blake?'

'Yes sir. Venners, it's an engineering factory. She works in the canteen.'

'I know it ,'said Eleanor, 'thank you.'

Seventy-Six

A week later. The fingerpost to Oldeney. 'Are we nearly there? I'm tired,' Claire yawned as she peered through the windscreen.

Arthur was fast asleep.

''Ten minutes, darling,' said Lucy. 'Give Arthur a shake.'

Malcolm Truelove shook his son gently by the shoulder. 'Come on Arthur, time to wake up.'

We were followed by Joe's van advertising his pies and sausages and carrying the luggage - how that would go down pulling up at the front steps I shuddered to think

'That's a big wall,' said Arthur . 'Is it a prison?'

'No, not a prison. Here we are.'

'Wow!

The gates were impressive. 'What's that rumbling?'

'It's a cattle grid,' said Claire. 'To keep Bambi in.'

'Bambi?'

'They have a herd of fallow deer in the park,' said Lucy.

I slowed. 'If you look in the trees to the right you can just make them out.'

'Where? I can't see anything,' said Arthur. 'Oh, I see them'

'That's the stag,' said Claire. 'It's got pointy antlers, prod you up the bum.'

'It doesn't,' laughed Lucy.

'I'll bet it could.'

'And, we have a welcoming committee.'

'Where?' Claire wound the window down and stuck her head out. 'It's Martin and Graeme. Yoohoo,' she shouted and waved. The twins reciprocated.

'Do you want to ride in, Claire?' said Graeme.

'Yes, please,' she scrambled out of the personnel carrier, ran to Apple and gave it a hug. Graeme lifted her so she could get her foot in the stirrup and waited until she mounted. 'Come on Arthur, it's fun.'

'I've never ridden a horse before.'

'Come on Arthur, if Claire can do it .. I promise you won't fall off.'

With help from Martin Arthur was in the saddle. Shown how to hold the reins and with the twins holding the harnesses, they set off with us following.

'Claire is with Graeme the younger twin,' I said.

'How on earth can you tell?'

'I can't really, but Graeme's pony, Apple, is the lighter. Arthur, is on Dapple, Martin's pony.'

'Martin, he's the Earl? The one who was stabbed?'

'That's right.' I stopped as we crested the slope. The scaffolding had been removed. There was silence for several seconds as the panorama was absorbed. 'Good God, is that the house?'

'Eye-catching, isn't it?'

'Magnificent. What's it like inside?'

'Wait and see.'

Seventy-Seven

We stopped at the foot of the staircase. Claire and Arthur continued to the stables. Claire now riding without Graeme holding the harness.

Givens made a beeline for Joe. 'I'm sorry, sir, you can't park there.'

Joe smiled and said. 'I've got the luggage.'

Givens turned and snapped his fingers. 'Christopher, the luggage, quickly now.'

Carol and Bard came slowly down the staircase, Carol carrying something we hadn't expected. Lucy climbed towards them. 'Where on earth did you find that?' she said and laughed,

'Under a gooseberry bush, where else?' she said. 'Victoria Charlotte Elizabeth, meet your Aunt Lucy,' she said handing her over. '6lbs 4os,'

'Your Ladyship, Madam?' Said Katherine holding Arthur up in the air.

'Yes, Katherine? ... Ah, I see. We shall either be in the Drawing Room or on the Parterre.'

'Madam,' Katherine and Helen departed with their charges.

'Every time?'

'No., if we have no visitors I take my turn, even Bard. And bathtime is our pleasure; even the boys. An introduction to human anatomy, without pressure.'

Van parked out of sight Bard and I left the Parterre to join Claire, Joe and Malcolm Truelove who were heading our way followed by the twins.

'Daddy!' Claire came haring towards us. 'I was riding without Graeme holding the reins.'

I scooped her up. 'I know, we saw you. Was it fun.'

'Mmm,' she nodded vigorously.

I made the introductions.

'My first name is Martin the same as this one,' he indicated the grinning Earl. 'To save any confusion, friends refer to me by my university nickname of Bard.

'And the Earl?'

'In a family setting, Martin. If you're talking about him to the staff, His Lordship or the Earl.'

'And I'm Graeme or Sir Graeme,' he said with resignation.

'Can we take Claire and Arthur to the swings?'

'There are some drinks coming. And if you're going to climb, Claire will need a harness, something for her legs and to keep her hair under control. Give us half an hour.'

In spite of the little Earl being out of action for some time there had been several changes to the playground since the wedding. The main addition was a platform of split sweet chestnut about eighteen feet up a massive oak tree, with a zipline rigged to a conifer some forty yards away. Bard had even constructed a safety net from sheetbends – the same knot used to construct fishing nets; supported on spas.

Bard climbed first. Unhooked the seat, suspended from the eye of a pulley block, in turn from a line round the trunk of the oak; this was their playground.

To me it looked a bit Heath Robinson, even though the twins were happy to use it. Martin insisted on demonstrating first, followed by Graeme. It looked simple enough. Claire went next. If *they* could do it so could *she*. Lucy wasn't so sure. But ...

Lucy and Carol each holding one of our twins and Katherine holding Victoria were standing to one side, Helen behind.

Claire weighed just over two stone and looked incongruous in an old pair of the twins' too-large jeans, fastened with the smallest belt they could find. Her hair, usually free flowing was tied back with a ribbon. Hand over hand Bard hoisted Claire up to the platform.

'Weeeee!

Bard unhooked her from his line. Claire stared up into the tree and the zipline way above her head.

'What are you doing?' said Claire as Bard clipped two tethers to her harness and onto the zipline.

'These are to make sure you can't fall.' He indicated the swing. 'Now hold these two ropes and climb over the seat and sit.'

'Keep your bottom on the seat and hold tight. I'm going to count from five to one and let you go. All right?'

Being up in the tree was exciting although she couldn't see any deer. 'Yes, she said and nodded then began to swing; it was just like her swing at home. She swung harder.'

'Three-two-one. Go'

Below everybody was watching. 'Just look at her,' said Lucy. 'You'd think she was on her swing at home. Not a care in the world ... Oh my God!'

Claire leant backwards and slipped from the seat, her weight, such as it was, pulling her hands from the swing until she was suspended from the tethers.

'Daddy!'

'Hold onto the tethers, Claire.' I shouted.

Easier said than done. Claire's lightness plus there was no pulley to assist slowed her.

'Hello daddy,' she said looking down at me. 'Why am I stopping?'

'Are you hurt?'

'No, daddy. Why did I stop? Martin and Graeme didn't stop.'

I took hold of her hands and walked her down the zipline to where she could put her feet on the ground. 'Because you're a little girl that doesn't weigh a lot and, you weren't sitting on the seat.'

'Are you cross with me?

'No, I'm not cross with you,'

'Can I have another go?'

'Yes,. But Arthur is next.'

After that it was plain sailing. I went up to the platform to give Bard a hand. Even Claire climbed up the ladder instead of being hoisted. Last to have a go were Joe and Lucy. I think they enjoyed it more than the children. Malcolm Truelove and Carol declined.

A meander back to the House to freshen up before a light lunch on the manège followed by riding lessons for the non-riders. A tour of the walled-garden, stables and fire station to follow. Joe left to return to Huddersfield. The climax being a tour of the House. To say it was magnificent was an understatement.

We stayed for three more days. Being looked after as if it were a free five-star hotel. Hours of horse riding, Playing on the swings and the zipline, or simply enjoying walking through the magnificent parkland. Any stress we'd brought with us lying in the woods.

We left with an open invitation from Carol to return anytime. The Trueloves stayed. For us life had to carry on. On a personal level I needed to get back to work and I missed my karate club. Claire knelt on the rear seat waving until they were out of sight.

Seventy-Eight

The news that Colin Greatorix had suffered a major heart attack came as a shock. Hospital visits restricted to close family.

An even bigger shock was that I was now a detective sergeant; taking over Collin's workload and stepping up my involvement in wrapping up the Collins investigation. Detective sergeant with four years' service?

Lucy would be pleased if only because I wouldn't be working nights on a regular basis.

Inspector Marshall would have another newly promoted sergeant. Paul McAndrew from Huddersfield; he lived only a mile or so from where Mum lived at Salendine Nook.

Chief Superintendent Cartwright looked me up and down. 'It's an unusual step to have a sergeant, still in his probation, moved sideways to CID in a case such as this. But Mr Wallace asked the Chief Constable specifically for you. Mr Barton asked for my thoughts. With regret,' he said and smiled. 'I had to agree that you were up to the job. Once exigencies permit, arrangements will be made for you to attend the Senior CID course at Wakefield.' He looked across at Peter Cartwright. 'He's all yours, knock him into shape.'

Peter smiled. 'No promises, sir, but I'll do my best.'

INSPECTOR MARSHALL put his pen down, sat back and smiled. 'Short and sweet?'

'It caught me by surprise. Sorry it had to be Colin's condition that made it possible.'

'Tragic. It doesn't sound as if he will return to duty, even if he survives. He's got twenty-eight in so he will get a full pension. Financially he and Mary should be all right.'

'I rang the hospital from home. He hasn't regained consciousness, not looking good.'

'Well there's nothing we can do. Oh, we're having a whip round if you want to donate.'

I put a fiver in the box.

'One final point, Brian. You've a reputation of doing everything yourself. You're a manager, albeit a junior one. Having the ideas is what you're good at, but you must learn to delegate. To build a team, especially in CID. A lot of what you will be doing is a ball-ache. There's as much kudos getting the evidence trawling through dross, as the flashy arrest. It's the evidence that gets the conviction not the arrest. You will be overseeing, so you have that element of control. The way to get noticed is to make decisions and stand by them unless a senior officer thinks otherwise. Even then don't be afraid to justify your actions. Unless they pull rank.'

'Yes, sir,' I said, and smiled the comment releasing some distant memories. 'Superintendent Valentine made the same point when he was a DCI and I was attached to his unit in the Wainwright case.'

There was an answering smile. 'Did he? You were young in service then and enthusiasm should never be stifled, merely guided. You've earned your promotion, now you have to help others shine. Anyway you're looking well, is your back all right?'

'An odd twinge now and again, otherwise fine.'

'And your leave, there was no address on the form. Somewhere nice?'

'Incredible. Perfect peace, apart from Claire, and seven year old twins. Horse riding, Ziplining and rustic swings. Wonderful walks through parkland with its herd of Roe deer. And wonderful hosts.'

'Anything to do with the last job where you rescued those children?'

'Helped to rescue, sir. Yes, Oldeney Carr House. The House is incredible.'

'They don't take paying guests perchance.'

'Er, no. Lady Carol told me there was so much interest after the fire she is considering opening the House as well as the grounds, but nothing further.'

'It's on the Beverley Road out of Brid?'

'It is.'

'Might put it on the itinerary next spring.' He stood and held his hand out. 'It's good to have you back.'

Seventy-Nine

10**.30am Tuesday. Nickleby had been remanded to police cells pending enquiries.** What had been going through his mind in the interim was anybody's guess.

It was a standard interview room. 15' x 12'. Windowless. Too warm. One table complete with ink doodles and initials scratched in the surface. A single chair on one side, Two on the other. A fourth chair behind the inward opening door. Nickleby seated in the single chair. A constable either side of the door.

I followed DI Cartwright and held the door for Mrs Watson then nodded to the two officers, one of whom remained outside. Mrs Watson took her seat, opened her shorthand pad and prepared to write. I took my seat nearer the door.

'Mr Nickleby, I am Detective Inspector Cartwright.'

'I am Detective Sergeant 547 Blake. The lady on my right is a stenographer who is recording this interview. I cautioned him... do you understand?'

'I do. Does the lady have a name?'

'She does; but that does not concern you.'

He gave me a half-smile. 'I didn't realise that you were a detective.'

'There's a lot of things that you don't realise, Mr Collins,' said the DI.

Collins took a deep breath and gave me a quizzical look. 'Was it the photograph that gave me away. The motor-cyclists. I left a finger print on the glass, didn't I?'

'You did,' I said. 'That linked to a handprint for which we were looking for an owner.'

He looked confused. 'But when a con dies any records are destroyed. What do you mean?'

'Normally that would be the case. However, yours appear to have been overlooked. But in any case, the handprint and the fingerprint on the photo frame glass told us that it was the same person. i.e. you. The check at New Scotland Yard told us who you really were.'

He gave us a long hard look then closed his eyes and groaned. 'Handprint? ... The car!. My left hand! Oh for fuck sake. My bloody gloves. Ah well.'

'You don't deny shooting Kenny Summers, Detective Constable Jack Roberts, Detective Constable Cameron MacArthur or David Nevin, with your Lipari pump-action shotgun,' I said.

'Don't recognise the name David Nevin.'

'The driver of the Morris 1000 who drove passed you at the scene of the triple shooting.'

'Oh him. No I don't' deny that either. If he had been driving a half-decent car he would have been ok. But ...'

'Do you admit to shooting Kenny Summers, Detective Constable Jack Roberts, Detective Constable Cameron MacArthur?' I iterated.'

The smile was humourless. 'Yes, I admit I shot them. Satisfied?'

'What part did Christopher Grogan play?'

He laughed. 'Chris? Not the sharpest knife in the drawer, but he's a grafter. Work his socks off. Had those plates off in no time.'

'But left the excise licence on the windscreen, and it had a police radio.'

'Yeah, thought about those later. Too late to do anything about them. That's what happens with a rush job.'

'Harry Fields?'

'Who else? That's who I worked for.'

I exchanged glances with Peter Cartwright. This was not what we expected.

'You're being remarkably candid this morning Mr Nickleby. Any particular reason?'

'I'll cough the ones you can prove. No doubt Chris has helped. I don't begrudge him that. There'll be a price on my head. So?'

'A price, why?'

'Harry doesn't like loose ends. There was a witness to the shooting. I couldn't find whoever it was. He thought it was you.'

'Hence the pressure on PC Lassiter and your visit to Sergeant Blake's home?'

'Bad move. But you don't argue with Harry. Not if you know what's good for you.'

'You're right, it wasn't me. The identity of that person is confidential, and will remain so.' I smiled. 'As a matter of interest, you shot two police officers, Field's bookkeeper and David Nevin. How much did you get paid for terminating four lives?'

'You might as well know. His original offer was £5,000; but there was only supposed to be Kenny Summers and one copper. In the end I got paid £12,000.'

'And you have no conscience about killing?'

'There's no profit in conscience. But I'm surprised you're still here.'

'Why is that?' I said knowing the answer.

'I passed details of your house to Harry. He's usually quick off the mark.'

'Oh, he did,' I said.

'But?'

Peter Cartwright lifted his hand from the table. 'Are you familiar with a Detective Inspector Beamish or Detective Chief Inspector Webster?'

A soft humourless smile crossed Nickleby's face. 'Better known as Bellamy and Frobisher. Yes, I know them,' He paused and gave me a quizzical look. 'You're trying to tell me that Harry gave them your contract. That's impossible.'

'It's not impossible,' said Peter Cartwright. 'Bellamy is unconscious in hospital; Frobisher is singing like a canary.

'I don't believe you.'

'You should,' I said. 'They told me they'd never been to your house before, yet they knew where the cellar was. Did you supply the details?'

'Harry has a copy of the plans. But how?'

'That would be telling.'

'You're serious? You've taken then both out?'

'I had a bit of help with Frobisher.'

He was chuckling to himself. 'You shot them?'

'Nope, just me and a colleague.'

It was clear he didn't believe us. 'You'll be popular in the Smoke. Those two made a packet scaring shitless those who crossed Harry.'

Eighty

My in tray was empty. Next the Truelove's.

I was met by Keith Fleming; two stripes on his arm. 'Hi Keith, I heard you were acting up.'

He grinned and nodded. 'Yes, thanks to you.'

'I might have mentioned your name but that was all.'

'Well, thanks anyway. They moved you sideways. Permanent?'

'It doesn't look like he'll be coming back.'

'It's tragic. He's been a good copper ... I need to get hold of Malcolm Truelove. Do you know where he is?'

'Yep,' I held my hand out. 'Your pocket book. For your eyes only.' I wrote the number in the index at the rear and handed it back. 'Just you.'

I dialled the number. Answered on the third ring. 'Oldeney Carr House, Givens speaking, how may I help?'

'Sergeant Blake. Givens, one of my colleagues, Sergeant Fleming, needs to speak with Mr Truelove. Do you know where he is?'

'One moment, sir,' I had to smile when he turned the phone away, I still heard the ensuing conversation. 'Your Lordship, Sergeant Blake is on the line, one of his colleagues needs to speak with Mr Truelove as a matter of some urgency. Do you happen to know where he is?'

'I will fetch him.'

'He will be here shortly, sir.'

I put my hand over the mouthpiece and saw Keith's eyebrows raise as I explained. 'Givens is the Butler. He was speaking with the

Earl, Martin, the seven year old twin of Graeme. They're a smashing pair of kids.'

A breathless young voice. 'He's coming. Is this about a murder?'

I had to smile. 'Now, you know I can't tell you.'

'Aww ... Here you are, Mr Truelove.'

'Thank you .. Sergeant Blake. Malcolm Truelove, how can I help?'

'I'll pass you onto Sergeant Fleming.' I handed the phone to Keith. 'I'll leave it with you,' I said and grinned. And left for Nickleby's' bungalow.

Eighty-One

PW Weatherly was at the bottom of the drive. 'Good morning sergeant. Have you taken over from Sergeant Greatorix?'

'I have. It's unlikely he will be coming back to work. Who's upstairs?

'A couple from forensic and DI Cartwright.'

I nodded and left her to her daydreams. Peter Cartwright met me at the door. 'Dropped in the deep-end,' he said and grinned.

'Nothing in his in-tray, sir. No distractions.' I wrinkled my nose. 'Good grief. that's decomposing flesh.' Just what had Collins been up to?'

Our thoughts were interrupted as Jack Hawkins, forensic biologist and his colleague almost ran from the house. 'Brian, you again? Inspector, will you get the house sealed until we can get proper breathing apparatus. Nobody can work in that atmosphere.'

'Where's it coming from, Jack?'

'Under the cellar floor. We moved a steel cabinet. Underneath was a manhole of sorts, like a drain cover. We moved it and you can smell what's down there. We replaced the cover and left.'

' I switched my radio on. 'Sergeant Blake, over.'

'You're a bit faint, sarge, but go ahead.'

'Is Sergeant Chalkley or Inspector Marshall there? It's urgent.'

Seconds later Inspector Marshall's voice. 'Yes, Brian?'

'Sir, Jack Hawkins from forensic is certain there's decomposing flesh under the cellar floor. From the smell I agree. We need someone from the council public health department up here yesterday. And can someone check with the planning department for the plans for the house that Collins built. And, does the Fire Service have full breathing apparatus.'

'Only been back for thirty seconds and causing havoc already.'

'Delegating, sir.'

He laughed. 'Very good. Leave it with me.'

Peter Cartwright was quizzical. 'Delegating?'

I nodded. 'Gave me the same chat that DCI Valentine gave me at Hecton.'

'Gotcha,' he said and laughed. 'Don't try to do it all yourself.'

'Right in one.'

'Ok, but why were you asking about planning applications?'

'Something that the Met DCI, Frobisher, mentioned. He was going to check out the cellar because Collins was known for hidden rooms.'

'But he came back and shot you instead; never got the chance to check.'

'So it seems.'

'This hidden room?' said Jack. 'Is there any further information?'

'No. I think Mr Wallace will have to contact Commander Jameson. Until then?'

'We wait.'

Ten minutes later a black Austin A40 pulled up at the bottom of the drive. PW Weatherly pointed us out. The leader, a portly man around five feet six, wearing a sombre three piece suit. His companion, tall, slim and similarly attired arrived; both out of breath. The leader smiled. 'Bit of a tow, I'm Phillip Kitchen and my colleague Carl Smethurst. Public Health. What's the problem, gentlemen?'

'DS Blake and DI Cartwright. This is the house owned by Nicholas Nickleby.'

'Oh,' he interjected. 'He's the man you arrested for murder.'

'He is. That is his real name, locally he was known as Nicholas Collins. And as this is an active investigation ...' I left the point hanging.

'You want to keep the information away from the Press.'

'Correct, the last thing we need is a panic.'

'I understand. Souls of discretion we are, rest assured.'

'Doctor Hawkins and his colleague will explain. Doctor?'

Eighty-Two

Phillip Kitchen and his colleague stood at the top of the drive facing into the wind taking in deep breaths of untainted air.

'Yes doctor. We will provide equipment and staff. There will be no need to trouble the fire service. And keeping this completely out of the public domain might prove to be difficult.'

'Press conference, Brian. I'll fix it up with Mr Wallace as soon as possible.

Dr. Hawkins, you're certain it is human remains?'

'No doubt in my mind, at least three individuals so far.'

'Once we establish when it was built we know where to begin,' I said.

Phillip Kitchwn glanced down the drive as a car drew up and discharged the occupants. 'Unless I'm mistaken this is your Mr Wallace and Inspector Marshall. We will leave you to it. There will be team here within the hour.'

The public health team exchanged pleasantries with Mr Wallace and Inspector Marshall and left. 'I hear you've been delegating, Brian,' said Mr Wallace with a broad smile.

What could I say. 'Yes, sir.'

Mr Wallace turned to Jack. 'Dr Hawkins. There is no doubt? They are human remains?'

'No doubt at all, superintendent. How many, it is impossible to say. But at least three. From the dimensions of a femur we found the bones are adult. I need to contact the office. Could I use the phone here?'

'I see no reason why not.'

Jack and his colleague left.

'Brian, I understand from Inspector Marshall that, with your previous enquiries, you probably know more than anyone about Nickleby. Fill us in.'

'Sir. Mr Cartwright and I gleaned a great deal from our interview with Grogan. He is terrified that Nickleby would have him killed if what he'd told us came to light. Somewhere, Nickleby has the film he used to blackmail those he trapped in his Halifax honey trap. He's a planner, doesn't trust anyone. Nothing was discovered during the search of his home; the chances are he has a safety deposit box, and he's terrified of what Harry Field may do to him now things haven't worked out.'

' Re Grogan's statement it's a good point about the film, we need a fingertip search of the house to see if he has a key secreted somewhere, and checks with banks and others who offer a security service.

'I've been in touch with Commander Jameson to ascertain calls made to Nickleby from Harry Field's network. And I'm bringing in someone you know to interview this Josie; plus the others if we can trace them.'

'Someone *I* know?'

'Detective Sergeant Elizabeth Farthing.'

That was a surprise. 'Penny's accepted promotion? She told me she never would.'

'I know; but times change. Now, this conversation you had with Grogan's grandfather. What can we glean from that?'

'Apart from the grandfather, Thoams Grogan and Mary from the High Street Café, I spoke with eight of those who sold out to Nickleby because of implied threats. Now he's in custody they may be more forthcoming.

'Something else that Thomas Grogan told me, Collins appeared from nowhere but with plenty of cash. Mixed in the pubs and clubs as far west as Burnley and Haslingden and as far east as Elland and Brighouse. Burnley and Haslingden are twenty to twenty-five miles west.'

'Just how far has he travelled looking for business?' said Peter Cartwright.

'Exactly, sir. Grogan said it was in 1962 he began to acquire businesses in this neck of the woods and putting his own people in,. He lived in rented accommodation for a couple of years in Mytholmroyd but in 1964 had this house built. Having the official dates from planning and speaking with the contractor would help. I can't see Nickleby bumping anyone off until he had somewhere to stash the bodies.

'We know he murdered Gloria Rodgers in the Met on the 12th August 1959; which is when he came north and began to use the name Nicholls.

'We also know that he approached Ralph Jenner of Jenner's engineering, who may be able to add more detail.'

'Right, anything else?'

'Just one thing, sir. I contacted DS Martindale; I met him while on my CID course. Told him about Collins and asked him if he could find out from companies house the directorships he's held.'

'Heard anything back?'

'Not as yet, sir.'

'Good move. I'll contact him. Brian, re-interview all your previous contacts. This time I want statements. Go wherever the evidence takes you.'

'Sir.'

'We need a press conference this evening, sir; before there are any leaks.'

'Good point, Peter, fix it will you? Sort out an incident room. Brian, As Nickleby's arresting officer you'll be at the Press Conference.'

Eighty-Three

Telex or teleprinter messages had been circulated to every police force within a thirty mile radius of Sowerby Bridge, requesting all outstanding adult missing person records be checked for possible victims. Possible small business owners who had left their business within the specified time. Also occurrence book references involving anyone with the name Nicholas Nickleby or Nicholas Collins.

Mr Wallace had been in touch with DS Martindale, initially to ascertain what information if any had been gleaned following my chat. Further lines of enquiry were identified.

Eighty-Four

The parade room at Brighouse police station was bursting at the seams. Last in line I followed Mr Wallace and sat behind the table adjacent to the door. Settled, the buzz of conversation died. 'Good afternoon ladies and gentlemen and thank you for coming at such short notice. I am Detective Superintendent Wallace. On my left are detective Inspector Cartwright and on his left is Detective Sergeant Blake. On my right is Detective Inspector Bentley ...'

The doors burst open as a BBC film unit entered in chaotic fashion. 'Martin Greenfield. Sorry we're late superintendent; heavy traffic.'

'How long?'

'Two minutes, max' was the flustered reply.

'That's one for the Guinness Book of Records,' came a quip from the rear accompanied by laughter from across the room. 'First time for everything.'

'Ready superintendent, sorry,' he said.

I checked my watch: Three minutes thirty seconds.

'Good afternoon ladies and gentlemen and thank you for coming at such short notice. I am Detective Superintendent Wallace. On my left are Detective Inspector Cartwright and on his left is Detective Sergeant Blake. On my right is Detective Inspector Bentley. As you are aware, on the 19th September three men, two of them police officers, were discovered shot to death on the A644 between Brighouse and Cooper Bridge. As a result of enquiries two men are now in custody. We are not looking for anyone else. The man we believe to be the gunman is known in this area as Nicholas, or

'Nick Collins. He was identified by fingerprints. We now know that his real name is Nicholas Nickleby, his father was a devotee of the writings of Charles Dickens ...' There was a pause whilst the laughter subsided, ...

An arm went up. 'Excuse me superintendent, Jack Reagan, Crime Correspondent of the South Yorkshire Times. Wasn't Nickleby wanted by the Metropolitan Police for the murder of a prostitute in August 1959. Believed to have been killed in a road accident whilst being pursued by the Met Police?'

Mr Wallace nodded . 'I believe that was the case, but any related questions are not within our purview and will have to be put directly to the Metropolitan Police.'

'Thank you.' Reagan nodded. The scribbling continued.

'That is the background for this conference. Amongst the follow up procedures we are searching all the properties owned or used by the criminal or criminals implicated. In Nickleby's house we found, according to our forensic scientists, human remains which have been in situ for between six months and three years, and are adult.in origin. We know that Nickleby or Collins, if you prefer, was involved with major criminals and also involved in prostitution and extortion. He travelled widely across Yorkshire and Lancashire. As a result the information that we have has been circulated to all police forces within thirty miles of Sowerby Bridge. Teams of police officers are already at work across Yorkshire and the north of England. In addition, people who have missing relatives that fit the criteria I mentioned are asked to contact us. We would also like to speak with anyone who knew, or had dealings with Nickleby since 1959. I would like to assure those people that we will exercise the utmost discretion.

'I will take some questions but can't expand on the information you have. In the press release, you can collect that at the door, is a telephone number for people to call. I would, however, stress that this is not a number to call for missing persons outside of the date parameters I mentioned. Neither is it to be used to make new reports of missing persons. Those should be done through local police stations .. Now, questions.

Very few. None of them earth-shattering. They all had deadlines to meet.

Warrants had been sworn and at 9.00am teams of officers raided every known business owned by Nickleby including the Woodpecker Hotel.

Eighty-Five

0800 **the following morning.** I had a couple of crime files to check before the work began in earnest. The phone rang. 'DS Blake.'

I smiled to myself as I heard the voice of ACC Patrickson, North Yorkshire Police. 'Good morning *Detective* Sergeant Blake. How is your back?'

'Fine sir, thank you for asking.'

'You like danger in your life.'

'Not to that extent, sir. To be honest I thought that was it. Had it not been for one of my colleagues it might have been, although I had a cocked loaded revolver hard under his ribs. But who would have suspected a couple of senior CID officers?

'I can't argue with that. And congratulations on your move .. DS in a little over four years. Which brings me to the point. I have spoken with your Chief, Mr Barton, he had no objection to my making this call.'

'I'm intrigued.'

'I'm not trying to poach you. You wouldn't accept it anyway. Your career so far can only be described as stellar. Now, next Spring I am planning a series of one day courses for officers who have shown promise. I thought you might be willing to come and discuss your service. How you have achieved what you have etc. Nothing is yet fixed, I wanted run it passed you, see what you think. You would be paid senior instructors rates plus mileage, paid via your salary or, if you are so minded, as a separate income stream. In which case we would require an invoice. You could bring your wife and children; I've told my wife a lot about you and would like to meet you.'

'It sounds interesting. I'd want to discuss it with Lucy and my stepfather. Can I get back to you?'

'Not a problem. Let me know when you're ready.'

Eighty-Six

My first call was on Ralph Jenner. 'I missed the press conference but my wife mentioned it. I take it we're talking about the same man?'

'We are Mr Jenner. The reason for my visit is to obtain a statement about your dealings with him. Also, anything else that you are aware of regarding Collins, including others who had dealings with him, in whatever context. We know that he had numerous business interests including prostitution and extortion. The more information we get the better.'

He looked troubled. 'Prostitution and extortion?'

'He was involved with some pretty nasty people.'

'I'll certainly give you a statement. Come into my office.'

Statement obtained. Next on the list was Thomas Grogan.

Dr Deighton was just leaving. 'The news about his grandson has hit him hard, sergeant. Ten minutes, maximum. Try not to upset him.'

Grogan was propped up in bed when I saw him, at least he smiled. Mary from the High Street Café was sitting on the far side of the bed holding his hand.

'Thank you lad,' he said and grasped my wrist as I sat. 'Will Collins, or whatever his name is die in prison?'

'I should think so. We're putting the evidence together to make it happen.'

He nodded and paused for breath. 'What about Christopher, will he be safe?'

'As safe as we can make him, Mr Grogan. There are certain, shall we say, avenues, that we're looking at with the Metropolitan Police that should enable him to stay out of trouble.'

'Good. Now,' he said relieved. 'This isn't a social call, is it?'

'Afraid not. I need to speak with everybody who knew or had dealings with Nickleby. But first, I need a statement from you.'

'Do you want me to leave, sergeant?'

'No, Mary, I want you to countersign Thomas's statement, if he doesn't mind.'

He hadn't lost his sense of humour. 'Nay lass, it's to show that he wasn't beating me up to get what he wants.'

'Something like that,' I said.

It took longer than ten minutes but I had more than enough to be going on with. I stood to leave and opened my briefcase. 'I've something for you, but I can't give it to you, but, Mary can.' I handed Mary a half bottle of Johnny Walkers.'

Grogan's eyes lit up. 'That'll do nicely,' he said and took my hand. 'Make sure the evil bastard dies in prison.'

I smiled. 'I'll do my best. Take care.'

Eighty-Seven

Neil Farrer greeted me with a broad grin. 'You've got a visitor sarge, female. Bit of a looker.'

'Detective Sergeant Farthing?'

'You knew?'

'I was expecting her.'

'I didn't know we had any female DS's. I gave her a coffee; she's in your office.'

'Thanks.'

The door was open. She was gazing out of the window nursing her coffee. 'Penny!' she spun round. 'Good to see you again and congratulations on your promotion. But, you said you would never accept it; it came as a surprise when Mr Wallace told me.'

She placed her cup on my desk and came across and gave me a hug. 'Circumstances alter cases, Brian. I'm divorced.'

That was a shock. 'But...'

'My ex-husband had another family. Not married but two other children. A female called Valerie Groves; same class as we were from school. Discovered by accident when he should have been in Glasgow on business; I walked into them coming out of the Grand in Leeds. Playing happy families at the Panto. So... the children were growing up and the extra money would be good ...'

'And you've passed your Inspectors.'

'True. Now, Mr Wallace told me you'd have something for me.'

'How much do you know?'

'Tied up with a Harry Field, some big underworld creep in London. One Nicholas Nickleby – Collins. The triple shooting.

And, the murder of a Gloria Rodgers in London when he was believed to have been killed in an RTA back in 1959. Prostitution and procurement. Interesting.'

'Not forgetting extortion.' I said as a retrieved a file from my briefcase. I handed Penny two statements. 'Ralph Jenner, a local businessman crossed swords with Nickleby, and Chris Grogan, Nickleby's gopher, he was with Nickleby when the triple occurred; also in custody.'

Penny put the statements on my desk. 'I see. This Josie girl; mentioned twice, any connection between Jenner's daughter and Grogan?'

'Not that I can ascertain.' Have a look at this.' I handed her Jackson's statement. 'Jackson was the manager of the scrapyard at Todmorden, owned by Nickleby. Bought cheaply after the owner was crushed by a falling stack of cars when he refused to sell to Nickleby.'

'Nice fella,' she said and picked the statement up. I watched her expression change as she scanned the statement. 'Why can't you ever get involved in anything simple?' she said and laughed. 'Who's involved from the Met?'

'A Commander Jameson, and a DCS Yelland. I met them both when I was in hospital.'

Penny's expression dropped. 'Your back! I never asked how you were, so sorry.'

'I'm fine,' I said and smiled. 'And once the Met have unravelled Harry Field's telephone accounts we'll know a lot more. Speak with Peter Cartwright or Mr Wallace if you want further details ... You heard about the human remains found in a hidden room at Nickleby's house?'

'Yes, is that what you're doing?'

'Yeah, ferreting out anyone and everyone who had dealings with Nickleby; see if there are any mispers that we might link back to this enquiry.'

'Good luck with that. What about this hotel in Halifax?'

'Not sure what the latest position is. Peter will probably know.'

The phone began to ring. 'Sowerby Bridge, DS Blake.'

'DI Cartwright, Brian. Eight possibles so far as a result of the press conference. You'll be getting an additional DC.'

'Thanks. Penny's arrived and she's going to see Ralph Jenner.'

'Link?'

'His daughter, Veronica, is a friend of *Josie*, tried to get her involved in Nickleby's sexual exploits. Should open a few doors.'

'Penny there? Put her on.'

I held the handset out. 'Peter.'

'Sir? ... Yes, I read the statements. About to set off for Jenners.'

She put the phone down. 'How do I get to Jenners?'

'Turn right out of the door. About a hundred yards.' I opened my phone index at J. 'Here's the phone number if you want to check if he's in ... I'll see you back here for a bite; perhaps.'

Eighty-Eight

Not surprisingly, Hazel Granby had been shipped in as office manager. She'd have her work cut out with this one.

After five days we had what might be an answer to the remains in the cellar. Enquiries across the north of England, mostly from the western side of Yorkshire and the area around Burnley and Haslingden. had highlighted four recurring names: Those missing between six months and three years ago with business interests taken over by Nickleby.

1. Victoria Phipps
2. Geraldine Doughty
3. Anne Smith
4. Graham McNaughton

Those who report their loved ones as missing live in eternal hope that there is a simple answer, that their mother, father, son, daughter, sister, brother, aunt, uncle, cousin, lover or best friend, will simply walk through the door one sunny morning safe and well. But, when a detective sergeant knocks at the door wanting to re-examine the enquiry from thread to needle. This time requesting details of the family doctor etc, the scenario takes on a different atmosphere. Plus, we may still not be able to set their minds at rest. In all probability that would rest with the forensic scientists and a reinterview with Nickleby.

PENNY'S INTERVIEW WITH Veronica Jenner was a simple matter. Yes, Josie MacDonald had tried to persuade Veronica to participate in Nickleby's sexual activity; Twice a week at £10 a time, tax free and fun. She refused and gave Penny Josie's address.

Eighty-Nine

'You're winding me up. Sold as a prostitute. That's bollocks.'

'No, I'm not, Josie. I'm serious. He's done it before; more than once. More to the point he considered that you were nearly ready. A major criminal in London was waiting for the phone call. Nickleby would be paid a lot of money for you.'

Josie's face clouded over. 'But, that's slavery.'

'True, and for as long as your new *owner* decided as such. So, who introduced you to Nickleby.'

'Can't get used to the change in name. I always knew him as Collins.'

'All right, we'll call him Collins. Who introduced you?'

'Aunt Myrna, licensee at the Flying Fox.'

'Real aunt? not just a friend of your parents?'

'Well, I've always called her aunt, but she's a mate of me mum's.'

'Are you willing to give me a statement, help us to get the evidence to put Collins away?'

'Suppose so.'

'We'll go to the police station, fewer distractions there.'

'YES, SIR. I HAVE JOSIE MacDonald's statement. The Flying Fox pub, sounds like a bit of a knocking shop. Licensee is a Myrna Sykes, a friend of MacDonald's mother. Underage girls, perfect for mispers and absconders, lots of young single men. Rooms by the half-hour.

Apparently Nickleby was well known. If that's the sort of pub he was looking for ...'

'Good point. Last thing we needed. However, good work.'

'Thank you. I've the names of seven girls who sound passible; but none match those Brian has. Passed them onto MO. They will let me know at Sowerby as soon as possible. I've just dropped Josie off at her doctors. Arrange for a VD checkup. And this coming Friday might be a good day.'

'For a raid?'

'Yes, sir. Find out who the players are.'

'If you have the time, It's your op. I'll speak with the chief super.'

THE SEVEN GIRLS WERE checked out and statements obtained. All approached by Nickleby but none had been willing to participate. That kept the possibles we knew of to four.

Ninety

The Parade Room at Sowerby Bridge was full. 'All right, settle down, NOW!' said Penny. 'You're not here to gossip,' the chatter stopped. 'This op has been put together at short notice, so listen .. You are all aware of the incident of the 19th September when three people, including two detectives from Blackpool, were shot and killed between Brighouse and Cooper Bridge. Those responsible Nicholas Nickleby alias Collins, and Christopher Grogan are now in custody.

'Nickleby worked for a major London criminal, Harry Field, and amongst his priorities was prostitution ... if anybody needs to take a leak go now. Once I've mentioned the location, nobody and that means you, will leave the group for any reason. Nobody left. 'Good, we're going to raid the Navigation. That's where Nickleby used to operate. I have it on good authority there are regularly underage girls on the premises and in the past is has been a magnet for runaways and absconders.

'Once we go in nobody leaves until either I or DS Blake give the OK.

'PCs Wright and Coverly, you will cover the front door.

'PC Grayson, rear access, and no smutty comments.

'The following will work in pairs and go in first. PC Carlson and PW Weatherly.

'PC Smith and PW Kidd.

'PC Carlisle and PW Bradley.

'PC Mason and PW Andrews.

'You will check the four bedrooms, and be especially careful with the girls.'

'Some of these lasses are as hard as nails, sarge.'

'I have done this before. And when any cases get to court their briefs will not hesitate to mention police brutality. Young underage girls. Not wise to the ways of the world. Easily led. Never been in trouble before. You name it and they'll try it on. So be careful

'The rest of you I want full details of *everybody* in the pub; not just the public bar. But leave the licensee to me, I want warrant checks on everybody ... any questions?'

'Where's DS Blake, sarge?'

'Already there. Mount up, and those working in pairs make sure you're together. When we go in, go fast. The time now is, 20:55.'

Ninety-One

'This isn't the Navigation; it's the Flying Fox.'

'True, PC Wright,' said Penny. 'Come on everybody, shift, move it.'

One officer looked worried.

FRIDAY NIGHT. THE PUBLIC Bar was busy. I could see why Nickleby concentrated on this place and not just because of the young females.

I was sitting in a corner nursing my half pint of Websters when the door burst open. A line of police dashed in.

I stood held my warrant card above my head. 'This is a police raid, stay exactly where you are.'

'Fuck that!' the man next to me tried to barge passed.

I pushed him back into his seat. 'Stay there.'

Penny was behind the bar in seconds. The landlady prevented from sounding the alarm that rang in the rooms. Mark Carlson and Janet Weatherly were the lead. I stepped out and smiled at Weatherly. This would be a good measure as to how she might perform in future. 'Follow me.' I pushed the curtain aside and took the steps two at a time. At the top I stood to one side. 'You two,' I pointed at Carlson and Weatherly last on the right. Everyone else alternate.' So far so good.

With help from his shoulder Carlson had the door open. Both occupants naked. She on her back, hyperventilating, eyes closed, legs round the male whose arse was, according to Carlson, later, going like the clappers.

Carlson put his foot on the lad's backside and pressed. 'Come on chum, play time over.'

'Bastard,' he said trying to break free. 'Get your fucking foot of my arse, I'm cumming.'

He kept it there. 'If she has one call it lucky.'

'You bastard!' he said with some venom. Froze. Then relaxed. 'You bastard.'

The girl arched her back and dug her nails into his, screeching through gritted teeth. She opened her eyes and looked at PW Weatherly. 'Enjoyed watching that, copper? Learn anything?'

Janet Weatherly felt herself blushing. The girl laughed. 'You're blushing. The little pervert's a virgin. How sweet.'

'Come on, get some clothes on. Unless you want to go in the van in bollock order.'

'If she has a kid it's your fault. Besides she's my girlfriend.'

'It wasn't me with my prick up her fanny, so that won't wash. Girlfriend? What's her name?'

Silence.

'Girlfriend my arse. You paid for this room for a half hour. She's a tart and underage. Get a move on.'

'You as well,' said Weatherly. 'Get some clothes on.'

'All masterful now your boyfriend's shown you what to do.'

'He's a colleague, now move it.'

She lifted her handbag from the bedside table. 'Can I get a handkerchief?'

'Ok, be quick about it.'

'Don't wet yourself,' the girl replied. In one continuous movement she reached inside the bag with her right hand and pulled out a dagger-shaped paperknife in her fist, spun to her right stabbing Weatherly in the neck.

'See how you like a prick,' she ripped the knife out turned and lunged at Mark Carlson's unprotected back.

Janet put her hand to her neck and felt the blood. She hadn't learned much from the karate class yet, but she had two older brothers. She threw herself at her assailant, reached over the girl's head with her left arm, hooking her fingers up the girl's nostrils yanking the head back as hard as she could, before grabbing the right wrist and falling backwards across the bed. 'You're nicked.'

Carlson took one glance over his shoulder then snapped at his prisoner. 'Get dressed and do not muck me about. SARGE! JANET'S BEEN STABBED IN THE NECK.' Without waiting for a response he fished in his pocket. 'Here you are Janet, a clean hanky. Let go of this tart and press it as tight as you can against your neck. You'll be ok,' he made eye contact and nodded. 'Let go of her nose.' Janet relaxed her grip. Carlson seized the girls chin. 'Good. Listen you. One move and I'll forget you're a female.' He reached across with his left hand. 'Ok, I'll have this,' he took possession of the knife. 'Now let go. Janet, you as well.'

I burst in accompanied by PW Kidd. Carlson didn't look up. 'Need an ambulance, sarge. and someone to look after this bitch.'

'Kidd, get her dressed and cuffed. Separate transport. Book her in for Unlawful Wounding. She talks to no-one.'

'Sarge. You've done it this time, Katie. Get some clothes on'

'Sergeant Blake, urgent.'

'Go ahead, sarge.'

'Weatherly's been stabbed in the neck, need a ambulance.'

'There's a traffic car outside.'

'That will have to do. Ring RHI and inform them.'

'Will do.'

'Where are you, Brian?'

'Last on the right, sir.'

John Raymond, veteran member of the police first aid team, plus colleague Neville French, arrived. 'Neville, get a firm pillow to support her head and shoulders. Then stand behind and keep the pressure on her neck.' John Raymond smiled at Janet. 'Try and relax. We'll have you in hospital in two shakes. I'm just going to tuck your right hand inside your tunic. Mark's going to hold your left,' he looked up. 'Aren't you?'

'I can manage that.' He said smiling at Janet and taking her left hand.

Her grip tightened.

'Neville, hold that pad tight against her throat.' Pillow in place John looked at his colleagues. 'Ready? On three.'

Staircase negotiated they entered the Public Bar. The only sound the scraping of the tables as they were pulled out of the way.

'Where's my daughter?' said Myrna Sykes. 'What have you done with her?'

'Nothing, Myrna,' said Penny. 'Yet.'

DI CARTWRIGHT PERUSED the knife and bloodstain on the sheet. 'Quite innocuous under different circumstances.'

'Yes, sir. It's a deep wound and looks like venous blood. Could have nicked one of the major blood vessels.'

'Do you know what happened?'

'I heard Carlson shout. In the few seconds it took for me to get in he had it under control. The punter was getting dressed. Carlson had control of Sykes, given Weatherly his clean handkerchief to press on her neck, and had the knife in his hands. Quick thinking and a cool head.

'He told me that after Sykes stabbed Weatherly she tried to stab him in the back, or the neck. Weatherly had leapt on Sykes' back, got her fingers up her nose, yanked her head back and grabbed her wrist. If she hadn't managed to stop Sykes we could have had a real tragedy on our hands.'

'Until he shouted you had no idea?'

'No, the other three teams were leaving their rooms so I grabbed Kidd to come with me.'

'Carlson's from Brighouse.'

'Yup. He's a good lad.'

The DI furrowed his brow. 'Expressed an interest in CID at his last appraisal.'

'You could do worse.'

'You had Kidd book Sykes in for unlawful wounding.'

'Yup, just for something to write on the sheet.'

'What do you have in mind?'

'Minimum, section 18, wounding with intent.'

'Fits, but you were thinking attempted murder?'

'I was. Intention to kill or commit grievous bodily harm. Look at the knife, it's a lethal weapon. The principal thing against that is her age, although it's not unknown.'

'True, and both carry a maximum sentence of life. But until we have the full story.'

The DI's radio crackled into life. 'DI Cartwright, over.'

'Go ahead.'

'Just to let you and Sergeants Farthing and Blake know that PW Weatherly's parents have been notified and are being transported to the Royal Halifax.'

'Noted.

Ninety-Two

The medical team was waiting. With skill born of practice Janet Weatherly was transferred to the waiting trolley. With Mark Carlson still holding her hand Janet was rushed into A&E.

The trolley stopped. A tap on the shoulder. The Doctor smiled. 'You can let go now, officer. We'll look after her.'

'What? Sorry,' he said and let go, watching the doors swing to behind them.

Seconds later a Doctor burst through the door. 'Good, you're still here. What sort of weapon was used?'

'Like a very small sword, about the size of a letter opener, but it had been sharpened.'

The doctor nodded. 'Did you witness the actual stabbing?'

'No, sir. This was a raid on the upstairs of a pub being used as a brothel. Janet was behind me, if I'd been paying more attention it wouldn't have happened,'

'Don't be too hard on yourself, she's going to be fine. Look, why don't you have a coffee in the canteen,. We'll be here a while.'

'NOTED.' RADIO OFF. 'You know, Brian, there were doubts that Lassiter was not the only leak.'

'Yes, and you were going to put someone in the Navigation to see if there was advance warning.'

'I borrowed Bradbury from Brighouse to keep an eye. Sure enough the licensee announced that they would be a visit from the boys in blue. There was an exodus for the Flying Fox.'

'That'll teach them.'

'It was Cooper. First out of the briefing and last into the van.'

.'Cooper? Surprised at him, but he was a mate of Lassiter's.'

'Mr Wallace and Martin Chalkley are having a heart-to-heart with him. Let's hope that's an end to it.'

I stayed at the Fox to oversee the photographer and complete my pocket book. He was finished in under an hour. Premises secured and a bobby on the door I scrouged a lift back to the nick; call Lucy and typed my statement.

Ninety-Three

The Royal Halifax was more or less on my way home. Janet was out of theatre and of danger. Mr and Mrs Weatherly were leaving as I arrived.

'Sergeant Blake, can you tell what happened?'

'You are aware of what we were doing, Mrs Weatherly?'

'Not really, only that Janet had been injured.'

'It was a raid on a pub cum brothel.'

Mrs Weatherly blushed to the roots of her hair. 'But ...she has no experience.'

Her husband grinned. 'It sounds as though she has now, dear. She knew what she was letting herself in for when she joined. Is it serious, her injury?'

'Potentially. But PC Carlson acted fast and gave her a clean handkerchief, to press on the wound. One of the traffic officers was a first aider. However, the first I knew was when PC Carlson shouted. In the few seconds it took me to gain access to the bedroom he had it all under control.'

'So you weren't there?'

'Not in the room. I had four teams to supervise so I was outside in the corridor.... Have the doctors told you anything?'

'Not really, other than to say it was an emergency.'

'Par for the course. But is there anything else you would like to ask me?'

'What can you tell us about this PC Carlson?'

'Mark? He's a good lad. Has three years' service; provided he keeps his nose clean and passes his exams will certainly get promoted at some stage. But I'm not sure what *he* wants.'

'He seems very nice. Kept apologising for letting Janet get injured. Sounded very protective.'

I frowned. 'As far as I know they hadn't met before today. But when there are mixed teams, male officers tend to be more protective, and this operation was the largest that Janet has been involved in.'

'Perhaps it will be the making of her,' said her father.

'I had wondered if she would resign because of it.'

'I doubt that, sergeant,' said her father. 'She set her heart on joining the police and the stories that Jenny, Jenny Sendrove told her, didn't put her off.'

'Time will tell.'

'And PC Carlson did ask if he could come back tomorrow and visit Janet.'

'Asking for permission to visit your daughter. Who knows?' I said and smiled.

'Who knows indeed., sergeant. We'll let you get on. C'mon dear.'

After Janet Wetherley's parents left I had a word with the smiling ward sister. 'Back already? We've only just let you out.'

'Fraid so, sister. How is Janet?'

'Very lucky. Your first aiders did a damn good job. Whatever her assailant used could easily have caused major problems. But apart from being sore and having a scar she should make a full recovery. At the moment she's asleep. As I told her young man, call in tomorrow after ten-thirty.'

Ninety-Four

The next morning I made the short diversion to the hospital. Janet was conscious and I could pay a short visit after ten-thirty.

8.00am on the nail. Mini-conference in the parade room. Chief Superintendent Cartwright, Detective Inspector Cartwright, Detective Superintendent Wallace. Inspector Marshall. Bill Chalkley, Penny, me and John Bradbury.

'First,' said Chief Superintendent Cartwright, 'The injury to PW Weatherly. She is still early in her probation, has she been taken through procedures during arrest, in particular searching. Sergeant Blake.'

'At the scene of an arrest and a full body search when booking a prisoner in; and all property. I wasn't present in the room when the assault occurred. So I can't say exactly what happened. PC Carlson may be able to help in that regard.

'What I can say, sir, is the first I saw was PW Weatherly lying on the bed holding PC Carlson's clean handkerchief tight against her throat. Sykes was on her back on top of Weatherly. Carlson had Sykes under control with a grip on her chin and had removed the knife from Sykes' right hand.'

The DCS frowned. 'How long did it take you to gain access to the room?'

'Once I heard Carlson shout, three seconds, sir.'

'Three seconds?'

'Yes, sir. I instructed PW Kidd to get Sykes dressed, cuffed and booked in for unlawful wounding.'

‘I understand. And the two Traffic officers performed the first aid and together with Pc Carlson transported PW Weatherly to hospital. In the circumstances that is highly commendable. But what does Carlson say in his statement, Sergeant Farthing>’

‘I have Carlson’s statement here,, sir,’ said Penny removing it from the file. ‘This is what he says: *I was supervising the male getting dressed and had my back to PW Weatherly. I heard the female say “Can I get a handkerchief?” Janet replied, “Ok, be quick about it.” The girl answered, “Don’t wet yourself.” A couple of seconds later the girl said, “See how you like a prick.” I glanced over my shoulder and saw Janet on her back on the bed her left arm over the girl’s head and two fingers hooked up the girl’s nostrils, holding her head back and grasping the girl’s right wrist. Sykes was holding what looked like a small dagger in her hand.*’

‘Dagger?’ queried the DCS.

‘Yes, sir,’ I said. ‘It had been a letter opener, both edges honed to a razor sharpness.’

‘I see,’ said the chief superintendent. ‘Was there a handkerchief in this handbag?’

‘No, sir.’

‘This is a simple training issue , sir,’ said Mr Wallace.

‘I agree. I have to call the Chief in,’ he glanced at his watch, ‘thirty minutes. I will raise the matter then, if he doesn’t beat me to it ...’ The DCS paused. A playful smile crossed his face. ‘Sergeants, what should we charge? You first Blake.’

‘Any unlawful sexual activity is over. There’s no rough-house. Sykes has two previous for prostitution, but not in this area. So she’s looking at a fine. She’s either confused as to whether there is a handkerchief in her bag, or being duplicitous and using the comment about the handkerchief as a distraction, intending to use the knife from the start. The bag was on the bedside table, six or seven feet from where Weatherly was standing. Penny will you stand by that chair,' I said pointing. 'We know what happened. Sykes takes the knife in her right hand, her body blocking what's happening and, in one movement turns and delivers the blow with a straight arm, so ...' I rotated clockwise with my arm straight and stopped my blow adjacent to Penny's neck. 'Then she pulls the knife out and goes after Carlson. Only to be stopped by Weatherly. There was no need for any violence at all. It was gratuitous. She must have known how sharp the knife was and could have aimed for anywhere on Weatherly's body. She chose the neck.'

'You're thinking Attempted Murder.'

'Yes, sir. Section 18 fits like a glove; no problem. The level of intent and recklessness is, in my opinion of a different level altogether.'

'Interesting. Farthing?'

'Section 18 is nailed on, sir. And whilst I tend to agree with Brian, Sykes is a juvenile, I think that has to be taken into account.'

'So you think Section 18. Wounding With Intent?'

'I think that Attempted Murder would be the more appropriate charge had she been older. In the circumstances, Section 18.'

'Chalkley?'

'I'm pleased It's not my decision, sir,' he said as they all laughed. 'But seeing you've put me on the spot; I would keep it simple and stick with Section 18.'

The DCS was enjoying this. 'Care to answer, Blake?'

'Sir. Child murderers aren't exactly two-a-penny. But Mary Bell was only eleven when she strangled those two pre-school boys. So, there are precedents. What the outcome of the trial will be, remains to be seen.

'Had Janet Weatherly succumbed to the assault last night, or indeed so in the next 364 days we wouldn't hesitate to charge murder. Sykes is fifteen.'

The DCS took the floor again. 'You have all passed your Inspectors exams and you may be making that decision in the fulness of time. Mr Wallace?'

'The correct charge would be attempted murder. Whilst I accept your point Farthing and you, Chalkley, we should not look for reasons to reduce the charge too soon. Leave that to others. And any future prosecutor could apply to the court if necessary.'

Now, Bradbury, What happened at the Navigation?.

'The call came in. The licensee made the simple announcement that they were expecting a visit from the boys in blue in the near future. There was an exodus, mainly young girls heading for the Flying Fox.'

'Out of the frying pan.'

'So it would seem, sir.'

'Mr Wallace. Cooper?'

'First out of the briefing and last on the van. Couldn't really argue. I've suspended him. Discipline have served the necessary papers but I'm certain there is more to come.'

'Keep me posted. And last Farthing. It was well planned and almost perfectly operated. But what was the end result?'

'There were over fifty in the pub when we arrived, sir. Four warrants executed, Two each non-payment and non-attendance. The man who tried to barge Sergeant Blake out of the way? Clive Grayson. The prison service want him back. He was allowed out on compassionate grounds to attend the funeral of his brother. It's a pity he didn't have any siblings. Did a runner from the cemetery and that was two years ago. It was his first visit to the Fox. He wasn't happy.'

'I'll bet he wasn't,' said Mr Wallace. The laughter settled.

'As far as the sex offences are concerned. One couple, just unfortunate. He's twenty-one she's twenty. His family aren't religious. Her family are staunch Roman Catholics and her father holds the view of, I'm your father and as long as you are under my roof you will not marry outside the faith. They both have good jobs and just waiting until she is twenty-one. No money changes hands between them and Myrna rents them the room.'

'No offence,' said Mr Wallace. 'When do they plan to marry?'

'She's twenty-one in a month. So six weeks to two months'

'And the others?'

'We apprehended three, sir, although there were several others who have been spoken to. There were one sixteen and two fifteen year olds, one of whom is Myrna Sykes's daughter, Kathryn, generally known as *Katie.* She was the one who stabbed Janet Weatherly. Rooms £5 per half-hour. And the girls are kept busy. That's a minimum of £120 today, tax free. There was a separate drawer kept for hire of the rooms containing £535. In addition, £310. 15.6d in the cash register. Both amounts have been entered in connected property and the cash is in the safe.'

'It will be interesting to see what she usual enters for Thursday in previous weeks, always assuming that she has some system for recording the cash that goes through the business. You can bet it's less and she pockets the remainder,' said Mr Wallace. 'Sergeant Blake, see if you can get a judge in Chambers to issue a warrant for access to Sykes's bank accounts. First take Bradbury and carry out a fingertip search of the premises.'

'Sir.'

'OK Farthing, well done. We can get the Flying Fox closed but they will go elsewhere. Mr Marshall bring your licensing visits register, please.'

Chief Superintendent Cartwright closed the register. 'At the earliest opportunity, Mr Marshall I want a sergeant to visit every licensed premise in the subdivision and advise the licensees of what has happened here. Mr Fowler will take care of his area. They will be informed that visits will be stepped up to ensure that the law is fully complied with and there are no underage children on the premises;

especially Thursday to Saturday. They will no doubt belly ache but so be it. Also please ensure that new probationers are reminded about searches and the dangers of not carrying them out thoroughly.'

'Yes, sir,'

'I will arrange for a Special Court a.m. tomorrow. Court papers to be completed today; no hiccups. I will apply for a remand in custody for Myrna and Kathryn Sykes to await committal proceedings. All other offences including underage sex, bail to court in four weeks.

'Yes, sir,' said Penny glancing at me. It was going to be a stretch. 'I've arranged for someone from social services to act as appropriate adult.'

Ninety-Five

A middle-aged Miss Vanessa Kinnock, from Social Services, arrived to sit in the interviews with Katie Sykes, Melanie Brookes and Pauline Maltravers. I don't know what she expected but she was totally unprepared for what was about to be discussed.

First was Myrna. Bearing in mind what we had found during the raid it was straight forward; although she did protest that Katie would be sixteen in two months.

The nineteen year old youth George Mathewson partner of Melanie Brookes was a straight forward admissions. He wasn't looking forward to his five minutes of fame in court.

The two teenage prostitutes were no problem.

Gregory Sutcliffe admitted his underage sex with Kathryn Sykes, and gave a statement regarding her attack on Janet Weatherly.

Last to be interviewed, Kathryn Sykes. Vanessa Kinnock acting as appropriate adult. Interview conducted by Penny and PW Doreen Kidd.

' ... and given in evidence,' said Penny. 'You understand, Kathryn?'

'Of course I fucking do. What's the matter,' she said to Vanessa Kinnock in a patronising tone. 'Never heard naughty words before? You're not wearing a ring. Don't tell me the Social has sent a virgin. Bloody Hell.'

'All right Kathryn,' said Penny. 'Cut it out.'

'Well, look at her. You look like you need a good fuck. Slacken off a bit instead of being uptight. Mind you, a good man up tight would make you feel a lot better. You should try it.'

Vanessa Kinnock looked as though she was about to burst into tears.

Doreen Kidd slammed her hand on the table. 'Katie, that's enough. You're in enough trouble as it is.'

'All right. Yes, Greg paid Mum a fiver for the room for half an hour, and paid me a fiver for a fuck, satisfied.'

'You admit it?'

'Why not. It's a fine. Ten quid will cover it, it usually does.'

'Now, you asked PW Weatherly if you could get a handkerchief from your handbag.'

' I did.'

'But you didn't have a handkerchief in your handbag.'

'I know,' she said and smiled.

'Don't get smart, Katie,' said Penny. 'You're telling us you wanted to reach the knife in your handbag without raising suspicion.

' Correct.'

'Why did you want to reach your knife?'

'To teach that little pervert a lesson.'

'PW Weatherly?'

'Who else?'

'But you were at least six feet away.'

'Easy. Pull the knife from my bag spin round and reach out. Bingo. Just like that. A little prick.'

'You'd sharpened the blade.'

'Some punters get nasty. Got to look after yerself.'

'PW Weatherly wasn't a risk; you weren't going to be assaulted. So why?'

'Scare her a bit. Give her a little prick. She's like this one,' she nodded to Vanessa Kinnock.

'So you didn't care what injuries you inflicted on PW Weatherly, although she was simply waiting for you to blow your nose.'

Katie sykes paused and frowned. 'All I did was give her a bit of a prick in the neck. I didn't fucking stab her.'

'After you had given her this, *bit of a prick*, what did you do?'

She shrugged.

'Isn't it true you tried to stab PC Carlson?'

'Never got a chance. That copper grabbed me from behind, nearly ripped my bleedin' nose off. Little cunt.'

'Well, that *little prick* you talk about cut PW Weatherly's right jugular vein. She required emergency surgery and, had it not been for three police officers, PC Carlson and two road traffic officers she would have bled to death. You will be charged with attempted murder.'

'NO! It was just a little prick in the neck.'

Ninety-Six

Miss Kinnock was in the Well of the court. Chief Superintendent Cartwright took his place as prosecutor. The Chairman of the Bench, Major Draco Hambleton and fellow Magistrate, Mrs Tracey Grosvenor entered. Myrna and Katie Sykes were brought into the dock.

As the chief superintendent stood Draco Hambleton said. 'A little unusual, chief superintendent, an adult and a juvenile before the court together on an occasion such as this.'

'Mother and daughter, sir. Myrna Sykes and Kathryn her fifteen year old daughter.'

'Co-defendants?'

'In a manner of speaking, sir.'

'And both defendants have been charged.'

'They have, sir.'

'Very well,' he said and nodded.

'As a result of information received that the Flying Fox public house, situated in Canal Approach, Sowerby Bridge, licensee Mrs Myrna Sykes was using the premises as a brothel, in which underage girls were involved, Detective Sergeant Elizabeth Farthing put together a plan to raid the premises. An operation which was carried out successfully yesterday evening.

'Four upstairs bedrooms were being used. That element of the raid under the supervision of Detective Sergeant Brian Blake. Four teams, each comprising one male and one female officer were detailed, one for each bedroom. In each bedroom couples were found in the act of sexual intercourse.

'One couple were found to be consenting adults and no money changed hands. Of the other three girls one was aged sixteen and the other two fifteen years of age, including Kathryn Sykes; Myrna Sykes' fifteen year old daughter. When interviewed the males involved stated they regularly visited the Flying Fox because they know that young girls would be available for sex. I would point out here, sir, that there is no suggestion that Myrna Sykes had any control over the girls, merely provided clean rooms at a charge of £5 per half hour.

'In the last room on the right PC Carlson and PW Weatherly found Kathryn Sykes and Gregory Sutcliffe, nineteen years old.

While PC Carlson was overseeing Sutcliffe getting dressed, PW Weatherly likewise with Kathryn Sykes who asked if she could get a handkerchief from her handbag. Instead, when Sykes removed her hand from the handbag she was holding a dagger-shaped letter opener; both cutting edges sharpened. To all intents and purposes a small stiletto. In one movement Sykes swung her arm striking PW Weatherly in the neck; the knife damaging the right jugular vein. An injury requiring emergency surgery. Sykes then tried to assault PC Carlson whose back was unprotected, only for PW Weatherly to pull Skyes' head back and to seize her' wrist preventing any further assault.

'PC Carlson took control of Sykes and provided PW Weatherly with a clean handkerchief to try and staunch the flow of blood from her neck. He then shouted to attract the attention of Sergeant Blake. Then removed the knife from Sykes' right hand,'

'Did Kathryn Sykes say anything when she struck PW Weatherly?'

'Yes, your Worships. PC Carlson and PW Weatherly both stated that Kathryn Sykes said, "See how you like a prick.'

Major Hambleden snapped when Kathryn Sykes began to snigger. . 'Enough! Young lady, you are in enough trouble without you making fun of these proceedings. You have been charged with one of the most serious offences possible under British law. You struck an unarmed police officer, who was witing for you to get dressed in the neck with what the Chief Superintendent describes as s stiletto'

'If you strike someone in the neck with a bladed weapon, with sufficient force to warrant emergency surgery you must expect the maximum the law can deliver. Your life, no thanks to your mother, appears to be a disaster. Perhaps it is time you began to reflect on your future. The application is granted .. And in relation to Myrna Sykes?'

'Offences under Section 26 of the Sexual offences Act 1956: Allowing girl or girls between the ages of thirteen and sixteen to use premises for the purposes of prostitution. And under Section 33 of the Sexual Relations Act 1956 of managing a brothel. Myrna Sykes has two previous convictions in the past ten years.'

'Thank you.' He and Mrs Grosvenor got involved in a chinwag for several minutes. He looked up. 'Chief superintendent, your application is denied. These are somewhat minor offences and Myrna Sykes' previous convictions are historic.' He turned to the Dock. 'Mrs Sykes, the fact that we have denied the police application is nothing to do with any guilt. Instead you will be baled by this court *sine die.* That is until such time as proceedings are held. In the interim you will attend at Sowerby Bridge police station daily between the hours of 10am and 12 noon in person, from tomorrow where you will sign the relevant bail form. This will give you the opportunity to visit your daughter. She will need all the support she can get. Should you divert from this at all you will be brought back to the court and remanded in custody, Is that clear?'

'Yes sir. Thank you.'

'You will be taken back to the cells until the paperwork is ready and you can say goodbye to your daughter. One final thing. It would be unwise of you to contact or try to contact PW Weatherly, I hope you understand.'

'Yes sir. Thank you, sir.'

Ninety-Seven

Janet Weatherly, wearing a bed jacket over her nightie and surrounded by a marshmallow of pillows was propped up in bed. The dressing round her neck clearly visible. Out of uniform, even in these circumstances, she was pretty. Mark Carlson seated on a chair on Janet's left, holding her hand in both of his. What he was saying I have no idea, but they were both smiling.

They both looked up as the door opened. Janet tried to remove her hand. Mark was having none of it. 'That's right, Mark,' I said smiling. 'You hang on. Don't worry I won't be here long.' I pointed at the chair in the corner of the room. 'Do you mind?'

'No sarge,' said Janet, her expression suggesting otherwise.

I parked myself. 'It's good to see you both looking so well.'

'I don't mind admitting I was terrified.'

'Any sane person would be, Janet. In the few seconds it took me to respond Mark had it all wrapped up, and according to the sister in A&E they almost had to prise him away from the trolley.'

They smiled at each other. 'Janet's not the only one. When I saw ... I, I'm still wondering what I did wrong. Could I have stopped the attack?'

'No, you were on the opposite side of the bed. Kathryn Sykes knew there was no handkerchief and all she wanted was unquestioned access to the knife. It took a second and you coped brilliantly. You could drive yourself mad playing *what ifs*. So try and let it go. The main thing is you are both here. Kathryn Sykes is on remand pending committal proceedings for attempted murder.'

Mark lifted Janet's hand and kissed it. There was no objection. 'What was her mother charged with?'

'Remanded on bail for offences relating to prostitution. And at some time in the near future DS Farthing will want a statement.'

Janet took a deep breath and sighed. 'I suppose so.'

There was a pregnant pause. I smiled at them. 'You know, I met my wife in traumatic circumstances.' They both sat up and listened. 'I'd been at Pannal for about five weeks ... '

'That's some story, sarge.'

'And now you're married with three children,' Janet said and squeezed Mark's hand.

He reciprocated. 'I'll tell you what, Janet. You lie on your left side then I can snuggle up behind and put my arms round you. How's that?'

She blushed. 'You-will-not,' she replied in mock outrage. 'Not yet anyway.'

So that's what they were smiling about. 'That's what the consultant told Lucy and me. So?'

'And if a hospital consultant recommends it, who are we to argue.'

'I wouldn't recommend it in here, Mark. Sister might not be so accommodating.'

'Don't worry, he won't.'

'I'm sure,' I checked my watch. 'It's time I was off. There's not much wrong with you two, so be good to each other.'

'Sarge, before you go. Can we ask you a favour?'

'Of course.'

'You're a DS with less than five in...'

'I'm a DS principally because DS Greatorix had a heart attack and I've been involved with Nickleby- Collins since day one.'

'Sergeant Farthing did mention Collins.'

'The Fox was one of his hunting grounds, looking for young girls for the brothels run by a major London criminal.'

'Was Sykes in on his racket?'

'Remains to be seen. But to answer your question I'm a sergeant with four in.'

'But you were a detective and attended the Junior CID Course?'

'I did, and, according to DI Cartwright, you want CID.'

'Yes, I do, plus,' he paused and grinned, 'I fancy your job. Would you give us some coaching on answering exam questions?"

'Ok. And you want this as well, Janet?'

There was a degree of hesitancy in her reply. 'Certainly the promotion exams.'

'Janet, I might be jumping the gun and it's nothing to do with anyone except you two. If you want children don't let the job get in the way. A family is protection from the job. Now, leave it with me and I'll put some stuff together.'

I opened the door and heard the approach of familiar footsteps. I glanced over my shoulder. They hadn't wasted any time. Their lips were glued together, her left hand on the back of his neck. 'Ahem. The chief's here.'

There was a giggle from the direction of the bed. 'Good morning, Blake. Everything in order?'

'Yes sir,' I said. 'It appears that the young couple are adopting a mutual support system.'

He frowned, then smiled. 'Couple? ... Are they now. All good for morale.'

'Yes, sir,' I beat a retreat.

The chief pushed the ward door open. 'No, no formality. Relax. I just wanted ... '

Ninety-Eight

Myrna Sykes was not pleased to see Penny and me. 'What do you want now?'

'Can we sit?' I said as we pulled a couple of chairs from a nearby table.

'Help yourself,' she said and sat opposite.

'What can you tell us about Nick Collins?' I said.

The blood drained from her face. Her voice faltered. 'Nothing. I don't know anything.'

'I think you do, Myrna,' said Penny. 'In fact we know he was a regular here. He worked for a London villain.'

She closed her eyes and sighed. 'Field! Tell me something I don't know. Collins was a talent scout for Field's brothels.'

'You know about Field.'

'In my line of business? Can't avoid him. One thing you learn about creeps like Field and Collins, or shall we call him Nickleby, is you don't grass them up. If you're lucky you only get hurt, people disappear.'

'When did you meet Collins?'

'In Acton, Always looking for the youngest.'

Penny and I looked at each other then at Myrna. 'Katie?' said Penny.

She nodded. 'Not then, but when he walked into the Fox I nearly dropped, thought he was dead after that accident. He hadn't changed and still after the youngest. I'd found out that Katie had a few lads from school and one or two were a bit rough, at least I could make sure she was safe. Then I realised Collins was still working for Field. Wasn't having that.'

'How old was Katie when you found that out?'

There was silence. 'Not something I'm proud of, but that's a genie you can't put back in the bottle. She was fourteen.'

'So you suggested Mary Donoghue, didn't you? Anything to save your daughter from Field.'

It went silent.

'Yeah. That and me, just to keep Katie safe. I didn't know about the knife she carried, until ...'

'Ok, did Collins have sex with Katie?'

Myrna sighed. 'A couple of times; and he knew she was fourteen.'

'And the other girls, their ages.'

'I don't ask. They all look old enough and they're not virgins.'

There's no point is stressing the moral aspect in this. 'Collins is in custody and going down for life. So is Field.'

'I heard, but Field won't go down without a fight. Too many people with too much to lose, including coppers.'

Yes we know, or at least Sergeant Blake does.'

'That was you?'

'It was.'

'It was at Collins' house wasn't it? That's where those four sets of human remains were found. That says it all.'

'How do you know there were four?' I said. 'That hasn't been released.'

'Must have been, how else would I have known?'

'You tell us,' said Penny. 'It hasn't been released. But you're correct, so how did you know? Some of your regulars disappeared, a warning?'

There was no reply.

'Well Myrna?'

'Not regulars, travellers, but they weren't scum, not like some of them. Never caused me any trouble.'

?What were their names?'

'O'Donoghue – Christine and Joseph, and teenage twins – Patrick and Mary. She was a pretty girl. Collins kept on at them about a job in London. Patrick and Christine weren't stupid; they knew what Collins was up to. One evening about twelve months ago it came to a head. Joseph and Patrick offered him outside.'

'And?'

'Never saw them again.'

Their van, was it towed or a living van?'

'Towed. Used to park it up against the far hedge. Next morning it'd gone. Everybody assumed they'd left after the do with Collins.'

'How often did you see them?'

'Three, four times a year.'

'But nothing for twelve months.'

'Not even a whisper.'

'I don't suppose,' said Penny. 'You remember what they wore?'

'No, love, drab, dark colours – black or browns except Mary, she liked bright colours. One sweater in particular, always wore it, red, yellow and green hoops, long sleeves. Apart from that nothing stood out.'

Ninety-Nine

Information passed to DI Cartwright we left for the local travellers site and Michael Doohan.

'Bijou residences,' observed Penny as we entered the site. Vans around the edge, mostly new or fairly new. When you didn't pay any taxes there was money to spare.

The crowd began to gather as we decamped. 'I smell something unhealthy like pork gone off.'

'Yeah, and I smell scum. I'm looking for Michael Doohan.'

'I'm Doohan. Watch yer mouth, what do yer want?'

'Not you,' I said. 'Michael Doohan.'

'Who are yer?'

'Detective Sergeant Blake and Detective Sergeant Farthing. Now, where is he?'

'Nothing to do with you, copper.'

'I'm Doohan,' said an Irish voice behind me. 'What do you want?'

He was around sixty, six feet two and not an ounce of fat. 'We want to talk to you about the O'Donoghues.'

'There not here, copper. Fuck off and take your bitch with you.'

'That's enough McGurk, don't give them any more excuses to come here than they already have. If there is so much as a footprint on that car you'll pay for the damage and I will deal with you. Come in,' He turned his back on McGurk and returned to his caravan. Inside was spotless. He sat on a chair adjacent to the table under the window and waved us towards a couch. 'He was right, they're not here and we haven't seen them for over a year.'

'So we understand,' I said. 'Was that normal?'

'They never stayed but called a few times.'

'They were travellers. Any special reason why they wouldn't stay?'

'You've met one.'

'McGurk?'

He nodded but said nothing.

'I've met one McGurk. Not him. Younger. Gave your name.'

He had a wry smile. 'That would be Patrick. And if you've met Patrick you should know the other reason why they wouldn't stay.'

'Collins?'

He nodded again.

'O'Donoghue's daughter, Mary.'

'It was. Like bees around the honey pot, so they were. I would not want any McGurk as a son-in-law. As far as Collins was concerned he smelled wrong, something you couldn't define. The McGurks did work for him but Collins was bad news. Who was it locked him up? You?'

'It was. You knew that Collins wasn't his real name?'

'I heard. Something to do with a murder in London?'

'Yes.'

'Bad news. You can smell it a mile away.' He paused and thought. 'So, you two are involved with Collins. You've met the McGurks and you're asking about the O'Donoghues who haven't been seen for over a year. Is this something to do with that report of human remains being found at Collins' house?'

It was our turn to smile.

'Fair point.'

'I don't suppose you have any photographs of the O'Donoghues, Mr Doohan,' said Penny.

He stood, walked to a chest of drawers and removed a biscuit tin from the bottom drawer before handing Penny a 6x4 inch black and white photograph. 'Not a recent one, but it's a good likeness. They were a good family.'

'This hooped sweater the girl's wearing. Was it red, yellow and green?'

He thought for a second. 'Yes, it was.'

'Just for reference, how tall was Mr O'Donoghue?'

'Around five feet ten.'

'Did any of them have any injuries that may have damaged bones?'

He exhaled sharply. 'Bomes? It goes with our way of life. Big Patrick lost the third finger of his right hand perhaps thirty years ago, Mary fell out of a tree when she was eight or nine, broke a bone in her right leg. They gave her some kind of splint, they called it ...sounded like a boy's name.'

'A Thomas splint?' said Penny.

'That's the one. Nobody else had one. She was pleased until they teased her and called this Thomas her new boyfriend.'

'Eight or nine? I'll bet,' said Penny laughing. 'In that case she broke her right thigh.'

'That she did. Always had a slight limp after that.'

'Thanks. Do you mind if we copy it. We'll get it back t you.'

'Leave it with Myrna. Don't come back here just for that. Give me a bad name,' he said, laughed and stopped. 'You were the one locked Patrick up driving that bloody car of Collins.'

'I was. Collins made an unannounced visit to my home and left his car outside as a warning that he knew where I lived. That was stupid of him. The information was passed on. He was on his own when he visited my home, so his bumping into Patrick was a stroke of good fortune.'

Doohan nodded. 'Is there anything else?'

'Not offhand. We'll leave you to your own devices.'

Penny stepped from the caravan when Doohan said to me. 'You're the copper that was shot a few weeks ago.'

'Yes, thanks to the information Collins passed on.

Collins was mixed up in that business?'

'Up to his neck.'

There was silence as the two detectives drove from the site. Michael Doohan strolled towards McGurk. 'I want you off this site permanently, you have one hour.'

'You can't do that, we're blood.'

'I warned you about Collins the first time you brought him here. Did you listen?'

'He put a bit of work our way, Michael, what's the problem?'

'He was wanted for murder in London.'

'That's nothing to do with us.'

'Do you know why he paid Patrick £50 to drive that VW back here?'

There was no reply.

'No? Well I'll tell you.' He pointed at the detectives car. 'Minutes before, Collins had been at that copper's home threatening his wife and children.' There was silence. 'Oh, not directly, but by being there. Letting him know that he knew where he lived. What Collins didn't know was that the police knew who he really was. It was that copper who locked him up. Patrick told him that Collins had paid him to shift his car. Your Patrick is in his pocket and your family bring the police to our doorstep.

'You're the coppers new best friend are you?' McGurk sneered.

'No,' Doohan said and took a step forward. 'The only thing he told me was about the threats. I've got my own sources. How much did Collins promise you if your boys could get their hands on Mary?'

McGurk paled. 'I've no idea what you're talking about.'

'Don't lie to me. They used to sniff round her as if she was a bitch on heat. How much did Collins promise them?'

'Well?' He took a step forward.

'£200.'

'£200? You know that Collins used to supply girls to some thug in :London for his brothels?'

'Mary would never have agreed.'

'Don't be stupid. You think that would have made any difference? They were family, but that means nothing to you or yours. You know the police are trying to find out the identity of the human remains found in Collins cellar. How long is it since the O'Donoghues last paid us a visit or were seen at the Fox? Well, I'll tell you, twelve months. And twelve months since the O'Donoghues had a set to with Collins about Mary. You think there's a link? You have fifty-five minutes to get off this site. I don't want to know where you're going, or to see your faces again.'

One-Hundred

10.00am Friday 13th. The door to the windowless interview room opened. A handcuffed Nickleby entered escorted by two police officers. Gone was the confidence and the bonhomie. In its place was a hunted look.

Uncuffed. Officers waiting outside, Nickleby gazed around the room. 'Not much of a view, I'm disappointed.'

'That's unfortunate,' I said.

'Who's she,' Nickleby said looking at Mrs Watson busy taking notes.

'She take shorthand,' said Penny.

'I can see that,' Nickleby said. 'Does she have a name ?'

'Probably,' I said. 'But not one that is relevant.'

'And your colleague?'

'I'm a police officer,' said Penny.

'What a surprise. Anyone would think you didn't trust me.'

'You know who I am, that's 'all the matters. Take a seat.'

'All right,' Nickleby said, 'Why am I here?'

'We thought you might like some time out of prison,' I said.

He was not amused. 'Very droll. My brief has told me that you can't question me about things I've already been charged with. Just get on with it.'

'With limitations we can,' said Penny. 'But in this instance it's all nice and new. So I will tell you that you are not obliged to say anything unless you wish to do so but that anything you say will be taken down in writing and used in evidence.'

He frowned. 'What new stuff?'

'Patience Mr Collins and all will be revealed.'

You could hear the cogs spinning inside his head.

'Oh,' I added. 'This is for starters. The first of many interviews. What can you tell us about Myrna Sykes?'

'She's the licensee of the Flying Fox; regulars call it The Bat.'

'And what did you make of her?'

'In what way?'

'As a person? A licensee? A lover?'

'What?'

'You did have sex with her, didn't you?'

'Consenting adults, nothing illegal in that.'

'True,' said Penny. 'But how many times did you have sex with her fifteen year old daughter, Kathryn? But, she was only fourteen when you first had sex with Kathryn Sykes. At least that's what Myrna Sykes put in her statement. As did Kathryn.'

'I didn't know.'

'Mr Collins,' said Penny. 'Didn't know what?

'How old she was, She was a tall girl, pretty with a great figure, looked old enough.'

'Both Myrna and Kathryn say you did. But you just wanted to get laid. Isn't that the simple truth? You didn't care.'

'No. I thought she was old enough. Besides I wasn't her first.'

'Did she tell you that, or did you realise when you penetrated her?'

'She was confident. I assumed. Satisfied?'

'You are over twenty one years of age, the law expects you to be able to tell the difference.'

'Then the law's an ass.'

'A standing cock has no conscience., has it?' said Penny. 'You didn't care.'

'Now, according to Myrna you first met when you went to her brothel in Acton, West London.'

'I know where Acton is.'

'When she knew you as Nickleby.'

'And?'

'She said you always wanted the youngest.'

'I don't recall.'

'Maybe, but you do recall looking for girls for Harry Field's brothels. Myrna knew you involved, so surely you remember?'

There was no response from Nickleby.

'Come on Mr Nickleby, you can tell us,' said Penny.

'No?' I said. 'It gave Myrna a shock when you walked into the Flying Fox. She thought you were killed in that road accident in 1959. Thanks to Alex Frobisher there you were; large as life.'

One-Hundred-And-One

'Now, tell us about the O'Donoghues.'

'Nothing to tell.'

'According to Myrna there is ... Care to re-assess? ... No? ... Something you could never understand. As Kathryn's mother, Myrna was already aware of your link to Field when you were in London, and when Katie told her about your sexual proclivities she not only offered you free sex with her, she suggested that Mary O'Donoghue would make a good substitute for Katie.

'You even offered Patrick McGurk £200 if they would help in getting Mary to comply. In fact, whenever the O'Donoghues were on the travellers site, the McGurk boys were, 'sniffing round Mary as if she was a bitch on heat'.

'It all came to a head about twelve months ago when the O'Donoghues were having a quiet drink in the Flying Fox. You rolled in and started on them again. They were sick and tired of your pestering and offered you outside. They haven't been seen since.'

'True,' said Nickleby. 'They left. I haven't seen them since.'

'It is true, Mr Nickleby, said Penny, 'that you were the last to see them but it was not when you left the Flying Fox, was it?'

His face paled again. 'I don't know what you mean.'

'I'll refresh your memory, shall I?' I said. 'It was a comment made by

Frobisher just before he and Bellemy attacked me. 'Nickleby always had a hidden room in the cellar. I'll go and check it out'. And, although he claimed they had never been to your house before he knew where the cellar was.'

Penny lifted a box file onto the table.

'Once they were in custody I put in a request to the Planning Department for the builder's plans. Sure enough there was no additional room shown.' Penny slid a 10x8 inch black and white photograph across the table to Nickleby. 'As you can see there's a large steel cabinet against the left-hand wall. When our forensic scientists moved the cabinet guess what they found.'

'Surprise me.'

'Oh, it won't be a surprise.' Penny slid a second 10x8 photograph across the table. 'There was a manhole cover. When they removed it the stench of decomposing flesh was over powering which necessitated the attendance of the Public Health Department.

'When the contents of the cellar were emptied and cleaned this is what they found. But you already know, don't you?'

'If you say so.'

Penny slid the next photo across the table. 'This is the re-assembled skeletal remains of an adult male; approximately five feet ten inches in height.' I pointed to various aspect of the photograph. 'You can see at these places where the body was cut into pieces using a circular saw. And here,' I pointed to the right hand.

'The missing third finger; lost whilst stripping a motor vehicle engine some thirty years prior.'

Penny slid the next photo across the table. 'This is of an adult female approximately five feet four inches in height. And again where a circular saw was used ... And this,' I pointed to the pelvis, 'is called the sciatic notch. Compared to the same feature in males the female notch is much wider.'

'The third photograph,' Penny slid it across the table. 'Is of a teenage male and once again has been cut using a circular saw. This skeleton has a narrow sciatic notch.'

'Lastly,' Penny slid the photograph across the table. 'Is of a teenage female, as you can see by the wider sciatic notch. Also cut into pieces with a circular saw. You can also see here,' I pointed to the right femur. 'The fracture scar as a result of a fall from a tree when she was nine years old. These are unquestionably the skeletal remains of the O'Donoghue family.'

'If you say so.'

'How did they get into this room beneath your cellar?'

'You're the detective. You tell me.'

'I checked with the builder who drew up the plans; Terry Williams. He says you approached him to build the room and offered him £500. Have you anything to say?'

'No.'

'Where and how did you murder the O'Donoghue family?' said Penny.

'Don't recall.'

'But you did kill them then dismembered their bodies?'

'Seems like it'

'Why? Why did you do it?'

Nickleby shrugged. 'It's how I make my living.'

'Killing people?'

'Not necessarily. Harry tells me what he wants. If you agree there is no turning back; that's his contract. Succeed and get paid. If not you're lucky if you live. Word was spreading that the O'Donoghues were being awkward. It was affecting my income and Harry would have found somebody else. Couldn't allow that.'

'So, killing and disposing of the O'Donoghues wasn't sanctioned by Harry Field?'

'No. Call it self-preservation.'

'Getting rid of a blockage in the system?'

'In a manner of speaking. Yes.'

' And this was the night they disappeared?'

'Where did you kill them?'

'Don't remember.'

'Or don't want to?'

He shrugged.

'How did you kill them? By shooting?'

'Too noisy. A sharp knife.'

'Where?'

He shrugged again.

'Then dismembered them.'

'Must have.'

'All by yourself?'

'You've got what you wanted. Just charge me.'

'One more thing,' I said. 'You say that you've done work for Field for several years. Is there anything else you want to tell us, keep him inside? You can bet your bottom dollar he'll try and offload as much as he can onto your shoulders.'

He sat there for a moment then nodded. 'That's what he would do. Here's one for nothing. His ex-wife, Yvonne.'

'What about her,' I said.

'She was a nympho and always had some toff in tow; the latest some Rt. Honourable jerk; more money than brains. When Harry divorced her there were conditions. He'd ensure she had plenty of money. In return she's not to embarrass him. She was a lush, kept getting drunk in his casino bars and shooting her mouth off. He decided enough was enough, she had to go.'

'She became your contract?'

'Yup. The cover story was she and her lover were spending a weekend in Belgium then onto Italy. I forget where. No forwarding address and no further contact.'

'He reported her missing?'

'He did.'

'What was the truth?'

'Concrete boots for two in the German Bight.'

'You killed them and threw the bodies overboard?' Said Penny.

'He shook his head. 'No bodies.'

'Alive?'

'Yup. Harry was paying and it's what he wanted. It didn't do to ignore him.

'And he was there to ensure all went to plan?'

'Oh yes.'

'How deep is the water?'

'About 120 feet.'

'How many bodies did you get rid of for Field in this manner?'

It was six but he deserves more. 'Didn't keep a count but it's well into double figures.'

'The boat?'

'Harry's. Called Happy Daze, out of Dungeness.'

'I don't believe you. Your contract, you supply everything. The boat was yours.'

Collins grinned. 'Worth a try.'

Penny charged Collins with four counts of murder.

Mrs Watson typed the interview up. Penny and I delivered it to Detective Superintendent Wallace who called Commander Jameson.

It was transferred force to force by traffic car arriving at New Scotland Yard in three hours, DCS Yelland would have more than enough to get his teeth into.

DI Bellamy had still not recovered consciousness. DCI Frobisher was on remand and I was released and returned to being the sub-divisional DS.

At 2pm the next day I joined over two hundred fellow and former police officers to pay our last respects to Colin Greatorix. He had been a good copper and a great bloke. He would be missed.

I left one cemetery to visit another, Hecton, tell my biological father about my sidestep into CID. Not to rub it in but to keep him up to date. I wondered what rank he would have reached but he would have been delighted with my progress.

One-Hundred-And-Two

Detective Superintendent Wallace could taste the tension as he entered the governor's office. 'Everything is arranged; they will leave at two minute intervals. As they exit the prison each van will pick up a brace of traffic cars.'

'Do we know which Collins is in,' said Deputy Governor Graham Sidebottom.

'I do and it's all in here Mr Sidebottom,' said the governor locking the file in his safe.

'What about the police?'

'I know,' said Wallace. 'The van crews know and will follow their predetermined route. Force control have knowledge of the routes but not which vehicle contains Collins. They will only find out if something kicks off. Keep your fingers crossed.'

Wallace shook hand with them both and left. Operation Conflict was in play. What the next move would be was unknown.

ONE MILE TO THE SOUTH two pairs of binoculars were focused. A light began to flash. 'That's it, dash-dot-dash-dot, That's C.'

His colleague picked up his walkie-talkie. 'Control, target is number three, repeat number three.'

FOR THE FIRST TIME in a week the sun was shining. Barnsley bound traffic was light.

'Charlie, are you sure this is the right route?'

'Yup, A61 south from Wakefield. According to the map the water on the left is Newmillerdam.'

'Water, trees and carpark. Looks like a nice spot.'

'Never mind that. Keep your bloody eyes open. You heard what the superintendent said.'

'I did, but he's not here.'

A warning voice from the rear. 'Look out! Air cover behind, starboard side, coming up fast and low .. It's a bloody Scout.'

'What? That's military'

'I sodding well know.'

The Scout overshot, the sound of its engine becoming fainter.

'There was somebody in the back carrying an RPG.'

'Don't be so fucking stupid, Roger.'

'I carried one. It was an RPG.'

'Where the hell is it?'

'Never mind that, Stewart . Decamp into the woods I'll meet you at the far end. Tony, you're i/c. Now move.'

The eight officers, all ex-military and carrying side arms bailed out and ran into the woods to the amusement of a group of children. 'Are you playing hide-and-seek with that helicopter, mister?'

'Something like that, son,' said Tony. 'Don't wave and tell them where we are, promise?'

He nodded his head. 'Is that a real gun?' he said pointing at the Smith & Wesson revolver in the holster on his belt.'

'No. We don't carry real guns in public.' The sound of the Scout was becoming louder. Searching. 'Now be a good lad and walk towards that car-park. We have work to do.'

'X-Ray3 emergency.'

The pips began. 'Go ahead.'

'Decamped at Newmillerdam. It's teeming with civilians including children. There's a Scout military helicopter, one male in the rear with an RPG, searching the woods for us.'

'Confirm RPG.'

'Yes, RPG. Get onto the army, see if they've lost one. And somebody to take care of this. Out.' Into second gear and foot hard down. The movement caught the pilot's eye.

'Below. Left.'

'I see it, take it round.'

Desmond 'Des' Smith, former sergeant in the SAS had been in some tight corners in his time, but playing dodgeball with an RPG in a helicopter was up there with the best. Seeing the chopper rotate he drove the personell carrier across to the offside verge, decamped and vaulted the wall. The eighteen foot fall into a disused railway cutting wasn't in his plan. His ankle broke on impact. The pain lanced through him. 'Fuck!'

A quick look around, a good covering of large shrubs and trees. Dragging himself under a large elderberry bush ensured he was out of sight, unless the chopper blew the cover away. As always he carried two triangular bandages. Using these and a couple of large twigs he stabilised his ankle in a figure of eight bandage before dragging himself further under cover.

The foliage and bushes swirled. Loose vegetation blown away. The chopper descended into the cutting,'

'That's all I fucking need,' he hissed under his breath. Drew his revolver and cocked the hammer. 'Just you stick your head too close, sunshine.'

'IS THIS A JOKE, INSPECTOR?'

'No captain it is not. There are eight police officers in the Newmillerdam area being hunted by a Scout helicopter, and someone armed with an RPG. The officers are carrying sidearms only.'

'May one ask why?'

'They were taking a prisoner to London for interview and trial. A lot of people want to stop him.'

'Very well. Wait.'

WORKING BOTH SIDES of the cutting the remaining members of the team returned to where they had last seen the chopper. Tony Kaye raised his hand. The rest stopped and crouched. The chopper landed. Rotor idling. One man decamped, knife in his right hand.

'For fucks sake,' Kaye hissed over his shoulder, 'that's Craven.'

'Take him out.'

'If he's on foot then Des is there. Besides there's a pilot somewhere.'

HE EASED THE BRANCHES out of the way. 'Peek-a-Boo. Well, what a surprise. Hello Desmond, fancy seeing you here. How are the mighty fallen.'

'Gerry Craven,' he said in a drawl. 'Gerry after a piss-pot, and Craven like the coward you are. You make as much noise as a bull elephant. From the stench I thought I was back in Africa,' he smiled through the pain. 'Still carrying a knife?' He sneered. 'You don't have the stones. Just a gutless twat. Always have been, always will be.'

Craven raised the knife. 'All right, enough of the compliments. Where is he?'

'Where's who?'

'Don't piss me about, Desmond. Collins, the man you were taking to London.'

Smith smiled and shook his head slowly. 'Wrong again. No passenger, only us poor squaddies. We never had a Collins on board. You screwed up. But you should be used to that, screwing up. Remind me, what was it? Ignominious discharge? Never learn do you?'

He glared at the man responsible for his being kicked out of the army. His blood boiled. 'You bastard!' Craven took a step forward. Smith's .38special round obliterated his right eye.

THE PILOT PICKED UP the loaded RPG, exited the chopper and strode towards his fallen colleague.

Right, don't trip and shoot yourself,' said Kaye. 'More to the point, don't bloody shoot me.'

They broke cover. 'STAND STILL!' shouted Kaye.

The pilot stopped and turned towards them. A broad grin broke his scowl. 'Peashooters? against an RPG? You're not serious.'

'You've never fired an RPG before, have you?' said Kaye laughing. 'You left the safety on.'

The pilot paused and glanced at his RPG.

A second shot rang out.

PATRICK WEATHERILL hid his anger well. In over thirty years in the prison service, now prison governor he had never felt such betrayal. 'Why, Mr Sidebottom? Why have you thrown your career away? Not to mention bringing the service into disrepute ... Well?'

Detective Superintendent Wallace interrupted. 'I think, Mr Weatherill, that this interview ought to be carried out elsewhere.'

'SUPERINTENDENT?' SAID Sidebottom as the prison gates closed behind them. 'Was Collins killed?'

'No, he was taken to London by train last night which is why you were kept out of the way this morning.'

'But?'

'Mr Weatherill had suspected for some time that confidential information regarding prison inmates was being passed to unauthorised individuals. He contacted me, hence the plan; kill two birds with one stone. Only the third van contained police officers. In spite of Mr Weatherill's comment about knowing which van Collins was being transported in, the only person who knew, was me, except the person who opened the envelope Mr Weatherill locked in his safe. You were the only other person who had a key to the safe. Shall we leave further discussion on this matter until the interview. I have several questions I would like you to answer.

The End

Don't miss out!

Visit the website below and you can sign up to receive emails whenever Jon Mason publishes a new book. There's no charge and no obligation.

https://books2read.com/r/B-A-ZRTW-EGBNH

BOOKS 2 READ

Connecting independent readers to independent writers.

Also by Jon Mason

Blake Detective Series
Dance With the Devil
The Blooding of Brian Blake
Nemesis
Counting The Dead
Death in The Slushpile
Macello

Watch for more at www.jonmasonbooks.com.

About the Author

JON was born into post WW2 Yorkshire in England. His brother Stuart was born in 1938. His father, demobbed from the RAF where he had been a Dispatch Rider, returned to the tailoring industry. His mother had spent the war years x-raying wheels for battle tanks.

They lived in a small, inner two-bedroomed terrace house. There was no damp-proof course, double glazing, central heating or hot water on tap. The tin bath hung from a nail under the stairs and the lavatory was across the back yard..

Leaving school in 1962 he joined the West Riding Constabulary as a Cadet and as a Constable in 1965. His initial training carried out at No3 District Police Training Centre, Pannal Ash, Harrogate, in the then North Riding of Yorkshire.

Over the next three decades he gained experience across much of what the police service has to offer. 1965-70 on uniform beat patrol. From 1970-75 in the Road Traffic Division as an advanced driver and also where he was firearms trained. From 1975-77 Force Control where he learned his radio and computer skills before being promoted to the Western Area Control Room in January of 1977, Twelve months later he was seconded to the fledgling Computer

Development Unit working with Ferranti International in the development of Stage 4 of a resource handling and incident recording system known as Command and Control (Not big Brother) and the setting up of the Communications Training Wing at the West Yorkshire Police training school. December 1983 saw him transferred to an inner city sub-division where he spent the last 10 years of his service as uniform patrol sergeant where he also worked closely with the Air Support Unit, Custody Officer and the last four years as the Station Sergeant.

In May of 1967 Jon and his fiancee married. A marriage which so far has lasted for over 56 years. They had two children, tragically Andrew, the elder, died of a heart attack in January 2018 - he was 48. Their daughter is still going strong.

Prior to retirement Jon qualified as a fitness instructor and subsequently head-hunted to work in a new community based cardiac rehab programme where he had the opportunity to study cardiology at Leeds University Medical School and exercise physiology at Carnegie. He also studied bio-mechanics.

All that knowledge and experience Jon brings to his books.

Read more at www.jonmasonbooks.com.

www.ingramcontent.com/pod-product-compliance
Ingram Content Group UK Ltd.
Pitfield, Milton Keynes, MK11 3LW, UK
UKHW040632021125
464526UK00004B/4

9 781916 757127